ROSS

Additional copies may be ordered from the publisher for educational,
business, promotional or premium use.
For information, contact ALIVE Book Publishing at:
alivebookpublishing.com, or call (925) 837-7303.

ISBN 13
978-1-63132-200-6

Library of Congress Control Number: 2023905862

Library of Congress Cataloging-in-Publication Data
is available upon request.

First Edition

Published in the United States of America by ALIVE Book Publishing
and ALIVE Publishing Group, imprints of Advanced Publishing LLC
3200 A Danville Blvd., Suite 204, Alamo, California 94507
alivebookpublishing.com

PRINTED IN THE UNITED STATES OF AMERICA

10 9 8 7 6 5 4 3 2 1

ROSS

PATRICK J. HAGAN

Alive Book Publishing

To the "Love of My Life,"
Margaret Mary Lynch Hagan,
for all she has meant to me
over our years together.

MY ROSS BACK STORY

by Ronan O'Neill

To fully appreciate my continuing story as presented in *ROSS*, the reader should be aware that many of its characters first emerged in my two biographical sketches of my earlier life as suggested by my deceased psychiatrist and friend of many decades, Dr. Margot Arnaud. *SAUSALITO*, featured me as a younger Ronan O'Neill, my family, and a number of my formative experiences, with considerable focus on the women in my life. My second effort, *MILL VALLEY*, emphasized my legal career growth, as well as my family, and other people close to me, in new or changing relationships.

SAUSALITO began with me, Ronan, arriving in that Northern California bayside town in 1971 as a junior Coast Guard officer assigned to observe a major oil spill investigation. I had recently returned from the Viet Nam War, was highly decorated but still suffering the traumatic effects of combat. On arriving, I first met Carolyn Tyne, an aspiring young model with whom I almost immediately became casually involved, and eventually we ended up sharing what was to become her Sausalito apartment.

My reactions to the oil spill investigation and my Sausalito friend Joel Tinker's being in law school led to my decision to leave USCG active duty and to become a lawyer. While attending UC Hastings Law School in San Francisco, I fell in love with a school mate, Sandra Allen, and became engaged. Her father was the managing partner of a large San Francisco firm where I clerked during law school and was expected by that family to start my law career. However, my engagement ended abruptly when Sandra reacted violently to my decision not to join her father's firm. Immediately thereafter, I experienced a serious emotional crisis, which might have been far worse as I stood on the Golden Gate Bridge unclearly pondering very negative thought patterns about my future. But the fortuitous and timely appearance of an old college girlfriend, Mollie Phelan, brought me through the worst of that crisis. With the initial help of my psychiatrist, Dr. Arnaud, my mother Kate, and Mollie, I became more able to confront my fears and moved forward with my life.

Following law school, my friend Tinker provided me the opportunity to join Klein Kelly, a small Oakland law firm, and I quickly began to thrive there as a defense litigator hired mostly by insurance companies. I married Mollie, who was then an IBM systems analyst and very quickly became a much sought-after computer applications developer. I achieved some initial significant prominence in the Northern California defense bar at a time when asbestos was fast becoming a medical and legal pandemic. As a result, within less than fifteen years after my initial arrival in Sausalito, I had become immersed in nationwide high-stakes litigation, often collaborating with my friend Tinker who had relocated his practice to Washington, D.C. As *SAUSALITO* ends, Mollie, our four young children and I had relocated to the nearby town of Mill Valley, from which my second novel draws its name.

In *MILL VALLEY*, Mollie and I enjoy an almost blissful decade with our family. I continued a mostly long-distance relationship with Carolyn, without actually meeting her son, Patrick, until near the end of this book. Meanwhile, Carolyn has become an even more successful model on an *haute couture* international level. Mollie's career as a computer applications designer becomes increasingly successful. She changes employers and her job becomes bi-coastal. All of this while I was coping with a burgeoning practice of huge, potentially high dollar outcome actions on a national scale. During that same time, our firm's local asbestos caseload increased markedly in size. I was able, over time, to expand my diverse team to include a somewhat beautiful woman lawyer with prior legal experience as well as a scientific background. Soon, I fell into a long-term romantic relationship with this Martha Walsh, who became our team's resident expert in Science and Medicine, and my frequent travel companion.

Desert Mutual insurance Company (DMIC) designated me as National Coordinating Counsel for all of its CAL Board asbestos litigation, which became national in scale. I continued to litigate against, and at times with, Sandra Allen, my former *fiancée* and her father who represent a larger target defendant in many of the same cases. Also, with input from various members of our joint national CAL Board defense team, I was designated to undertake the development of a novel defense to the massive US Environmental Protection Agency-driven litigation to remove all asbestos-containing products installed in buildings, which gave rise to more than a few of those mega-cases. I tried the first phase of such a case against the Los Angeles Unified School District (*LAUSD*) with mixed results in the face of some political duplicity.

My work allowed me to meet key figures on the world stage of international public health in our quest to defend CAL Board and develop a novel defense. These assignments lead to my travelling even more extensively; and, in the case of the iconic European scientific experts, providing high-end hospitality as entertainment. (These leaders of their respective scientific communities were rarely expert witnesses and would accept no fees for their time because they believed that might appear tantamount to being bribed.) I was also retained by DMIC to coordinate and manage a London search for their missing old reinsurance policies, placed with Lloyds syndicates, to assure that company's continued liquidity. This assignment led to my meeting, and later becoming romantically involved with

Madeline Myles in London.

This continuum of my life, as I set out in *Mill Valley*, culminates in a bitter phase as Mollie is suddenly taken seriously ill, not long after she meets and befriends Carolyn and her son when they come to visit Carolyn's long time West Coast home in Sausalito. This book ends with Mollie being rolled into emergency surgery.

ACKNOWLEDGEMENT

To Bruce McDonald and Jane Wells for all of their editing assistance, and encouragement, and to Kristin and Phillip for their technical help.

PROLOGUE

The ever-tortuous months of Mollie's cancer battle were relentlessly devastating for her, our four children and Kate. As time shortened, Mollie's circle of caregivers widened to include Carolyn and her son, Patrick, Ingrid, our au pair, and at least in spirit, Tinker and Elaine in D.C., my team at the firm; and even some of my clients. Everyone tried to be supportive, but nothing they could do, or say, made any real difference: Mollie's cancer was relentless.

Mollie's initial surgery was brutal with pieces of her most private areas being removed to stop the spread of the cancer; even then, she needed radiation and chemotherapy with the devilish results of weight and hair loss, as well as ever-increasing weakness. Worst of all: even with all of these efforts, nothing proved availing to relieve Mollie's ever-worsening pain as her condition deteriorated.

Mollie was home, as she desired, bedridden in Mill Valley. She had several "talks" with me. Her first was about her last few years and trips to New York for APP, INC, as her employer was then known. She had come to regret being away from her family and me so much, and to miss so many of her children's extracurricular activities.

In telling me about this, Mollie said she got to thinking when she started to have those awful pains that she hoped it was not God punishing her for neglecting her family, and me. I told Mollie not to think anything like that. She knew too well her family history for cancer. That's all that was happening here. (I did not go into anything about her perhaps waiting too long to voice her complaints. After all, she was probably having her earliest pains during, or maybe even before, our first family trip to Europe when we went to London and she did not want to spoil our family's long anticipated event. If that was the case, no point in causing her any added feelings of grief or guilt!)

Carolyn, of whom Mollie had grown increasingly fond before her illness and despite their relatively brief period of friendship, turned down some choice modeling assignments and moved out to Sausalito to be close to Mollie. She got her Patrick into 9th grade at the San Francisco University High School in Pacific Heights, just across the Golden Gate Bridge from her Cote d'Azur condominium in southernmost Sausalito.

Carolyn was like a saint in the way she came to Mollie's aid over those harrowing times! I remember multiple occasions, not sure how many, when Carolyn would sit on the edge of a chair and hold Mollie's hand, sometimes stroking her fingers, as Mollie lay stretched out on the family room couch, too frequently in obvious pain. At times, they seemed to carry on whispered conversations. Carolyn always tried to stay for at least one meal and she would often make it (a pretty good cook for someone whom I thought probably ate out with great regularity).

But it was those whispered conversations that I began to think about. After weeks of treatment with little or no improvements, I believed Mollie began to formulate a firm belief that this was really the beginning of her end. But when I tried to talk, too often she put me off with her pain or her exhaustion. I could see no gainful purpose to pushing myself on Mollie, especially for Mollie's sake.

Then, one day, Carolyn came to me saying that Mollie does not want me to think she's "giving up," but would I arrange for Father Seamus (from St. Anselm's in Ross, our parish, because its priests all came over from Ireland and were much more "our types" than the diocesan priests in the Mill Valley parish) to start visiting Mollie. So, I did that: and, starting the next day, there were often more whispered conversations to which I felt strangely, but perhaps rightly, to be politely excluded.

As her condition continued to progressively deteriorate, Mollie's second "talk with me" came some weeks after her first. She told me that she wanted to stop all of her treatments as they only made her feel increasingly worse. Instead, she just wanted pain medication, as much morphine as she could tolerate and still be aware of her surroundings, especially of her family. Mollie confided that she "knew she only had weeks, maybe only days, left." While holding back tears, I promised to do as she asked.

Then, she asked me to sit down and said she wanted to talk about me when she was gone. She was blunt (I think it was partly the pain): she knew that I had achieved a reconciliation of sorts with Sandra, whom she had met on a few occasions. Mollie said, "Seeing you on that Bridge rail in my mind's eye, I can never forgive what that woman did to you. Do you understand me?"

I nodded affirmatively, and Mollie continued, "If I were not there, you might not be here. But one person would be. That's your son Patrick. I do not mean our son. I mean Carolyn's, with you. I do not know if she would have told you when she was pregnant or not, but I am almost positive that she did not tell you because of Sandra! Do not bother to deny it. And I may not be right. I have not asked Carolyn or you. I love you too much and I am honestly quite fond of Carolyn who is an incredibly caring person. Besides, I was all but out of your life at that time. So who am I to criticize? He is a lovely boy."

I could see Mollie tiring. Still, she went on, "Carolyn has told me repeatedly that she's a Lesbian, that she has Vera on her farm in Connecticut, and that Vera loves Patrick as if he were her son. But Carolyn's here, now. She brought Patrick, saying it was just temporary. Now, listen carefully and please do not interrupt: I talked to Carolyn and explained to her much of how I feel about Sandra and how she treated you. I told her my concerns. I trust her as if she is my best friend, next to you. Perhaps, in these final moments, she is that. Ronan, do not wait long after I am gone. Ask Carolyn to marry you. Give her a little time. I don't think it will take much. I firmly believe she will say, 'Yes'. You, not to forget my children, need someone to look after you. Carolyn seems to me to be that best someone once I am gone."

With those last words, Mollie's head began to droop and she appeared to sleep. I put my arms under her and lifted: Mollie weighed little more than half of her former healthy weight. Upstairs, I laid her on her side of our bed, on her back. I pulled up her covers. I changed, brushed my teeth and climbed in next to her. I rolled on my side and as gently as I could manage, put my arm over her and held her, feeling her life slowly ebbing away. I started to cry very quietly and as I began to nod off, I went to lift my arm. But with that movement, I felt Mollie's hand try to hold my arm in place.

I slept.

— — —

1

MY WORK DURING MOLLIE'S ILLNESS

Although I kept everyone who mattered in my life generally aware of Mollie's illness, and my primary need to attend to her during that time, my level of business communications could not completely stop.

By virtue of my being National Coordinating Counsel for CAL Board, Inc. (CAL Board), appointed as such by its very long-time primary Insurer, Desert Mutual Insurance Company (DMIC), I was delegated to be in charge of all of that company's asbestos litigation in U.S. courts. This involved what many people call "personal injury" cases of various conditions or diseases, occasionally even a death, claimed to be caused by CAL Board's various construction products usually during the installation process (referred to in the insurance industry and by the defense bar as "bodily injury or 'BI' cases"). These BI filings numbered more than 1,000 open matters in various state and federal courts, about half in California. Many of these cases historically named CAL Board as a Defendant, often without any research to investigate if the claimant plaintiff was ever exposed to any of our clients' products (I had made some considerable progress on this issue with the lead plaintiff attorneys in Northern California, but not as yet elsewhere).

The other major cases were the "BUILDINGS Litigation," largely a product of the United States Environmental Protection Agency's (EPA's) rulemaking process requiring the removal of all asbestos containing materials (ACM) from any buildings where human exposure was a possibility. As of that time, these EPA Rules had resulted in extremely high risk litigation, with no settlements and expensive litigation for both sides. Many of these lawsuits were either class actions or joinders of similar large entities. As a prime example. at that point in time, most of them involved school districts, of all sorts. A few cases had resulted in court ordered dismissals, but the plaintiff lawyers were learning how to avoid those. Much of my time was spent on these massive matters since any negative outcomes could prove extraordinarily costly both to DMIC, and ultimately CAL Board, if its insurance ran out.

I discuss the status of those pending major matters or locales here briefly (and also to inform any first-time reader):

Northern California asbestos-related bodily Injury (BI) cases: That number of open cases by then had passed 500 and new filings once again were increasing, with the unfortunate added factor that the quality of those case being much improved from the perspective of the plaintiffs' injuries. Mercifully, Reggie Fox, now a full partner at Klein Kelly, was in control and had the confidence of Austin Smith, General Counsel for our client, CAL Board, and Manny Garcia, Head of Major Claims for DMIC, the primary casualty insurer for CAL Board. My involvement, in terms of actual participation, in these Northern California BI cases was relatively minimal during this timeframe.

Southern California BI Cases: This number was increasing and we needed meetings with those plaintiff attorneys: however, the volume was less than 200, all in Los Angeles (LA) and Riverside Counties. Phil Hassard, a junior partner, had relocated to Pasadena and had these largely under control. He was in the good graces of Austin and Manny; but these would need my attention sooner, rather than later.

SCHOOLS BUILDINGS Class Action: Time was running on discovery. Mary Smith, another junior partner, and Martha Walsh, a senior associate, were attending meetings and interacting with Joel Tinker, my former US Coast Guard buddy and Klein Kelly partner, now with a growing firm in D.C.; and, when needed, associated with me. Martha and I had been selected by the lead defense counsel for all of the defendants in this class to act as lead counsel in recruiting, preparing and presenting expert witnesses on Science & Medicine for the defense of this case and other BUILDINGS cases which follow.

COLLEGES Class Action: This BUILDINGS litigation was in abeyance as the initial plaintiff, Clemson University, had been ruled to be an arm of its State of South Carolina causing the loss of federal court jurisdiction. No appeal followed, but based on their counsel's representations, we expected a private college to be named the next putative class representative in a new filing in the not distant future. I was not needed until then.

Los Angeles Unified School District (*LAUSD*): Another BUILDINGS case, but a single plaintiff, albeit huge!. Martha, who spent quite a bit of time in SoCAL, was taking the present lead, with my coaching {along with Mary and Tinker} for our new-ish second tier defendant KK Small, an extremely large Los Angeles-based construction products distributor, brought in after the first phase trial and the plaintiff dismissing our earlier client, CAL Board. Martha and I were trying to leverage our former client's positions to get our new client dismissed from this matter. So far, no success, but we did appear to have the *LAUSD* counsel somewhat stymied on how to move their case forward against specific defendants. The need for my help was minimal.

SoCAL BUILDINGS Cases: This growing case load was looming as a potential trap. The number of filings was increasing, especially as larger school districts began to file for themselves. I was needed here to try to rally defense leaders to adopt a previously successful course of action. The problems then included: the introduction of a whole new cadre of defense lawyers representing many defendants, some new to this type of litigation. Apparently, some, if not many, of these new firms saw this litigation as an opportunity for their own enrichment. Another major issue was the potential for joinders in a single action among school districts in high population counties in SoCal. I felt compelled to leave Mollie's side and go to Philadelphia for a key meeting on national defense coordination, including these cases.

DMIC LLOYDS Coverage Activity in London: Working with the leaders of DMIC, Quincy Franden-Jones, a London barrister, and Bradley Campbell of Thornton, Campbell & Thornton, London Solicitors, on the very eve of Mollie's illness onset, we had sent a letter, over Bradley's signature, to Cheshire & Booth, a London Placing Broker connected with a vast array of placements of annual casualty insurance coverage, including reinsurance, with many and varied Syndicates at Lloyds which specialized in a wide variety of coverages, including reinsurance, and which were thought of, by those unfamiliar with this coverage market, e.g., the general public, simply as LLOYDS. An unexpected response to that letter mandated that I travel to London without significant delay!

When I could find no way of avoiding Philadelphia and London, with the help and understanding of our lawyers, my CAL Board colleagues, Alicia Gomes in Philadelphia, Lead Counsel for the National Coordinating Counsel group, and the Brits in London, along with John O'Sullivan of DMIC's willingness to be flexible, we put together a schedule to accomplish all of this in one "long week," with the understanding that I might have to depart at any moment to be with Mollie if matters worsened sufficiently in my absence. Martha and Mary, from Sir Richard Doll's office, made the London arrangements and Lily, my assistant, dealt with the hotels, trains, cars and flights (overseen by Martha with whom I was in daily verbal touch, but had not seen for many weeks).

Carolyn had been gone intermittently for a week or two, but she managed to arrange to be in the area for that entire time I might be gone. (When Carolyn left the area for a "shoot," her Patrick would pack a bag and come to stay with our boys.

Carolyn had a car service take him to school in Pacific Heights and bring him home after his sports practices or other extracurricular activities.)

My mother, Kate, who was fairly devastated by Mollie's ordeal, moved in while I was gone. Kate wanted to help Mollie so badly, but her advancing years essentially allowed her only to care for herself, with little reserve of strength or stamina to be of much further assistance to others. Our *au pair*, Ingrid was incredibly helpful, acting as so much more than an *au pair*. We even were able to contact Yolanda, our nanny from the childrens' youth, and she agreed to help out. (If only we both did not work so many hours, perhaps we would have had neighbors or nearby good friends to assist; but alas, we did not.)

So it was that I felt compelled to embark on a trip that I only wished I could forego.

2

PHILADELPHIA FOR
COORDINATION MEETINGS

Martha Walsh and I met at the TWA Lounge at SFO. (We both got upgraded to First Class because our last minute tickets were full fare coach, upgraded to Business at purchase with miles, and because of our accumulated status over the past few years, now allowed even Martha to up-grade to First on her own. She was quite pleased with this capability to fly "in the front of the plane.")

When she first saw me, Martha started to do an intake of breath, but seeing my eyes at the last second, caught herself. She came up to me and said, "Ronan, are you certain that you should be making this trip?"

Me, "Yes. Why?"

Martha, her voice rising ever slow slightly as she spoke, "You do not look well. You've lost weight. So much weight! This situation with Mollie is really taking a toll on you!"

I took a deep breath and said, "Things have been bad. So very bad. We can talk more in our seats."

With that, Martha reached out and squeezed my arm, shaking her head ever so slightly. "Oh, Ronan," was all she said at that point.

— — —

Later, when we were settled in our favorite seats, 1A & 1B, before take-off, (Our "flying office" as I referred to those roomy seats) with coffee and a pack of scones each, I leaned toward

Martha and said in a whispered voice, "Mollie is doing poorly, but she will be surrounded by care givers, most of them being those that love her. She knows the import of this trip for me, the firm, and our clients. Plus, she loves London, and by my going, she said it would be a proxy for us as a couple. She even said to make sure that the two of us go to Wheeler's and have Dover sole while thinking of her." With those words, I had to stop talking, otherwise I was going to break down and cry.

Martha reached across the console separating us, took my hand and squeezed it, again saying, "Oh! Ronan" Then, "However are you dealing with this? I will do anything I can to help you. Help Mollie! Help your family?" Then, Martha began to choke up. I squeezed her hand for a second, then moved it back to the console, took a last sip of my coffee, and put my head back on the seat back, as if to sleep. The plane began to taxi, and soon we were airborne.

The flight attendant asked Martha about breakfast and that caused me to open my eyes. During my sleeplike hiatus, I had come to the conclusion that I needed to get a much better grip on myself if the reasons for my leaving Mollie were going to be justified by my conduct. With that thought, I ordered breakfast. I tried being conversational with Martha, perhaps made more uncomfortable than I expected to be by virtue of our hidden life as each other's secret lover, "Martha, I do need someone with whom to talk. Please remind me when we are truly alone to tell you about Carolyn."

Martha, "Who's Caroline?"

Me, "Later, please. Her name is Carolyn, not Caroline." A pause, then I said, "Why don't you tell me what you know about why the *Mullen* case strategy is being so widely rebuffed by so many SoCAL co-defendants and what you've been able to learn about who are the real decision makers for each of those new defendant entities?"

That got us going until the food arrived and we managed to

maintain some momentum as we ate. In the course of breakfast, I realized how little I had been eating. I made this mental note: you will need your strength to weather this crisis. You cannot allow yourself to lose your self-control or your self-esteem. Put your grief on hold as much as you can and do not show signs of weakness to your potential enemies. With that, I went back to Martha and our preparations.

A few minutes after noon, D.C. time, the flight attendant with whom we had flown before, stopped and asked if either of us wanted a drink. Martha looked at me, I thought for a second and said, "I'll have a Stoli on the rocks."

Martha said, "make mine a double, please." And looking at me, said, "His too!"

We had two doubles and a light lunch and I felt surprisingly better, at least physically, by the time we disembarked at Dulles International. We retrieved our bags and the driver who was waiting for us had a baggage cart to assist, so we were on our way to the Mayflower as quickly as one could exit Dulles in those days.

In the car, the driver was separated by glass from our conversation when Martha pushed a button. She said, "Please tell me about Carolyn!"

"Well, at this moment, Carolyn is probably sitting next to Mollie holding her hand. They have known each other little more than a year. Carolyn used to have her primary residence in Sausalito. That's where I met her. In fact, she was the first person in Northern California whom I was to meet. That was 1971. She was perhaps 18 and I was almost 27 in my last year of active Coast Guard service. It was on the roof deck parking area of the Cote d'Azur in Sausalito, when I asked her for directions to Tinker's apartment, where he lived during law school. We introduced ourselves, and she showed me the way to Tinker's door. Knowing that Tinker was in law school and probably had to prep for the next day, she asked if I wasn't busy later, could we perhaps meet for a drink at the No Name Bar on Bridgeway. After dinner, Tinker did need to prep for classes the next day. You remember that drill. So, Carolyn and I had those drinks together.

While I was on that very first trip, Tinker and Elaine got engaged and I met Sandra. Ultimately, I decided to go to law school and ended up at Hastings. Tinker and Elaine were going to get married soon after I was arriving, but they wanted me to have the second bedroom in their apartment. I was a little nervous about that. When I arrived with my things, who should be on that same rooftop parking lot but Carolyn. We had been failures at writing to each other. I was only slightly better with Sandra.

Carolyn smiled and seemed happy to see me. I told her I was going to go to law school. She asked if I was going to move in with Tinker knowing that his roommate had just graduated and left the area. I told her about the upcoming wedding and my discomfort. Carolyn told me her roommate was moving to Paris and she was desperate to find someone over twenty-one to move in with her as she was too young to sign her own lease in California, being just 19. So, she asked me on that spot. I agreed. We were roommates of sorts for almost three years, until I got back together with Mollie.

Carolyn was a great roommate for law school because she was gone so much. You see Carolyn became a very highly sought-after model, first bathing suits, then lingerie, then fashion, and finally high fashion.

Martha looked at me and her eyes grew wider, and she said, "Carolyn Tyne?"

"Yes."

"You lived for three years with Carolyn Tyne?"

"Yes."

"Why didn't you marry her?"

"I do not think she would want me to answer that. You see

Carolyn is, above all, a very private person. She is warm, considerate and a wonderful mother. She wanted to bring her son out to California last year for him to see where she got her start. She still owns that same apartment at the Cote d'Azur from when it went through a condo-conversion and she bought it. She uses it as her West Coast headquarters. She wanted her son to meet some people from her earlier life and I was the first one she thought of. Her son, Patrick, calls me Uncle Ronan. We stayed loosely in touch over the years. Mollie was never much into fashion. So, she did not know Carolyn by name. But Mollie came to be very fond of Carolyn, very quickly, and of her son, Patrick."

At this point, the car pulled in front of the Mayflower and we got our usual warm welcome from Clayton and highly efficient service up to our usual rooms on the eighth floor. It was about 3:30, with dinner set for 5:30 at Duke Ziebert's, a block away on the other side of Connecticut Avenue.

I made a series of calls, speaking to Mollie, Carolyn, Kate and Ingrid at home, with a promise to call back after our dinner meeting. At the office, I spoke first to Reggie about the BI cases in NorCal, then Lily, then Sean Kelly (Jerry Klein was out), then Mary, but no one could find Phil. I then called Austin Smith to let him know I definitely was going to the Philadelphia meeting. He wished me well and asked after Mollie. Manny and I were in frequent contact about the claims and cases, especially CAL Board's. (I was waiting until tomorrow to call John O'Sullivan about the DMIC/London portion of this trip.) Lastly, I called Martha at about 4:40. She let herself into the living room of my suite and took a seat on the couch while I occupied the chair.

She looked at me and said, "Now, I think you look like you'll live. This morning you looked so badly. I was truly worried for you. You really must eat. Your family needs you. You know they do, and will." Pause, "Is there anything else about Carolyn I need to know?"

I looked at Martha steadily, "When the time comes, if it does, there may be. But for now, you know the basic story of how she comes to be in Mollie's life at least as much as she is in mine. Shall we be the first to dinner?"

— — —

On the short walk back from a somewhat exhausting dinner discussing the key planning items for tomorrow's National Co-ordinating Counsel (NCC) meeting at Alicia Goines' Philadelphia office, I looked over at Martha who failed to respond to my question about leaving tomorrow morning. Her head was slanted a bit downward and she seemed lost in thought. Then, she stopped suddenly, grabbed my arm and spun me toward her. Her face was directly in front of mine, and said, "I know that you are hurting right now, that your mind must be locked in on Mollie and her fate, that it's taking all the strength you can muster to make this trip and do what you know needs to be done. I am certain that you feel that these critical tasks can only be done by you. Look at my eyes: I love you now more than ever, and I feel for you. I know you will not do anything with me on this trip, and I know it is to show your love and total commitment for the 'Love of Your Life.' But understand, if you need anything from me, do not be afraid to ask. I'm here for you and I will do anything I can to help you get through this ordeal." With that she let go of my arm and her hands went to her sides.

Before she could turn away, I said, "Thank you! I needed something like that at this moment."

— — —

The next morning, Martha and I arrived at Alicia's office in Liberty Place shortly after 9:00. She was up to date, doubtless from Martha, on what was going on in my life, and offered her sympathy. With that as well as coffee and pastries, we moved to the business at hand; what were the lines of authority and politics for dealing with the SoCAL BUILDINGS cases and their new, mostly local, counsel.

Alicia explained again her client's position that all the final strategy and tactics ran through her. Ours was the same for CAL Board, running through me. Wallboard appeared the same, now running through Sandra after her father's death and his firm's break-up. (But not 100% clear.) US Gypsum and WR Grace seemed to follow the same model, at least that's what their NCC counsel said at these meetings. But first in South Carolina, and now in Southern California, the effectiveness of their chains of command seemed less than clear. The same might be said of other companies in certain other jurisdictions. Alicia and I thought that this needed to be resolved very soon to get back to continuing to create a united defense front that would not undermine those of us who were willing to strive for dismissals of these cases early in the litigation process by motions to dismiss.

We agreed that Alicia would address the politics first and that I would lay out the tactics, and from that point onward we would play off each other, hopefully garnering some allies as we moved forward.

Things grew heated early on as several of the National Coordinating Counsel felt their authority was being questioned, but Martha who had been present for the SoCAL BUILDINGS defense counsel meetings set that record straight in no uncertain terms and things became more positive moving forward. In due course, with some limited arm twisting, we got all of the NCC's present to agree to utilizing the *Mullen* briefing model for demurrers in all of those SoCAL state court cases (*Mullen* was a class action case to remove all asbestos containing products from all single and double family homes in California filed by a war widow in a Northern California jurisdiction. It relied on U.S. EPA Regulations requiring such removal as its basis and did not plead that she had removed any such product, or, for that matter, that the products of all of the defendants in her suit were present in her house. Plus, this arguably embodied millions of homes, just in California.). We realized that the proof of NCC influence on local counsel itself would come at the next SoCAL defense meeting.

The NCC meeting was moving to a protracted end, but we had to leave early to catch our train. Alicia called for a short break. Several of the other attorneys, at that point, came forward with well-wishes for Mollie. (Not clear how they found out.) On the MetroLiner to D.C., Martha drank coffee and I had a bottle of water.

As soon as I got to my room, I called home. Mollie was awake and we chatted for a few minutes: I reported that the purpose for my attending that NCC meeting appeared to have been accomplished, or at least for my reporting to Mollie that was the case. Whether or not that turned out to be accurate actually awaited that next SoCAL defense counsel meeting at the end of next week, which Martha would attend. After Mollie, I spoke with Ingrid, on her way to collect the children from school, then to Kate, about whom I was worried would try to do too much, and finally to Carolyn. I asked her how Mollie was really doing and Carolyn reported she was having a fairly good day, but the radiation and chemo had really worn her down, so Mollie's stamina was virtually non-existent. I told Carolyn how grateful I was for all that she was doing to take care of her "new friend." To which Carolyn said, "I feel like I have known Mollie for more than this past decade, and most of that time I was either jealous or envious of her, and I cheated on her with her husband. Once we met in real life, she turned out to be one of the nicest, kindest, most genuine people I have ever met. And with her voice welling as if tears were about to start, Carolyn ended, "I love her. Now, Good Night!"

I called Martha. She came right over to my room. I thanked her for her speech last night, telling her how much I appreciated it. Then, I reached for Martha and pulled her into a gentle hug, holding her there for a long moment, pushed her back, kissed her forehead, and said, "Let's go get started on drinking. We can get a head start on Tinker and his boys!" Carlton got us a taxi to Georgia's. I talked to Martha about their great Southern Fried Chicken (still using bacon fat!).

— — —

The debriefing in D.C. that evening was intense with Martha, who was spending increased time in SoCAL on those BUILD-INGS cases, especially in my absence, contributing significantly. The main issue was what do we do if there are two courses of action proposed by local defense counsel as available despite the consensus from today's meeting?

My position was straight forward, quoting Admiral Lord Nelson's command at the outset of his British fleet's battle with the French in his war-turning triumph at Trafalgar: "Go straight at them!" In other words, we, and those who are with us, will go forward with the full *Mullen* approach, confer with plaintiff's counsel, divide up the briefing and file a Demurrer to each case as it came due. Martha was openly anxious about the aggressive tone we were taking as were Tinker's partners. But to me, and Tinker agreed in due course, the deciding factors were first, we have the NCC consensus (even if it does not include the newer smaller defendants) which should be persuasive in itself; and second, the precedent of *Mullen* and its success, including that heretofore granted Motion on Judicial Notice of key demo-graphic facts to be presented for each of these cases; and third, a Demurrer involves no real risk to their clients, other than some added money, if unsuccessful.

Finally, if holdouts still remain, we go forward without them. We changed topics to our UK scientific experts and Martha be-came far happier on that theme.

— — —

Back in my suite, after the needed phone calls and good
nights and a Bon Voyage or two, I felt depleted. Our flight the
next day was a daytime flight from Dulles to Heathrow, departing at 6:15 a.m. Our meeting with Cheshire & Booth on our proposed reinsurance document search was Thursday at 10:30 in
their offices in the "Old City" of London, a few hundred yards
from the Lloyds Building. DMIC's Chief Operating Officer and
its decision-maker on this project, John O'Sullivan, was arriving
early on Wednesday by flying a "Red-Eye" from Sky Harbor
Airport in Phoenix. Our plan was to meet him for a drink at his
hotel, The Berkeley, and then for drinks with Bradley Campbell
and Quincy, who were to join us about 7:00 that evening for a
final preparatory dinner. In the end, this was going to come
down to the persuasiveness of Quincy, the highly burnished reputation of Bradley Campbell of Thornton, Campbell & Thornton,
the seriousness, but reasonableness, of Desert Mutual Insurance,
and whatever *gravitas* Martha and I could bring to that meeting
tomorrow. (The decision to bring Martha proved somewhat pivotal. It was proposed by Bradley Campbell who openly stated
that her unexpected presence might have a disconcerting effect
on the brokerage people who rarely, if ever, dealt with women
across a conference table. He failed to allude to the fact that John
O'Sullivan and I were undoubtedly of Irish lineage, but of uncertain allegiance, especially significant in those days as the Irish
Republican Army (I.R. A.) was still very much in play.)

3

CRITICAL LONDON MEETINGS

So it was that we all came together in a private corner of the Berkeley's Dining Room, the evening of our London arrival. Quincy, much to my surprise, admitted that this was his first meal at The Berkeley, which elicited what I thought was a slightly smug grin from Bradley. We quickly agreed as to who would generally do what at the meeting (as the client of all of these others, John was advised multiple times that he should not address the broker's people unless it was suggested that he do so by one of the two British advisers with my concurrence). If we needed to confer among ourselves, Bradley should ask for a brief recess. But what we should strive to attain was an agreement to continue to negotiate on this trip, even if they did not seem ready to give us access to their policy records storage. Terms and conditions could begin to be worked out, but only if we could just get to some threshold agreement.

Much of this had been discussed in a fragmented sense in the course of drafting the initial letter and other preparation. (This is why lawyers spend so much time: being thorough and considering the alternatives, and their derivative options!) John O'Sullivan pushed his chair back at the end of dessert. It was 10:00 p.m. and I thought he would like to get his rest. Instead, he said, "My favorite hotel bar in London is not the American at the Savoy, but the Red Room at the Grosvenor House. Mr. O'Neill and Ms. Walsh are staying there. They are doubtless the most in need of rest, so I suggest we repair to that bar for a few nightcaps on Desert Mutual. That way they only have an elevator ride."

John rode in our taxi. He turned to me and said, "If these

gentlemen do not have the spine to ask for what we need tomorrow, Ronan, we are counting on you to push ahead. We do not want to lose what may be our only opportunity for reinsurance having gotten this far. Moreover, we really feel a need to get a sense that we are moving toward a resolution, and not merely stagnated in a protracted negotiation, at which we are given to understand, the British are experts."

— — —

After two more drinks, small talk and even some sports talk, Martha and I did go up to our rooms. I made the needed calls. Nothing was amiss, but no one said anything had improved. Mollie sounded sad, especially when I told her we had not gotten to Wheeler's, as yet. I couldn't cheer her up.

I called Martha. She came in the connecting door wearing her robe. I looked at her. She held the robe closed, and asked, "Is there anything I can do for you?"

I said, "Will you sleep with me? Just sleep? Hold me? I feel so exhausted and so concerned about all that comes next!"

Martha took my hand, led me to my bed, had me lay down, pulled covers on me, then went around to the other side, got under the covers (no robe), and laid up against me with her arm around my shoulder, and said, "Go to sleep. Try not to worry. Things are in God's hands. I'm here for you. Good night."

— — —

Bradley had arranged one of their firm's cars to take John, Martha and me to the offices of Cheshire & Booth. Martha and I were the first to be picked up. We were at the driveway of Grosvenor House at 9:55. The doorman tipped his cap and said, "Your car awaits you."

The cap must have served as a signal because the car, a Rolls

Royce judging by its hood ornament, pulled to a stop, the doorman opened the rear door, and I followed Martha into the rear
seat, tipping the doorman as I passed him. The driver, Stephen,
allowed that the car belonged to Thornton Campbell, and he had
been fully instructed in his duties. With that the glass moved
soundlessly between the compartments, leaving Martha and me
isolated. In a matter of more than a few turns, we were in the
driveway of The Berkeley and picked John up before 10:10. He
greeted us pleasantly and we were left to wonder about the end
of last evening for but a moment, when he said, "Our Brits, like
so many I have met over the years, all seem to have an almost
infinite capacity to absorb alcohol. They might have kept me in
the Red Room until its close, but for your both leaving. Ms.
Walsh, I do believe your parting took some of the air out of the
room. Still, we managed two more rounds, although Quincy
may have snuck one more in whilst the tab was being closed.
On matters of substance, you all missed nothing. How was your
breakfast?"

Bradley and Quincy were in the Cheshire & Booth waiting
room when we arrived. The time was 10:25. Bradley went up to
the receptionist and told her that our party was now fully in attendance. In turn, the receptionist picked up a telephone hand-
set, spoke a few words and told us that someone would be out
to meet us. In less than a minute a gentleman of average height
with a head full of very black hair stepped up and, appearing to
know Bradley, addressed him, "Good morning, Bradley, would
you be kind enough to introduce your guests?"

With a slight bow to each of us, he introduced first John O'-
Sullivan to Stanley Booth IV, Vice Chair of the firm bearing his
family's name. Mr. Booth proffered his hand and John shook it,
both bowing ever so slightly. My turn came next, then Martha
and last, Quincy. All with the slight bow (even Martha). Mr.
Booth turned and we followed him but a few steps into a highly
polished, windowless room of what appeared to be somewhat

darkly stained mahogany. A slightly oval conference table, seemingly with a capacity for twenty or more chairs, had five occupied on the far side of one end. Mr. Booth stopped at each of his people and gave us their name and title, then introducing each of us flawlessly. The last gentleman, who was as tall as me, with curly brown, slightly receding hair was Frederick Piece, Jr. of Piece Fields, Solicitors, apparently well- known to Barry as well, and of about the same age.

Barry sat across from Frederick Piece, John across from Stanley Booth, then me, then Quincy and last Martha. To my surprise, the first to speak was Stanley Booth, who said, in essence, "We have all read the letter from Mr. Franden-Jones and you, Barry. Some of us, more than once. Although this might come from Frederick, I feel we will have a better start if it comes from me. Even though we are not prepared to agree with all of you on very many points of agency law that you postulate in your letter, we are mindful of the vast difficulties facing the market now and doubtless in these forthcoming years. If we are to agree to negotiate something with you all, we must of needs have a non-disclosure agreement from the outset bearing in mind that all of this can be reduced to litigation, but that these conversations are needed to avoid that potential option, and must be a nullity for future use if we cannot get to a resolution. Agreed, Frederick?"

"I could not have said it better," was his short reply.

Bradley, "Do we need to caucus?"

I looked at John who glanced at me, and he nodded to me. I said, "I do not think a caucus on the principle itself is needed, but perhaps on the draft, if you happen to have one handy?"

Frederick Piece looked at me, nodded and said, "Clearly, Mr. O'Neill has read that if we opened with the need for an NDA, but we have no draft, we are not taking them seriously. We have one and will share it for review at the next break. It is not that long, nor do I believe it to be controversial. Why don't we move

onto the next topic agreeing that all that follows is covered by
that as yet unsigned NDA?"

The five us glanced quickly from one to the next, nods were
affirmative, and we proceeded.

— — —

The Cheshire & Booth people were far more forthcoming
than any of us had expected. We caucused briefly before beginning lunch. While Bradley and Martha reviewed the three-page
proposed NDA, I ventured a thought, "When Mr. Piece made
that observation about having a draft NDA prepared, I had a
flash for a moment, now it has returned. Suppose we are not the
first entity, American or otherwise, who has seen the need to go
down this path; and suppose that the DMIC letter seemed more
reasonable than others. Perhaps these gentlemen are trying to
find or identify, or even create, a path which offers them the
most safety, the least cost, and especially the highest probability
of avoiding future high stakes litigation. What with business clo-
sures, failures and deaths, this entire market is fraught with
peril. Let's try to push our 'advantage' to see how much head-
way we can gain today. What do you think, John? Quincy?
Bradley?"

With that, I nodded toward Martha. She filled the dead air
with, "Bradley and I see this agreement as essentially fair. It
would pass muster in California if these are considered settlement talks which is not expressed, but can be readily inferred
from the language."

Bradley chimed in, just as Quincy was about to speak, "In
light of this perhaps inspired proposition you advanced Ronan,
and assuming you are essentially accurate, then our accepting
this NDA on its face would create the basis for moving toward a
more detailed historic document storage organization disclosures
today, or if they need to parlay, by tomorrow perhaps. Quincy?"

Our barrister chimed in with, "Barclay and I have minds that run in the same direction. Too often negotiations become stymied by artificial barriers. I think we should try this out by accepting their NDA, with the sole caveat that both sides consider these 'potential settlement negotiations' to satisfy California and some other states' laws."

As we were talking, John was reading his copy of the NDA. He did not make a mark on it, and uttered, "I was worried about not making enough progress. I hear what you are saying, Ronan, and perhaps you are correct. You too, Bradley and Quincy. My only concern is if they are chess players, they may be so many moves ahead of us that we could be entrapping ourselves. One way to test my thesis might be to ask them for some sign of good faith."

Martha said, "Bradley and I can speak to the NDA and its basic acceptability as a position, not an acquiescence, using the settlement discussion as a stalking horse. Then, Quincy and Ronan can probe for something rising to the level of good faith, to show that both sides are willing to push for a successful outcome. John, how about that?"

Lunch gave an opportunity for strangers to learn a bit more about each other (these were the days before the internet). The Cheshire & Booth camp seemed reassured hearing that John's family had migrated to America from the south of Ireland four generations ago. They were less comfortable with my lineage. O'Neill was known to be of Ulster lineage, but largely Catholic to the core. When I told them of my family's emigration in the 1880's, entering through the port of Baltimore, and many of them staying there or moving north to Pennsylvania, my uncles fighting in the First Great War, and my father being in the U.S. Navy in the North Atlantic and African waters, then with Eisenhower in London, they all seemed vastly assured.

After another two hours of talks ensued, the Cheshire & Booth people, having accepted our acquiescence in the proposed

NDA with the addition of a single clause, asked to adjourn these meetings until tomorrow at 10:00 to allow them time to confer before making their next offer.

We walked to Bradley's office, only a few blocks away. We rode the same elevator up to the top floor and walked to the rear of the building to Bradley's magnificently appointed office with its spectacular view, and to a greeting from his assistant, Madeline Myles, "Very nice to see you again, Mr. O'Neill, and you, Mr. Frandsen-Jones. You must be Mr. O'Sullivan and you, Ms. Walsh. I am Madeline. May I get you some refreshments?"

Bradley looked up from his desk and said, "After today, I believe gin & tonic is in order. A very large one for me, Madeline, if you please."

When Quincy joined in quickly, we all did (and I dislike gin, but then I had never had Hendrick's, or had a gin drink as good as that one made by Madeline). After toasting what we hoped was a successful first day of meetings, John O'Sullivan said. "I was worried, and still am, but I feel somewhat assured about our direction. I do hope these feelings are not misplaced. What do you think they will offer?"

Quincy allowed that it could be some convoluted plan to keep us away from their documents themselves. Besides that, he was less certain. Bradley thought it would be something with some substance, but offered nothing concrete. I raised the issue of all of their documents that have no relationship to DMIC or its placements (we needed to have a position on that). Also, whatever they offered, would they let us try it out?

But with the second drink, the interest began to shift to dinner and what might come after tomorrow's meeting. I knew John O'Sullivan would not like to lose any momentum now that these opening negotiations seemed to be going somewhere. That would have to be a point to be mentioned before we broke up for the evening. Bradley intervened on my musings, "I asked our lunch chef to put together a few appetizers to hold us until dinner. Shall I ask Madeline to put them out now? Would you all like to dine together or get a good night's rest after last evening?"

Cold clams in an excellent sauce, potted shrimp and an Italian bread with a garlic combination spread provided a repast and several of us switched to a marvelous white French Burgundy, which Madeline offered to all. I looked at my watch, saw that it was after six and decided that at least I should head back to the hotel to make my calls. I advised the others and told Martha that she could stay with the others if she wished. She did. Madeline offered to call a taxi, then walk me out.

At the elevator, Madeline took my arm and turned me slightly to face her as the door closed, saying, "Bradley told me that your wife is very ill. I feel terribly for you. If you need anything whilst you are here, please do not hesitate to ask. Bradley is quite fond of you, and you know about me." As the elevator door opened, Madeline went first. A taxi was waiting at the curb, and the sky looked ominous. The temperature had dropped. The driver pushed the door open for me and I entered. Madeline leaned in to say farewell and gave me a light kiss on the cheek, "I hope your wife recovers and that I see you again under better circumstances. Take good care!"

— — —

My calls went to home first, then to Carolyn who was not there, and finally to Kate. My mother would never admit to it, but her strength and stamina were slowly beginning to slip. She was a bulwark in seeing to Mollie in my absence, but she did appreciate all that Carolyn and Ingrid did for Mollie as well. In the midst of a call with my partner Mary at my office, Martha knocked on my door. She looked like a drowned rat: dripping wet. I quickly finished with Mary and turned to offer Martha assistance, helping her out of her coat and placing it over a chair to dry. She undid her blouse, and turning her back to me, asked me to undo her bra clasp. Then, holding her clothes in place, turned her head, smiled a wicked smile and said, "I will be dry and tidy in about twenty minutes. Can we do a light dinner and talk?"

As the rain lashed the windows, we decided to go to the hotel dining room for our light dinner. Martha called down and we had a table within minutes. Martha and I had the new Grey Goose, a French vodka that was delightfully refreshing. We got extra ice on the side. Martha, "If you want to talk about her health, please feel free to tell me about Mollie. The few times I have met her, she has never been anything but wonderful to me. I do hope she is not suffering terribly."

I examined myself for a few seconds, Then, "Martha, I have avoided talking about Mollie outside of the family, and very little there. But you must promise that whatever we say will go no further. (Martha nodded.) I am afraid Mollie is dying and her treatments have become little more than a distraction for her at this point. I do not know what to do. I may have to stay home for some time when we get back. Worst of all, I have incredible difficulty bringing myself to talk to Mollie about the very real possibility of her end approaching. I am beside myself with pain for her: the anguish is overwhelming."

When my meal arrived, I could hardly eat. Martha said, "I'm so sorry I asked. I was just trying to help. Please forgive me. AND please try to eat. We'll need you to be strong for tomorrow."

Martha held me for a while when we went back to our rooms.

— — —

Cheshire & Booth were as ready for us the next day, as were we for them. In four plus hours, we had a tentative agreement.

The previous day's NDA was enlarged to include non-disclosure of any type for all documents unrelated to DMIC, any of its related entities, all of their coverages, syndicate names, lead underwriters, names, and any other entity in any manner related to DMIC coverage, either directly or indirectly, the related agents for any of those aforesaid entities as well as any Lloyds entities related to DMIC coverages in any manner whatsoever, either directly or indirectly, for all time. This new inclusion mimicked, but exceeded, that similar paragraph directly applicable to all DMIC related documents, and was intended to protect all entities unrelated to any DMIC document search in perpetuity.

That amended NDA became an intrinsic component of a term sheet memorializing that Friday's agreements, including the years of all underwritten coverage brokered in any manner by Cheshire & Booth, then by the master categories for the storage of various underwriting documents relating to coverages, e.g., marine vs non-marine, and the sub-categories within each, then by the syndicate or entity retaining or otherwise interacting with Cheshire & Booth (this latter being hopefully by alphabetical sequence, but known to be not always the case). The years of DMIC's needed search were explored for the existence of documents and assurances were given in writing as to the probability of those documents existing. Then, the term sheet went on to cover the initial test protocol of a search to ascertain the correctness and potential complexity of a search for the missing coverages to prove up all of DMIC's various missing reinsurance. (We saw no need to look behind the "reinsuring syndicates" as that should prove to be the task of each implicated syndicate requiring funds to meet its own obligations. Those identities were also said to be maintained by an official office at Lloyds.)

The drafting took until almost 4:00 with a short break for box lunches as drafts were written, edited, negotiated and rewritten. All documents were agreed to be tentative and subject to

revisions based on the test search, and other heretofore uncon-
sidered circumstances. Stanley Booth IV signed for Cheshire &
Booth, with a written assent from Frederick Piece, Jr. John O'-
Sullivan signed for Desert Mutual Insurance Company, with the
assent by Bradley Campbell.

Duplicate originals were created and as they were sent out
for copying, a man in livery appeared with a tray of fluted
glasses, followed by another man carrying a large bucket with
four bottles of fine champagne. Glasses were filled, toasts made,
and to outsiders, it might appear that friendships were being
forged. I wondered what would happen based on the putative
test search. At any rate, we had an accomplishment: more than
my greatest expectation for an opening gambit.

— — —

Our negotiating team had drinks at the American Bar in the
Savoy Hotel, then walked a few blocks down Fleet Street to that
local Wheeler's where the three Americans had Dover sole and
the two Brits had fish & chips. Our taxi dropped John at the
Berkeley Hotel and we proceeded directly back to Grosvenor
House to pack for our twelve hour flight home the next day, due
to depart at 11:00 a.m.

Martha asked for one last drink in the Red Room before re-
pairing to our rooms to begin packing. We both had a double
Johnnie Walker Black on a few ice cubes, and Martha toasted our
effort, "Ronan, you were magnificent. I learned so much from
watching and listening to you. I could see you bring our preparation into play at crucial junctures. We ended up with so much
more than we had anticipated. Still, what do you really expect
from the test search?"

I had fended off any predictions at the team dinner, as did
the others. Even Quincy, who amongst us knew more about the
Lloyds market itself, had no real experience with this area of our

current confrontation. My answer, "I know that we don't know. I know from what Quincy did tell us that the terminology being used in the term sheet was essentially accurate. But our inability to get any realistic estimate of the number of pages of stored documents is quite unnerving. Plus, the level of organization, as they seemingly defined it, does not provide very much reassurance as to how our search team will actually go about locating the DMIC coverage documents. That said: one thing we really do need to consider is who will comprise our search team for the test. Any thoughts on that?"

Martha said, "Maybe we can save that one for the flight home tomorrow and I'll sleep on it tonight. Why don't we get going. You have a lot of calls to make."

So, Martha signed the check adding a tip and we rode up together. At her door, Martha asked, "Do you want me to hug you tonight?"

I thought for a second and said, "Yes."

The calls were long with home, especially Mollie, who drew nothing positive from my telling her about dinner at a different Wheeler's. I could sense, despite her not expressing any complaint, that her suffering was increasing virtually every day. Ingrid and Kate sounded anguished. They put Carolyn on the line next, before I could talk to any of the children. Carolyn said, "Oh! Ronan, you must get home tomorrow. Mollie is distraught without you. I must tell you this, and I do not want to, but I do not think Mollie has much time left. I am so afraid for her. I hope you think it OK knowing I am a Lesbian, but I think if I sleep with Mollie tonight, that might help her a bit. Would that be OK with you?"

I had no other possible reaction after absorbing Carolyn's words, "Of course, you can sleep with her. I so much appreciate your doing so!" We said a few more things and I inquired further as to how my children were reacting. Each woman had a differing view, but all agreed that the older two were beginning to suspect the worst was imminent, but they were less clear about the twins. At that point, I spoke to each one of them from the twins to the oldest. I told them nothing specific, but did tell them to be ever so nice and considerate of their mother who was very sick.

When I hung up, I was about to cry, but Martha entered through the connecting door. She was in tears, "I heard you with Carolyn when I started to come in a few minutes ago thinking you were finished your calls. Oh my God! This is too sad for words." She came over and burying her face in my shoulder hugged me as she shuddered with tears. Then, "Please clean-up for bed. I will hold you very tightly tonight!"

She did.

4

THE LOVE OF MY LIFE

That Saturday night after flying from Heathrow to SFO, I was on heightened awareness for Mollie. She was delighted to see me and I could see her perk up visibly as I bent over the couch to kiss her on the lips. I was careful not to touch her so as to cause any needless pain, but putting my hand right next to her side as we kissed, I could feel her shaking ever so slightly. As I pulled back, I could see her tears, but they were barely visible through my own.

I sat next to her and told her about our last dinner at a different Wheeler's and how I could not stop thinking about her. Mollie would not let go of my hand. She squeezed it. I squeezed back, as softly as I could. I asked if I could go speak to the children and she said, "Yes. Would I please send Carolyn in?" I did.

Robert was almost 13 and in 8th grade. Maeve, our oldest daughter was 14 and in 9th grade at University High School in the City (a year behind Carolyn's Patrick). We sat in the kitchen in the breakfast nook. Kate was with the twins. Both of my older children looked incredibly anxious. I began, "Your mother is very sick...." And with those few words, Maeve broke down and started crying uncontrollably.

Robert said, "She thinks Mom is going to die and she's been getting worse every night since you've been gone. I didn't know what to tell her."

I moved my chair next to Maeve so I could put my arm around her shoulders and leaned her head on my shoulder. At first, I only made sounds to try to comfort her, but I knew I had to tell them and this was the time. I picked Maeve's chin up with

my hand and tried to wipe her tears with a tissue that had mag-
ically appeared in my free hand. I helped her to sit up straight,
and tried again, "Her doctor has done everything he can for
Mom. So have all the other doctors, and the hospital, and I do
not want to tell you this, but you must know I have to. The like-
lihood is that your mother is going to die, fairly soon."

Maeve just stared at me through red, tear-rimmed eyes.
Robert's hands were clasped fast on the table, then his head
dropped onto his arms and I could hear his sobbing, while his
head and body shook. Maeve, barely able to say the words, in a
croaking voice, "I knew it. Oh my God, I knew it." She just continued to stare at me, her body wavering, even quivering

I moved between them and put an arm around each and the
three of us had a good cry.

Then came the even harder part, "Look. You are both old
enough that we thought you should know. The twins, Patrick
and especially Meaghan, are too young to know until the very
end. That's not to say that this is going to happen right now, but
it does seem that it will be soon, unless we get a miracle. So, your
Mom knows I am telling you. She is heart-broken, but we feel
you will be stronger for knowing now and by getting yourselves
prepared for when that dreadful moment comes. Now, you
must not tell the Twins. You can try to let them know that this is
serious, but that's more than enough. Leave it to me to tell them
when I feel it can no longer be avoided." I paused, then, "Mom
is with Carolyn. Do you like her?"

Maeve. "She's fine. Mom thinks she's great. She is always
nice and her Patrick is wonderful. What shall we say to Mom?"

Robert perked up for my answer, "You don't need to tell her
anything. You know how much she loves you, each of you. She
knows you love her. Just try to make her comfortable and tell
her about those things that she always finds interesting, like
school and your activities. The hardest part will be when you go
to tell her 'Good night' each night."

Next, I saw Kate and gave her a great hug, followed by hugs and kisses with the twins. Kate had their minds focused on school and I did nothing to disturb that mood. I stopped and asked Ingrid how she was doing, told her how much we had always appreciated her, and how much she would be needed in the days and weeks ahead.

Then, Carolyn left Mollie and Ingrid went into the family room where Mollie rested lying on the couch, and one of the them could help her to the facility nearby, when needed. Carolyn looked at me and said, "We need to talk." I followed Carolyn into the office that Mollie and I shared. "Mollie told me what she says she told you right before you had to go on this crucial trip, and I do believe for your career and the fortunes of your family that it was crucial. But, Mollie has been devastated here without you. Firstly, you cannot leave her for very long, if at all, until this is over, and I fear that will be all too soon. Second, she told me about my Patrick. Mollie, being Mollie, believes that my life has been one long sacrifice for Patrick, and indirectly for you. That's not as true as it may sound at the moment. But third, and please let me finish, she told me she asked you to marry me. I think you know all this, but I want you to understand. I am not at all certain what I shall do. Please do not look at me that way! And you must promise me now, again, that Patrick will not find out that you are his father. He is still far too young!"

"Oh, Ronan! This is so much more than I bargained for. Perhaps this is penance in advance. At any rate, know that I love your Mollie, now a bit my Mollie, and I still love you. I will be here for you as long as I am needed, but at some point, I must resume my career. Your turn: you have been very patient."

I had been thinking as I listened that Carolyn had given vent to a great many feelings, and the last thing I wanted was to upset her as she had been so much a stalwart during Mollie's tribulations, so I reached out, "Carolyn, let me start by saying that I love you, and always will. I love Patrick. I would do nothing to hurt him or you. I think you already knew that. I understand about your career, and the sacrifices you have made to be here now. They are no small thing. As to all the rest: I believe we must approach each event in its own time. Now for me: Mollie must be my primary focus, then my children, then my home and my family. As to that last group, after all you have done, my children and I will always consider Patrick and you as part of our family. As to 'any us,' that will need to await the end of this phase of our lives, however much time that may cover. I hope you think that fair?"

Carolyn reached down and took my hands in hers, looked up at my face, seeking my eyes, and said, "Ronan, you seem very wise at this moment. I do not know how you do it, but you convey such appropriate feelings for those about whom you care. I must be away for four days. Can I count on Patrick being OK here with you all while I am gone to New York? I must go to do this shoot: a cover for *Vogue* with a high fashion layout inside, and I will need to see Vera."

"Of course," I responded.

— — —

After dinner, which I ate next to Mollie, she asked me to carry her up to our room so she could watch me unpack and get ready for bed. As she watched, she reminisced in a low, but not sad, voice about our many business travels, but mostly about our two trips to England. When I went to say a nighttime greeting to the children and hopefully provide some level of reassurance to the twins, Ingrid helped ready Mollie for her night's sleep, including her medications.

I got into bed and laid down next to my Mollie, putting my arm as lightly around her as I could. She snuggled back into me ever so slightly and I heard her say, "I will love you for all eternity."

— — —

On our eighth night together, we followed the same formula as the preceding seven nights, but with one difference, as I heard her barely whisper, "Good-Bye, Love of My Life. I will Love You for ALL Eternity."

I squeezed my Mollie ever so lightly, and whispered, "God go with you, Love of My Life. I shall be with you for all Eternity."

— — —

That next first light, I was awake and got up, went around our bed, put my arm under my Mollie who weighed next to nothing, held her for a last time, cried for her, composed myself, went and got Ingrid and asked her to come to our room. Together we sat Mollie fairly upright, made certain that her eyes were closed, so that she looked like she was resting. Ingrid fixed her hair, and I went to get Kate in the guest room. She was awake and ready. She embraced me and I wondered how many mornings she had awakened already in preparation for this moment. I asked her to go to our room to console the children as I brought them in to say their first eternal good-byes to their mother. First, it was Maeve I sought, but Meaghan seemed to know and came with us. Robert's door opened and he followed. Our Patrick was the last, and I went to get him. He was the second born twin and the baby of the family. He took it the worst, but not as badly as I thought it could have been.

I called Carolyn and she brought Patrick. I called my partners and Lily, Mollie's brother, Brad, and lastly Martha.

A pall of sadness descended over all of us, but in memory of OUR MOLLIE, I could not allow it to persist. In three days, we scattered Mollie's ashes from the stern of the USCG Cutter Cape

Hatteras into the air of the Golden Gate and watched as the
breeze caused them to disburse easterly toward the Bridge. At
that moment looking up at the Bridge, I swore I could hear Mollie calling my name, "Ronan! No, Ronan!" as she had those
many years before.

At four o'clock that same day, we held a memorial for Mollie
at Marines Memorial Club to celebrate her life.

— — —

My problem was Mollie's life was over, but mine was not.

— — —

*The next day I spent two hours with Dr. Arnaud. During the weeks
I have related above, other than Mollie's requiem services, I did not see
Dr. Arnaud. However, we spoke with some frequency, and thanks to
her record keeping, I have related the first part of this book about Mollie
with more clarity than otherwise would have been possible. Dr. Arnaud
was, as always, an enormous aid at that most trying of times.*

— — —

5

ADJUSTMENTS

In the days following Mollie's funeral and memorial, I was at a loss emotionally. Kate tried to bestir me. So did the two older children. Carolyn had left the evening of the memorial for a shoot in Paris and another in New York City. We talked briefly on a few occasions, but the time differences played havoc with that. (Also, she went to check out her Connecticut property and to visit Vera during her brief free time on her New York City shoot.) Carolyn's Patrick was terribly troubled. (He had thought his father dead before his birth, so he had never faced the crisis of losing a close loved one.) In preparing all of Mollie's children for her death, we all, including Carolyn, had done our best. But, somehow, Patrick, not much older and with no experience of significant loss, seemed omitted from much of this. As a result, he seemed to have greater difficulty coping in those initial days, much the same as me.

So, it was that he came to me with questions that I was not expecting about death, Heaven, Hell and the like. He even asked about his father's soul, once we broached the subjects of faith, hope and the supernatural. As a net result of those days of early mourning, I began to shift my attention from myself to the younger generation, trying to satisfy, as best I could, their varying needs at this most troubling time; especially Patrick Tyne, who appeared to have little or no religious upbringing to provide him with any emotional foundation, including whatever insulation against death Christianity might provide.

— — —

Less than a week after Mollie's last rites were completed, I received a call from Reggie Foxx, my team's second ranking partner, seeking a lunch with Mary, Phil, Martha and me at the Buckeye, nearby my home, the very next day. That lunch meeting began to accelerate my healing process by getting me back into some kind of working groove; which, in turn, started to cause me to cut back on so much self-reflection. It was a late lunch and all four of those lawyers had cleared their calendars for the balance of the day. (They had all been at Mollie's Memorial and stood on the Bridge to watch her ashes scattered.) This day, however, they acted as if I needed a major boost to my spirits, which started with cocktails. Many orders of Oysters Bingo, a house specialty and a favorite of Mollie and me, stood up well to the drinks. The talk about the office started off lightly, including some good-natured banter. The main course arrived and we ate grilled halibut, poached salmon and shrimp scampi family style. Crisp, cold white wine was great and the shift in our conversation to more serious matters was hardly apparent. After almost two hours, I realized I should not drink any more. I was out of practice. When the check arrived, I reached for it, but our server handed it deliberately to Reggie, who said, "Sean and Jerry thought this was a good idea, so this lunch is on the Firm. Everyone wants you back, but we all know that there is so much you still need to do. Sean and Jerry said, and we support them, do not come back until you're ready. We'll continue to take care of business; and, as I'm sure you know, by their presence at the Memorial, that your clients understand. Now, do you want a ride home?"

My response, "CDR Foxx, Mary, Phil and Martha, thank you all for being here and for all of your support. I have asked our retired first nanny, Yolanda, to come back for a few months while we all sort things out. As you may know, Mollie became very fond of Carolyn over the last year or so.

"Carolyn is travelling for work, and will return on Sunday.

Her Patrick is staying with us, for now, and Carolyn may move in for a while to help. That's unclear. At any rate, I need to commit. So, plan to see me in a week from next Monday. I may not be full time right away; but, as we all know, the legal system waits for no one. Please thank Jerry and Sean. But mostly, thank you all again for this lunch. Please know how much all of this means to me. I appreciate each of you!"

— — —

That Sunday, I brought Patrick Tyne to await his mother at the Cote d'Azur. We arrived shortly before Carolyn, and when she entered, she was almost startled. Her arms were full of packages, and she fumbled with her keys and purse. Once she put all of these things down, she turned and her Patrick rushed into her arms, a not so little boy any longer, five inches or more taller than his seventy inch tall Mom. They embraced for what seemed like long minutes. Both may have cried a bit. Patrick backed away and looked at me. Carolyn looked strained, tired and saddened. She put out her arms to me and I went to her to be held. After a short time, Patrick joined in for a three-way hug. Carolyn was getting a bit squashed by two large men, so she shook herself free, saying, "I was not expecting you both to be here waiting for me. I was hoping to freshen up, get somewhat organized, and make my way to your place, Ronan. Patrick, could you grab my other two bags while I talk to Uncle Ronan for a minute or two?"

Patrick found where Carolyn had sat those keys and departed, allowing that he would like a breath of air for a few minutes. I asked, "Are you alright that we were here?"

Carolyn said, "We really do need to talk at some length in the days ahead. I have signed some new contracts which will give me more freedom to spend time out here. They pay extremely well. I cannot get Mollie out of my head. But more important to me, I have resolved that I cannot lose you again. We have a great deal to work out. It's so soon, and there are so many issues. Am I on the right track with you?"

With that, Carolyn took one step to me, we embraced and I kissed her, saying, "I agree. There is so much to discuss in the days and weeks ahead. You do know I do love you deeply."

I left when Patrick got back with Carolyn's baggage. They said they would be no more than an hour behind me. When they arrived, all four children, Ingrid and Kate were there to greet Carolyn. Even Kate had begun to think of Carolyn's Patrick as part of the family, he was spending so much of his time with us.

We had a cook-out, but no basketball in the driveway quite yet. Kate left before dark. Ingrid asked if she should make up a guest bed in Kate's room for Carolyn who nodded agreeably (no doubt being on Eastern time) and with that the children all began to retire. To each one, I would bid, "Good night, (a name), and God Bless You. Sleep well and see you in the morning."

Patrick Tyne was the last to leave and I said the same Good Night and Blessing to him. Carolyn waited until he was upstairs and asked me about the blessing. I told her about his lack of religion and how we had been talking –nothing too serious. She allowed that with her difficult childhood, religion had escaped her and she had never done anything about it; but now, she might be ready to give it a try. Then, she stretched and said how tired she was, and would I mind if she went to bed. When she rose, I got up and we came together for a hug and a kiss of affection. She moved toward the first floor guest bedroom. I turned out the lights and went upstairs to "our Bed." My last thought before sleep claimed me was that perhaps we all would need to move, as this house would always be "Mollie's house."

— — —

Carolyn was out and about a great deal her first few days

back in the area. Moreover, she was not at all chatty about what she was up to. Late on the Friday morning before the Monday when I was to return to the office, and while I was reading a package of mail from the office, Carolyn asked me, sounding quite serious, if we could, "Talk Now, Please!"

I put everything down, she sat across the family room game table from me and I gave her my undivided attention. Carolyn sat up straight, more erect than usual, which captured my attention even more. She began, "Ronan, I have spent more time thinking than I have been given to doing for most of my life, that is until these last months. Not that I have not planned in my past. I am a somewhat natural planner and some of what I am about to say will bear that out, so please try to hear me out without too much interrupting, if you can." Carolyn squirmed, I almost laughed. I had never seen her acting anything like that, almost nervous. She continued, "Ronan, I want you to marry me when you are ready." My jaw dropped and she held up her hand, "If it proves possible, I will renounce my Lesbianism. Not because I want to, but as a demonstration of how much I love you. Vera is extremely unhappy, and Lisette just does not believe I can do it. But they both say they understand. Go ahead, I am sure you feel the need to speak already."

So, I did, "Just so you know I too have been thinking about our marrying as a potential event in the foreseeable future. But please rest assured that I would never ask you to renounce who you are, or those you love. How could I? Think about us, especially me, the entire time I was married to Mollie. None of what we did meant I loved Mollie any less. Why should this change for you now? But thank you for your agreement to do so without having me figure out how or when to ask. By the way, do you have a timeframe in mind?"

Carolyn squirmed again, then, "I am not surprised about how you feel about my lifestyle. You have never come close to criticizing me, or my sexual preference! The next thing is where we would live. Now that you have told me how you feel, I shall keep the Cote d'Azur for Vera and Lisette, when or if they visit. It will be my separate property and I will hold it in joint tenancy with Patrick. Ultimately, it will belong to him, if he wants it, and if he ever learns about his true parentage. But I would want us to have our own home, so as an advance on your wedding present now, I am giving you a half interest in a house on which I will be closing in a few weeks. It's in Ross, just off Shady Lane. Seven bedrooms and eight baths, plus numerous other rooms, quite old. But sitting high enough to escape any potential floods from Corte Madera Creek. It will need some real work. I plan two in-law units on the ground floor for Ingrid and Kate, as necessary. I suggest we marry no later than when it nears the time to move in. There: I am finished for now."

"How can we afford a place like that?" I responded.

"Well. You could sell this house when we are close to moving and that would help, if you want to. But if you do not have trusts for each of your children, that might be a better time to set them up. You see, I have enough money to cover everything. Please recall that Patrick already has a trust, fully funded for his welfare, whenever something happens to me. So, with my new contracts and a somewhat lighter workload, I will earn just under one million dollars this year and I will need all of these write-offs!"

I think my jaw dropped. Carolyn was so many moves far ahead of me.

— — —

That very afternoon, I had a session with Dr. Arnaud, whom I had begun to address as Margo at her request. When I explained all that Carolyn had been up to, the good doctor allowed that Carolyn had surely loved me for many years: perhaps at first not even realizing it. Perhaps when she began to come to that realization, Sandra was there.

Then came Patrick, but Mollie had seamlessly replaced Sandra. "Somewhere, along her life's journey, Carolyn became ever more fully aware of her love for you, Ronan. You can only reciprocate now by letting Carolyn show you her manifestation of that love. She appears to care for you and Mollie's children, even Ingrid and your mother. Moreover, you were right: Carolyn did come to love Mollie. Please be careful, Ronan. Please be very careful, whatever you decide, do not let Carolyn get away somehow."

— — —

6

CENTRAL WESLEYAN COLLEGE and SOCAL

At the end of my first week back in the office, CAL Board was served with a new and more than slightly redrafted class action complaint in federal court in South Carolina, doubtless intended to replace the previously dismissed *Clemson* unverified Complaint. The matter was assigned to Judge Blatt, formerly the senior partner of Lead Plaintiff Attorney Ron Motley's original firm, and whom some of the locals allowed was a mite envious of Mr. Motley's financial success on much of which the judge had missed out by his moving up to the bench. Still, I had the sense that a plaintiff firm judge was not a great omen for this putative class action.

Mary was in the office. Martha was in Riverside. I asked Lily to send a copy to Tinker and to Josh Smoulders, our South Carolina local counsel in Greenville, and asked Mary to set up a call for Monday at 10:00 as I would be getting back to work ever more full time. A quick perusal of this complaint brought by a small religiously affiliated college, Central Wesleyan, revealed that it had a class definition which sought to exclude colleges and universities which derived operational funding from one, or more, state entities on an annually recurring basis. I read that definition twice, but was not certain what they were trying to avoid if anything more than a Clemson-like financial situation. (Certainly, the class could be substantially smaller as would its members, but identifying the class members, based on this definition, might not prove reliable, if even possible!)

The next Monday when we all talked about the class definition as pleaded, no one had a sense of certainty about what was

not meant to be in it, but it certainly appeared to exclude the gi-
gantic state founded, or funded, institutions (probably a certain
loser to try as a named plaintiff, and by extension, too risky to
try to keep in the class itself). Certainly, this new definition was
unclear and would be subject to a motion to dismiss for uncertainty. Yet the better issue was what also could be attacked in
the motion to dismiss. The major hole, an earmark of the *Mullen*
decision, appeared to be that Central Wesleyan had not pleaded
that it had suffered any actual injury, and thereby damages, as
of its pleading date! (That failure begged another point: if Central Wesleyan did plead that it had suffered injury, could it then
only represent those institutions similarly injured, and what
would be the legal yardstick for that similarity?) So, on we debated in a call lasting almost two hours. What to do next? Would
the defense meet again? What firms would be defense liaison?

   With money at a premium for Desert Mutual (and without
discussing that detail with those on the call), I suggested that
our team should not be poised to take on that lead pleading role.
I suggested to Josh that he get a hold of the "Leaders from the
Clemson matter" and get their thoughts on the "What Next?" as
well as someone getting a date certain for all defense interests to
file their responsive pleadings. We also would talk in a few days
about pleading options and the impact of Judge Blatt. We broke
after that with a promise from Josh to get back to me very quickly.

— — —

   LAUSD seemed under control from a litigation perspective
as its plaintiff counsel struggled to find a financially viable
methodology to undertake product identification in the verita-
bly total absence of documents from their client's contractors,
sub-contractors and material suppliers. Our latest client was in
the supplier category, but most, if not all, of its sales went to various types of contractor entities at construction sites, not to

school districts. Moreover, our client did not retain documents past fifteen years because of California statutes barring long-tail litigation of construction cases.

Martha had an excellent grip on *LAUSD*, but she wanted help on all of the other school district cases as the defense in those was not moving to proceed with a united front. A meeting was set up for San Diego for the following week, and she wanted me to attend to make a final effort to convince those newer defendants of the wisdom of trying a Demurrer first before committing to an Answer to the Complaints. These were interesting cases as San Diego, Orange, Riverside and San Bernardino, all had numerous school districts which had joined with each other in bringing their individual county-wide suits. (We were given to understand that each of those counties had school districts which were not interested in joining those lawsuits, but instead planned to rely on a recovery from the nationwide SCHOOLS class action venued in Philadelphia.) I called Manny and asked if I could join Martha for those meetings in San Diego in a last ditch effort to create some consensus in favor of a joint responsive pleading to each of these new SoCAL initiatives. Manny agreed, but in our call, he asked if I was getting to the point where I might be ready to go back to London to see if we could create an actual plan, with a start-up date, to get the search for DMIC's reinsurance documents at Cheshire & Booth up and running. I thought for a moment and then asked if I could have just a few more weeks to smooth things further at home. He said there would be no problem with that.

When I called Martha and told her about what Manny had said, she seemed to perk up just a bit, and asked if she should set up meetings with our Euro-experts? Much time had passed since we had visited with them, and especially Dr. Bignon to whom we owed a briefing. So, I allowed that made good sense and she should see what she could put together out at the three or four week mark.

— — —

Many other tasks were taking small parts of my time as I tried to get back up to speed, but the SCHOOLS class and another National Coordinating Counsel meeting loomed on the horizon as well. At this point, I realized that the resumption of frequent traveling was going to be hard on me, and perhaps harder on my family. How was I to deal with all of this?

— — —

I called Carolyn. She was in town staying for a few nights at her Cote d'Azur condo in Sausalito. I asked her if we could talk and she asked if I would like to come over to her place on my way home. I asked if now was OK? She agreed. Thirty-five minutes later, I knocked on her door. I asked about Patrick and she told me he was spending the week at my house to allow her to get her work done. We chatted for a few moments. Then I got to my point explaining my dilemma about travel and the children. I was sitting ninety degrees from her in a chair while she sat at the end of a sofa not far from me. She patted the sofa seat next to her and I moved there. Carolyn turned her face to me. Held my chin with a firm left hand so I faced her straight on, and ever so slowly, she brought her face up to mine and kissed me. We stayed that way for what seemed minutes. She pulled back ever so slightly, and said, "I can move in now if you want. All you have to do is ask."

We made love there on her couch. When I sat up, I asked, "Will you move in very soon?" She told me next week. I smiled and asked her to follow me home by thirty minutes or so, to allow me to tell Kate, Ingrid and Yolanda. I suggested that together, we tell the children all at once. She kept nodding her head, and when I looked at her eyes, tears had formed.

She pulled my face down to hers, and said, "I am so in love with you! Whatever you want!"

— — —

As soon as I got home, I asked Kate and Ingrid to join me. Yolanda had gone home for the day. I got them seated for a minute, and using a direct approach telling them Mollie's plan, Carolyn's acquiescence in it, and that I had agreed with Mollie, and now with Carolyn, that we would marry when we were about to move into our new home. But details of that move could wait until we told the children: should I wait for Carolyn? They each said "yes," because Carolyn's Patrick was upstairs with the boys!

So, Carolyn arrived and we caused everyone to be assembled in our family living room. Kate and Ingrid were strategically deployed among my children. Carolyn sat next to me, with her Patrick on her other side. I began with Mollie's wishes. The tears started with Maeve and Meaghan. Not long after them, came Patrick. When I told them that Carolyn and I were going to marry, it was like a bolt of electricity hit each of my children. I paused for a few seconds. Carolyn spoke, "I love your father. I loved your mother. I honor her memory and always will. I can never replace her. But I will try to do my best for your father and for each of you."

Meaghan got up and went over to Carolyn and gave her a hug. Maeve followed. Then Patrick, and last, Robert. (Only Robert never cried during this time. Everyone else did. I decided then and there that I would need to follow up on this soon with him. I wanted no hard feelings among the children. This was all going so fast for them!)

We waited a few days to tell them about the move. That caused its own set of issues!

— — —

When I told Margo about all of this, she was intensely supportive of both Carolyn and me, and especially of our candor in dealing with the children. Moreover, she stressed the need for continuing reassuranes with regard to our residential move as each child had evolved roots and friendships in Mill Valley and the move might prove quite hard for each one of them.

7

ON THE ROAD AGAIN

It was the foggy season in San Diego. We got good rates at the Del Coronado. As seemingly always, Martha had arranged adjoining rooms with a connecting door. Mine was the larger corner room with a breathtaking view down the beach and out to the ocean. The bellman had dropped Martha first and then brought me to my room, a mini-suite of sorts with a very usable, large sitting area. After waiting long enough for the bellman to explain my accoutrements, hang my clothes and get ice, Martha knocked on our connecting door. I walked over to it, flipped the lock to open and ushered Martha into my rooms. She asked, "Can I check out your view from the deck?"

Martha loosened her blouse and freed it from her slacks. As she went out on the deck, she dropped her top on a chair inside the deck door. As I looked at her, I could see she was wearing a swimsuit under her outfit, at least a swim top. After a quick survey, she returned to the door, looked at me, and asked, "I am at a loss as to what happens next. For several years, we would have at least been in each other's arms by now. After all you have been through, I guess I am trying to tell you that I am willing to wait, or do whatever it might be that you want of me. You have always been thoughtful, even kind, now it's my turn."

Martha's face had the outline of a shy smile. I looked at her for at least thirty seconds, then rose, went over to her, took both of her hands and drew her into the room, sitting her in a chair facing mine. All that while, I smiled, but did not speak. I pulled my chair closer to hers, then leaned down and gave her a full kiss on the lips, and said, "Martha, in spite of all that has happened, I have never stopped caring about you. I want you to know that, and it means I still love you, and still want you. But a great deal has been going on which must be unknown to you." Taking her hands in mine, and looking her square in those beautiful eyes, I continued, "For reasons you do not need to know in detail, Mollie disliked Sandra intensely. Mollie was afraid that when she was gone, Sandra would make an effort to win me back and succeed. Mollie saw that as nothing more than an eventual emotional disaster for me based on when Mollie fortuitously found me after Sandra had finished trying to have her way with me after law school."

Martha's eyes had widened, and she started to talk, but I held up my index finger to stop her. "When Mollie realized she was probably going to die, she devised a plan. You know that Mollie became increasingly fond of Carolyn. She convinced Carolyn that when she died, that Carolyn should marry me. You see, Carolyn has always been a Lesbian, but she had one man of whom she was fond and with whom she would have sex. That went on over many years, unknown to everyone. Except now you know that man was me. Carolyn agreed with Mollie to do what she asked, but never told Mollie about "the two of us." Maybe Mollie even knew, but she wanted to protect me. Mollie got both Carolyn and me, without either of us knowing about the other, to agree to that marriage. Now, Carolyn has asked me, and out of love for Mollie, and the others in my family, I have said, 'Yes.' That leaves you. I hope you can understand all of this, forgive me if you can, and we can continue to go forward as we were. I still love you." I only had to wait a few seconds, and Martha was in my arms, weeping, laughing and kissing me.

We made love, showered together and went to "the Del's" dining room downstairs. Martha seemed so carefree. I think she felt relieved with all of this.

(*I could not wait to tell all of this to Dr. Arnaud.*)

— — —

The meeting with the Southern California defense attorneys proved interesting (much like those in South Carolina, not all of them felt obliged to listen to their National Coordinating Counsel — I wondered how their clients dealt with them!).

We went round and round on the need to proceed by Demurrer first, or potentially waive it. Several of them felt a summary judgment motion at a later point in time would prove much easier to win. But the problem was that class certification resolution would probably occur before that summary motion might become possible and most judges who granted class status would be far less inclined to grant summary judgment as it would mean essentially reversing their own earlier certification decision. Several of the recalcitrants were persuaded, but US Gypsum and another smaller player stood steadfastly against the joint demurrer. I suggested that the rest of the defense would proceed without them, but they should advise their clients forthwith about the positions which they were adopting. They claimed insult from this statement and stormed out of the meeting. The rest of those present divided up the assignments, with Martha and I agreeing to help coordinate those filings.

— — —

I called Manny two days later and gave him a rundown on what was transpiring in my personal life since Mollie's Memorial service, which five members of Desert Mutual and Austin Smith of CAL Board had attended. That he was shocked when I mentioned remarrying was not a surprise. When I told him who it was, he said, "Is that the fantastic looking woman who tried to stay in the background?"

When I told him it was, he could be heard swallowing hard.

So, I explained to him about Mollie's last wishes. That made him say something to the effect, "My God, what a wonderful wife and mother to think those thoughts and act on them while she was dying. Ronan, you are a very lucky man!"

Then I told him I was ready to go to London in two weeks and he became happy.

— — —

Carolyn moved in just as she said she would. We talked about the decision to wait to marry until the move to Ross. After a long week of dealing with the subcontractors, Carolyn was becoming frustrated with several of them who were not committing to get their tasks done, which would hold up the whole project. It seemed they did not like working for a woman who was acting as her own general contractor. She asked me what I thought. I replied that I was not in a hurry to move, and since this was all her project she should do what she wanted. I did suggest that since we were clearly going to cohabitate in front of the children, that I thought we should have a small family wedding now. Surprisingly, she agreed. I asked about St. Anselm's and she agreed, adding that her Patrick had told her that he wanted to be baptized a Catholic. That being so, perhaps she could do that too?

I called Kate and told her all of this. She was actually pleased, and as I was hoping, asked if she could help. I took her up on that, and she was back in 15 minutes to set an appointment with Father Seamus Coyne, the pastor, which she would attend with Carolyn and Patrick to make all of the needed arrangements. So, I asked her to look into the wedding as well—just family! My goodness, Kate hadn't seemed that happy since the Twins were born!

Carolyn was delighted to have Kate involved. In no time, they were closer than I could have hoped. But after all, Carolyn was a very nice person. That said, she fired the two recalcitrant subs and the others helped her hire other subs of equal skill to those fired but willing to work cooperatively with both Carolyn and the other subcontractors. Carolyn clearly knew her own mind, and willingly acted on it!

— — —

I called Quincy and talked with him about having Bradley Campbell try to set up a meeting with Cheshire & Booth that would facilitate evolving a test search protocol for trying to allow us to begin moving forward toward an actual search for the DMIC reinsurance documentation. I gave him some time frames. Martha worked with our experts on their availability to coordinate our time while in London. John O'Sullivan, true to his word was a model of flexibility when it came to scheduling. In the end, I would be gone eight days and nine nights. Martha could only be there for three of those days as she was needed for a hearing in *LAUSD*. The rest of the time, I would be on my own.

Finally, I scheduled myself to attend the next National Coordinating Counsel Meeting in Philadelphia as well as a meeting on the Central Wesleyan COLLEGES class in Charleston, along with Tinker and Josh. I was beginning to feel like I was getting back to work, but I also had a sense that my heart was not in my work in the same manner as it had been before Mollie's illness and death.

8

LONDON COMPLICATIONS

As my black taxi pulled up to the Grosvenor House, I had a chilling sense that somehow Mollie was with me in spirit on this trip. I was given a nice small suite high up enough that the traffic noise was tolerable. I could see an adjoining door which might admit Martha when she arrived on the morrow for meetings with our British experts. I decided to go to Richoux for a small meal to tide me over until the next day. Our favorite waitress was missing so I had no need to bring up Mollie's death. Back in my room, I called Carolyn. It felt strange after calling Mollie all those years. Still, when she answered, I was pleased to hear her voice and she was extremely solicitous of my travels having heard from Mollie and me how very fond we were of our time spent together in London. Instead, I talked about my snack at *Richoux* and what lay ahead as far as work in the next few days while Martha was briefly present and we could engage our experts. Carolyn told me about continuing progress being made on the Ross house and how the cooperation now on-going among the subcontractors might result in its being ready for us to move in during the upcoming summer to accommodate changes in the schools for the children. (Her Patrick was definitely resistant to transferring from University High School in Pacific Heights to the Catherine Branson School only an uphill walk from our soon-to-be new home; and Maeve had her heart set on staying in University as well! OH, My!) Unlike Mollie, Carolyn ended not only with an endearment but added a sexy thought!

When Martha arrived at 10:45 the next morning, I had

already consumed the better part of a full English breakfast after utilizing the hotel's splendid workout facilities several floors below the lobby, and was on the hotel phone with Quincy when I heard her knock on the adjoining door. I made my excuse to Q and said we would see him after lunch about 2:30 - 3:00 at his chambers; whereupon, I unbolted my side of the door and there was Martha, looking ready to go. I asked how she was feeling and she answered, "Horny! I've been thinking about you for the whole taxi ride in from Heathrow. Are you well rested?"

Rather than discuss my physical condition, I decided to show Martha on the spot (rather her bed), just how well I was doing physically. After almost an hour, we rested and began to discuss the day. I explained that Bradley was going to meet with Quincy and us at Twenty King's Bench that afternoon to have a final discussion on our approach to Cheshire & Booth tomorrow morning. John O'Sullivan was arriving late tonight, and would be present tomorrow as well. For the next two days we would spend three to four hours each with Julian Peto and the McDonalds, with Martha taking the last flight out on that third day. I would stay four more days for follow-up on Cheshire & Booth and the experts, as needed.

Later at our meeting, the biggest point, besides the search criteria and sequencing, was who exactly would undertake the initial test search. After much thought, we decided that the bulk of the work would be undertaken by Bradley's clerks who would bill at the lowest hourly rate available. However, since none of them had sufficient background to begin the task, at least two senior clerks needed to be part of that initial team. In addition, we needed people who are smart enough to follow the process and to work out what needed to be done to ascertain if this search could actually yield the desired result. Toward that end, after a consultation, Quincy allowed that Wilfred, their chief clerk might step up for a week or two, whatever the length of the test. This brought Bradley to think a bit outside the box, and after a telephone call to his office, he allowed that he would spare Madeline for a few hours per day for a few weeks in addition to the two bright senior clerks. That brought things around to us. Martha and I talked (She allowed how very busy she was. Of course, I was the same.) So, we decided we would wait to see the timing of the test search and let our calendars dictate who would participate, if anyone. Finally, we believed that for the test, and perhaps the initial portions of the actual search, that Cheshire & Booth must have one or more people with some familiarity of the document storage area, and one of them would need to be available to answer questions and provide whatever assistance would appear viable at a moment of need.

Satisfied with our efforts, we repaired to a nearby gastropub for a pleasant, but not late evening, with minimal alcohol consumption except for Q and Wil. Martha had made an outline of our agreed thoughts/plans, and stopping at the Grosvenor House's business office, she was able to get it printed and enough copies made for our negotiating team, with a few to spare in the event of a need to disseminate it. We faxed a copy to John at The Berkeley for his arrival and then repaired to the Red Room for a night cap. Martha allowed that if she was not to fall directly to sleep upon reaching her room, we should carry our drinks up to our room forthwith. So, we did that, but Martha fell fast asleep anyway. At least, I got to finish her drink, tuck her in and repair to my rooms for a series of calls, including to John O'Sullivan who had just arrived at the Berkeley Hotel. Our meeting with Cheshire & Booth was set for 10:30, so John invited Martha and I to breakfast at the Berkeley at 8:45 as it was on our route, and we could take a single taxi from there.

— — —

We were once again welcomed by Stanley Booth and his lawyer, Solicitor Frederick Pierce. They escorted the five of us into the same conference room as used for our prior meetings, but this time, there were more Cheshire & Booth people present. Now, Chairman Booth made the introductions and then passed out two sheets of paper identifying all of the meeting's participants. Solicitor Pierce then added that all of those present had signed the NDA and they were open to hearing our suggestions on how we might wish to proceed.

Bradley and Quincy explained what we thought was a reasoned rationale for a test process to allow us to evaluate how to go about a more informed document search. As the person most knowledgeable about the Lloyds' process, Quincy appeared to take the lead, but Bradley seemed exceptionally informed as well. Their presentation aroused what appeared to be guarded interest in, and perhaps some admiration for, the thoughtful process which they sought to employ. When they paused, one of those "others" present, asked about the staffing which they envisioned for the test. I began to speak, but Martha sought to intervene, so I went silent. She recited the people who we had decided to utilize yesterday, but a clear leader was missing. When she got to that point, she turned to me, and being mindful of our pillow talk of the night before, I allowed that someone most knowledgeable about Lloyds' process was the natural leader for the search process, but that he should be involved on a limited basis through the test as well as the real search. We had discussed this with John on the taxi ride to this meeting: the less expensive and perhaps safest choice was Quincy. We allowed we needed a brief caucus.

In ten minutes, we were back. Quincy admired the process in which we had designated him to be the leader, but he did not want to be present for the physical search at all times. We announced that the leader would be Quincy, and quickly followed on those heals with the need for a knowledgeable Cheshire person to participate at least at the beginning, and preferably during any follow-on, even if on a limited basis, to minimize

misdirection and the waste of time on false leads or misconcep-
tions. Having said all of this, Bradley picked up the gauntlet and
tried for a soft landing in tendering the discussion to the
Cheshire & Booth interests.

The silence which followed Bradley was present for more
than a few moments whence Solicitor Pierce suggested that they
all caucus. Our group moved to a smaller room which had beverages and snacks laid out. We kept discussion to a minimum
although none of us thought the other side would eavesdrop.

Twenty minutes passed until we were summoned to return.
Once seated, Chairman Booth began to address us, and so it
seemed many of the others in the room, saying, in effect, that
ours was the first approach of this type which seemed to be undertaken with restraint and a sense of fairness; the fact that
Cheshire & Booth wished to avoid litigation on this topic was
clear; but, they also realized that if a process could be developed
by policyholders for their own benefit with the cooperation on
his brokerage firm, then they might be able to use it with the follow-on policyholders who would surely be forthcoming. Thus,
they were incentivized to cooperate with us, and would be willing to provide assistance of the type suggested. This created an
atmosphere of potential cooperation and "the others" from the
brokerage house appeared drawn more deeply into the discussion by Mr. Booth and several of the other senior executives who
had attended our earlier meetings. After three hours, it appeared
that a tentative plan for the test search was gathering momentum and a draft document for refinement would be needed. A
plan to accomplish and disseminate that was finalized, and a
further drafting meeting was set for 10:30 on the next day with
Bradley, Quincy and me attending.

We repaired to Bradley's office to be greeted by Madeline
and a light repast, with cocktails in lieu of tea, to hold us until
dinner. Our discussions were cursory. I excused myself, and,
when returning from the Gents was briefly sidetracked by

Madeline. I told her that I probably would have to work tonight and perhaps tomorrow, but might be free thereafter and hoped we might have dinner.

Within another hour, a written outline for a draft plan arrived. We all read it and conferred. After sharing our initial thoughts, I felt we would do well to retreat to our own rooms, think about this project and meet for breakfast to come up with some consensus points, if possible. Of course, I had mentioned that Martha would have to deal with our putative experts tomorrow. John O'Sullivan also announced that he had confidence that we could go forward without him for the moment; and, that he would like our projection of Desert Mutual's potential costs associated with the test document search itself; finally, that he would depart after breakfast tomorrow. He hoped that we could provide that draft projection by the time he landed in Phoenix.

— — —

The next day flew past with some marginal progress. Cheshire & Booth gave some explanation of what happened in their course of document retention, as far as the current management knew: essentially all documentation which they possessed on any given policy was collected into one place and bound up with ribbon (much the same as British court documents). Historically, these were placed in their office's basement, a vast cellar, and also historically very dry. They were unaware of any actual documents until quite recently that captured any more information on these policy bundles. In other words, this broker was holding out an apparently disturbing picture of a complete lack of institutional knowledge needed to locate specific policies.

But they did go on to say that they believed that those in charge of that basement over the years did create some means of ascertaining what kinds of policies were in given locations, but that this process was subject to change as the persons in charge changed. However, the great misfortune was that no one knew whether this information was recorded; and if so, where it might be stored! Thus, some exploration might yield a road map of sorts. At least that was their hope!

— — —

Martha departed on the last flight of the next day. Madeline gave me her number if I wanted to see her on the weekend. I knew I needed to rest a bit on Saturday; perhaps, a "lie-in," as some Brits called it. But I spent so much time later on that Friday evening calling Carolyn, then the children, Kate and Ingrid as well as Lily, Tinker and Manny that I had trouble falling asleep, then sleeping. So, on Saturday morning, after breakfast, I called Madeline. She was about to go shopping, but was delighted to hear from me. After a bit of small talk, she asked if I would like to join her for a "walk about" that afternoon followed by a home-made dinner. I accepted.

Madeline had us walk through her neighborhood's back streets and stop in cute shops, stores and markets. She bought things for dinner, but not much. I asked about wine, and she produced a wine market and we picked out several medium priced reds and a nice Chardonnay. Eventually, we ended up back at her place which she described as a condominium-type residence. At least only a three-story walk-up. We had a drink and chatted about the day so far and about her.

Madeline Myles had grown up in Leeds, a manufacturing city with its commerce supplemented a good deal by regional farming. Her father was a minor executive for a large shipping concern, while her mother was a secretary. Madeline liked Leeds up to a point, but she wanted more from her life than what her parents had (she had two siblings who never ventured far). So, she had moved to London to complete her schooling, and then

began acquiring skills on computers and other business equipment while working a number of differing jobs to embellish her
experience, always keeping her eyes open for advancement. She
viewed her present position with Bradley as almost ideal, a wide
variety of assignments and often meeting interesting people,
such as Martha and me.

As I was about to ask her about the sexual encounter on our
first meeting, she moved right to that topic: she was late to her
first experiences brought on by her mother's insistence on cau-
tion to avoid STDs as well as pregnancy. It wasn't until she was
19 that she actually learned the details on various forms of birth
control. Once seemingly empowered, Madeline became curious
and engaged with a variety of people. She was not monoga-
mous, nor strictly heterosexual, although she thought she preferred men. What an interesting woman! She claimed that she
had learned quite a great deal about sex by following this
lifestyle. After dinner, she proceeded to show me some of the
things she had learned, I was both fascinated and grateful to her.

— — —

In the final days of my trip, I was busy seeing Julian Peto and
the McDonalds during office hours. Clearly, Martha was doing
great work getting them ready. Corbett McDonald was a font
of factual background on asbestos, the evolution of its uses and
its history. Because these experts were to be offered as independ-
ent witnesses when the time for their testimony arrived, we
could not provide them with anything in writing lest it appear,
on their cross-examination, that we were providing them with
a form of scripted testimony. Thus, our preparation had to guard
against undermining the independence of their testimony. We
also pointed out that they should not memorialize our meetings
in any form of writing. Any type of documentation on which
they might rely would be discoverable, and they had a vast

amount of that which they had either created or accumulated on their own. Thus, we did need to go back from time-to-time to review our positions being espoused through each of them to reinforce their putative testimony. As I was in charge of oversight on this project, those were my tasks during those days. All went exceedingly well. They were all quite sympathetic about Mollie, especially Alison McDonald who teared up when she first saw me on this visit.

Bradley, Quincy and I also expanded the outline for the test policy search to take place in Cheshire & Booth's basement, including an estimate of the types of people and what they would get paid. But the multiplier for any budget was the number of days spent searching, and that was little more than guesswork at that time!

Finally, Bradley, Quincy and I decided that we should ask the client about its financial tolerance to learn what we might postulate in response, but our sole goal ultimately remained to locate the key reinsurance policy bundles. I alone got the job for that "budget vetting meeting!"

9

TWO NATIONAL COORDINATIONG COUNSEL MEETINGS

While I was in London, Carolyn and her Patrick had begun their expedited course of instruction with Father Coyne to allow them to become Catholics. Carolyn was very clear that she wanted to be married at St. Anselm's (the church and rectory were in Ross, but the school and nuns, just three of them, were in San Anselmo, the town immediately to the west of Ross). Its church was a humble looking, yet pleasant, building that would not overwhelm this event. So, Carolyn invited Father Coyne, whom Kate confided was quite taken with Carolyn, and he allowed that he would be pleased to preside at our wedding. Carolyn, not dragging her heals asked him about dates. So, the Sunday immediately before I was to fly to Philadelphia for the National Counsel Meeting, Father Coyne called to ask if we could stop in and see him after the 9:00 mass.

Father Coyne told us that he had a wedding cancel three weeks away on a Saturday at noon, and he was offering us that opportunity. If we said YES on the spot, he would read, at the noon mass today, the first of three weeks bans announcing the upcoming marriage to the parish, in an antiquated tradition, so that anyone, parishioner or not, could cite a reason why the putative marriage should not go forward. Carolyn asked what about her baptism. He responded that he did not see why that could not happen for Carolyn and Patrick next Sunday after the noon mass, if they were willing and could have their necessary attendees present. Carolyn was beaming — she was so happy. She looked at me, with a 'Are you really ready to go forward?'

look in her eyes. Of course, I could do nothing but agree whole-heartedly!

When we got home to Mill Valley, we called Kate to come over and told her we had news. All of the children having gone to 9:00 Mass were still at home, including Patrick Tyne. Carolyn called Ingrid and asked her if she could spend a few minutes at a family meeting at 2:00. When all were present and seated in the living room, I made a short speech about Mollie's desire that Carolyn and I wed, and as they knew, 'I had proposed and Carolyn had accepted.' Then, I turned to Carolyn and said, "The rest should come from you."

Carolyn, "As you all know, Patrick and I have undertaken a course of instruction to be baptized as Catholics. We met with Father Coyne today and he will perform that rite next Sunday after the noon Mass in the church baptistry. I am asking Kate to be my Godmother? (Kate smiled and nodded in agreement.) Patrick can decide whom he would wish to have. But I have more. Father Coyne also allowed that he had a wedding cancel in three weeks. He offered us that day and we have accepted. We really are going to be married!" And, with that joyous statement, Carolyn broke down crying! I hugged her tightly while everyone in the room gathered around us to offer congratulations.

Later that day, while we were alone, Carolyn asked me if I would be upset if she invited Vera and Lisette to our wedding. I allowed that as Patrick's "other mother" for all of those years, that she should also invite Vera to the baptisms as well. Then, I asked about Tinker and Elaine, a mistake because a bit of a floodgate of attendees was about to open with her agreement.

— — —

My first National Coordinating Counsel ("NCC") Meeting, after my lengthy absence following Mollie's death, was set for

Philadelphia at Abbott & Tweed, Alicia Goines presiding. Having flown to D.C. on Monday and spent Tuesday meeting with Tinker and his two partners as well as Mary, I was tired when I got back to my room after a two hour dinner. The first person I called was Carolyn. She had left a message for me at the Mayflower front desk.

Her voice was excited when she answered, "Ronan' you will not believe what happened this morning. (A pause.) I was telling my New York agent about our wedding. He interrupted to say that *Vogue* was interested in knowing if I wanted to be one of two models for their Bride's issue. Fred asked me to hold and in less than five minutes, he was back on the line. Ronan, *Vogue* wants an exclusive to photograph our wedding day: $50,000 plus all expenses and a week's honeymoon anywhere in Europe or the Caribbean! What do you think?"

I was nonplussed to say the least; I knew Carolyn was famous, but this was a shock! At first, I thought about our small family wedding (but I was having trouble deciding how far "the friends" part of that would go). Now, with lack of time and no place for a reception being major constraints, I did not want to be a complete "party pooper." So, I said, ending with a few questions, "Carolyn, Darling, sounds amazing, and a real coup for you. But where would we do it? Who would put the reception together on such short notice? Who would we invite?"

Her response, "Great minds run in the same direction. I have had trouble on who to invite as 'friends,' but when I called and asked Father Coyne if we could rent the parish hall behind the church for the reception, he told me that it would comfortably sit twelve rounds of ten plus a head table with room for a small band and they have a dance floor they can bring out. He was excited for the parish to get this publicity. So that's one hundred and twenty guests. I won't need half, that leaves you able to invite business friends as well. Oh, and your Mom is beside herself over the opportunity. She agreed to be my Matron of Honor.

She said she has contacts who she thinks can handle most of the reception details, including decorations, food, beverages and music. I cannot wait to tell the girls, if you agree. Think of the designer dresses they can wear as my bride's maids!"

I knew now why Mollie had liked Carolyn so much. They were so alike in how they approached a challenge. What could I say? I was so happy for Carolyn, and I told her so. She said she would have to go to Paris for an initial fitting of her gown and outfits, but would be back on Saturday. WOW!

— — —

On the train to Philadelphia the next morning, Mary got coffee and bought pastries at the station, and we settled down to enjoy our brief snack. Mary was one of "those friends" who would not have been invited to a small affair, but now, I began, "Mary, do you remember a woman named Carolyn who was present for Mollie's memorial service?" Her thoughtful 'YES,' brought me to move on, "Well, Mollie became quite fond of Carolyn before the time she became ill and even more so while she was ill, and then dying. Mollie wanted me to marry Carolyn so that our four children would have a mother figure, and for a few other reasons which do not matter so much.

So, I proposed and she accepted. We were going to keep it very small, but Carolyn's agent told *Vogue*, you know, the magazine, and they are going to cover the wedding. So, it will be bigger affair. Would you like to come?"

Her response surprised me, "Of course, but who is Carolyn?" When I told her that her name was Carolyn Tyne, that didn't seem to mean much. I allowed she was a famous fashion model, to which Mary responded, "How famous?"

When I explained that she worked for an agency in New York and Paris, and that her gown was coming from a Paris designer, and that she was on countless magazine covers, Mary said, "I guess I never paid that much attention to those kinds of magazines. Maybe I need to ask Martha about this? Will she be invited?"

When I answered, "Yes." Mary sighed and sat back.

— — —

When we arrived at Abbott & Tweed, I asked the receptionist if I could see Alicia Goines before the meeting started. I asked Mary if she would mind waiting, and she readily agreed.

"Alicia, good to see you. I asked to see you so that I could tell you something and ask you something, both in confidence." With that, Alicia sat and pointed to the chair immediately across from her at the small table where we sat, and nodded. I went on, "As you know almost six months back, I lost my wife, Mollie, after a protracted illness. She wanted me to remarry and picked someone out for me. We have agreed to marry in a very few weeks. Yesterday, I found out as did she, being a very high-end fashion model, and having arranged our wedding at a small Catholic parish north of San Francisco, it will be featured in *Vogue's* Bridal issue. My future wife's name is Carolyn Tyne. That's the first part; the second is, you've been a great business friend, so would you like to come?"

She looked at me for what seemed a full minute. "Carolyn Tyne, the fashion model? How do you possibly even know her?"

Me, "It's a long story. I've known her since she was 18 and starting out, living in Sausalito. We've been friends, and I lived in her second bedroom while I went to law school and dated someone else who will be here today. Hence the need to keep this quiet and private,"

Alicia, "How truly interesting. You know I'm Jewish. Any problem with the church?"

Me, "No."

Alicia, "Tell me where I can stay and I'll be there. Sounds like something that only happens once in a person's lifetime!"

— — —

The meeting itself hit most of the usual topics. I reported on our four experts. A subcommittee of three firms had been put together to come up with a plan to use our experts in cases where CAL Board was not a party, and they reported having a series of concepts which they should be able to report out at the next meeting. Tinker's firm having merged and grown had a conference room big enough to hold all the usual attendees, so the next meeting was set to be there with CAL Board's counsel hosting. Finally, we reported that the chain of command between NCCs and local counsel was becoming blurred in the COLLEGES class in Charleston and the SoCAL SCHOOLS joinders, so that decisions reached at these NCC meetings were not always being honored by local counsel in those other jurisdictions. This problem was discussed at some length, but no actual solution was reached to rein in those miscreants.

— — —

I stopped to see Dr. Arnaud on my way home from SFO that Friday. I felt the need to tell her about the upcoming marriage, and to invite her to the wedding, in person. Needless to say, she was delighted that I had acted expeditiously in asking Carolyn, and that Carolyn had accepted. She was shocked by the potential publicity, yet seemed to warm to the idea. When I asked about inviting Sandra, it was my turn to be surprised. Dr. Arnaud thought that if Sandra personally saw the marriage take place, that might well move her to get on with the rest of her life. But she tempered that advice by suggesting I run that putative invite by Carolyn before proceeding with it!

— — —

Carolyn arrived at SFO late that Saturday afternoon, looking radiant. Maeve and Meaghan went to the airport with me to pick her up. Clearly, Carolyn had become a great favorite of my daughters. Carolyn told them that their gowns and one for Kate would arrive early next week, and that the two of them plus Ingrid who was also to be a bride's maid to balance the three boys would have an initial fitting session on that arrival. Thereafter, the designer was sending one of his senior assistants to arrive the Thursday before that event to do the final fittings. Carolyn's notes on the initial fitting would assist for the final fit.

When we got home, I asked Carolyn again if she wanted her Patrick to be my Best Man, and again she said. "No. Far better for all concerned if it were Tinker. After all, my showing you to Tinker's apartment really did set this whole thing in motion!"

So, I called Tinker immediately and he agreed without hesitation.

— — —

That Monday I flew back to D.C. On the plane, Martha sat next to me as she was coming along to help discuss our experts with the South Carolina defense counsel. I had asked her to the wedding and she said, "Of course. How about if Mary, who told me already, and I come together? Would you like me to dress as a Dyke?"

I looked over thinking she was actually somehow insulting me, but then I saw she had a huge grin, and realized that her last line was said in jest! So, I went along, "Would you make a better one than Mary?"

But then, she said, "You might just be surprised!" After a "five-second face,", Martha started laughing non-stop.

I had scheduled dinner that night with Tinker who wanted to talk about the wedding. He was bringing Elaine. So, I asked about Martha; and since he knew her well, he agreed. That left me to explain about Sandra, if not in complete detail to Martha, which I did on the taxi ride to the Mayflower. Carlton was there and whisked us in. Robert showed us to our usual rooms. We made a few calls, and then set out for dinner at Duke Zeibert's Steakhouse, a block away.

— — —

Dinner turned out to be quite interesting: Elaine had been Sandra's roommate for more than a year in law school which led me to believe that she would think it a good idea to invite Sandra to the wedding. Not so. Elaine felt that Sandra still had a fix on me as a potential husband. Elaine said that Sandra never came out and said that directly, but whenever they talked, which was once or twice a month, hardly a call went bye in which Sandra failed to mention me somehow. Elaine found that a little disturbing as it had been going on for years.

I spent a few minutes pointing out the frequency with which our paths crossed in litigation, her father's death, and the break-up of his firm to justify Sandra's talking about me. But Elaine countered by pointing out that a great deal of what Sandra was telling her was of a non-legal nature! That caused me to raise Dr. Arnaud's logic on why to invite Sandra. Tinker chipped in saying that made a lot of sense, especially in light of what Elaine was saying. Martha said the words that needed to be said, "I have seen how Sandra looks at Ronan sometimes at the NCC meetings. Tinker, I think you're correct. An invitation, even if she fails to attend, might create a sense of 'final closure.'"

That hung in the air for a minute. I nodded affirmatively, and Tinker introduced a different topic: just how dressy was the wedding to be?

— — —

The next morning, Tinker, Martha and I caught the 6:45 from Washington National (now Reagan National) to Charleston and met up with Josh at the restaurant in the Omni in time for coffee. Josh had spent the prior night at the hotel, had a couple of drinks in the bar, and caught some "intel" for his troubles: COLLEGES Local Coordinating Counsel planned to push to Answer the Complaint and fight the "Class" itself in motion practice afterward, allowing for ample discovery.

We clung to our position that attacking the Complaint on a Motion to Dismiss was the only way to go and that "giving-in to a class certification fight," particularly at the outset, was setting the stage for a potential downstream loser. Especially, in front of Judge Blatt: if our motion failed, still better to build a record for appellate review briefing later on. So armed, we went upstairs to the meeting.

After our successful Motion to Dismiss in *Clemson*, we had more allies, including National Gypsum's local counsel, albeit probably reluctantly. The debate on how to proceed grew heated, but few counsel switched from their opening position. Finally, agreement was reached that CAL Board would lead a Motion to Dismiss filing with about 10-12 joinders and the balance would Answer the Complaint, with lead counsel seeking a Scheduling Order to allow briefing and a hearing on an expanded discovery order and on the motion in about 90 days to allow for briefing. With little time left, our team decided not to proffer Martha at this time to talk about experts on the BUILD-INGS class issues.

Tinker flew home. Josh, Martha and I spent the night. Martha had an adjoining room. Its door got used. Josh dropped us at the airport the next morning on his way while driving back to Greeneville. On the plane, Martha and I had a whispered conversation about our future. She seemed OK with my plan for the next while, but only time would tell!

10

SAINT ANSELM'S WEDDING

Our Saturday morning dawned cloudlessly. I had spent the night on the pull-out couch in the family room to totally avoid seeing the bride-to-be before she came down the aisle. Moreover, I did not know who would be giving her away. Ingrid and Kate were all abuzz, laying out a breakfast of baked goods, fruit and beverages, including my favorite coffee. The daughters had loved the whole fitting process with Carolyn. Especially, involving the French woman from Paris, with whom Carolyn conversed in apparently flawless French. The wedding was also a First Communion for Carolyn and Patrick who were both baptized as Catholics by Father Coyne just a week before (Kate was to be Carolyn's godmother and I was Her Patrick's godfather). The full liturgical Mass was to be at 11:00 with the reception to follow until 8:00 in the church hall right next door (I had not seen that very ordinary room decorated, as yet). All 122 guests whom we invited were planning to be in attendance. Tinker, driving my Mercedes sedan and staying at the new Marriott just past the *Dirty Harry* railroad overpass bridge by the new Larkspur Ferry terminal, picked the three boys and me up promptly at 9:45. We were out of the way so that Carolyn, Kate, Ingrid, Vera and Lisette, as well as the designer and her assistant, could attend to the gowns being worn by the various ladies.

Arriving at the church well ahead of the ceremony's outset, we had an opportunity to meet and greet the early arrivals. Manny from Desert Mutual was the first person I saw and with him was his very nice wife Alma, short for Esmeralda, who was

incredibly grateful for being invited. Several others whom I had
cleared with John O'Sullivan (who declined to attend due to a
prior engagement) were also present as was Austin Smith, General Counsel for CAL Board, and his wife whom I had never
met. She waxed enthusiastically for what seemed more than a
minute about the bride and how famous she was in the fashion
world using the phrase, "Quintessential All-American Girl."

All of my partners were present, some with a spouse. Martha
did come with Mary and both looked fantastic in their very
lovely dresses. Carolyn had a goodly number of friends, cowork-
ers and a few other models, but she had donated 16 people to
me to be certain no one important was slighted.

Then there were the *Vogue* photographers, scattered throughout the attendees, they seemed hardly noticeable. As the young
men were the ushers, Tinker took them under his wing and explained (once again) about seating the guests. As the time drew
toward 10:45, many of the guests started into the church. For our
relatively few attendees, the church was more than large
enough. The architecture, mostly ornate wood, including
columns, and stained-glass windows, was understatedly elegant. The lead photographer had been at work creating a set up
on each side of the church and each end of the central aisle to
capture the wedding itself, but mostly the bride.

By 11:00, everyone was seated. Tinker and I stood poised by
the altar rail. Father Coyne had yet to appear. Then I realized
that people were waiting for Kate to be seated. But she was
nowhere in evidence. The groomsmen, being youthful were
shifting about nervously. Then, the organist struck a chord. Father Coyne appeared a few feet away in what seemed newish
vestments. Ingrid started down the central aisle, moving slowly
and gracefully, followed by Meaghan, then Maeve, all of whom
looked to be arrayed in completely different gowns of different
pastel colors, all in step with Ingrid. Then I could see my mother,
Mary Katherine, appear at the entry door to the church, dressed

in an extraordinarily smart suit of deep blue. She held out her arm and there appeared Carolyn, radiant in a simple white gown which seemed to flow down and around her, giving her an appearance of otherworldliness. Her veil was simple and did little to hide her face, only caused it to be somewhat diffused as with her hair piled up and around her head. They moved slowly down the aisle. I was conscious of flashbulbs and cameras. Then Carolyn was right there in front of me, beaming her smile into my face and eyes. Kate handed her to me, pushing her veil ever so much more aside. The service began. It was all memorable (how little I remembered of my actually marrying Mollie), yet the bridal wedding picture in my office is that of Carolyn as she descended to the bottom of the staircase in our Mill Valley house in a pose reminiscent of Audrey Hepburn's initial appearance as a "Lady" for her very first event in *My Fair Lady*.

The rest of the day was largely a huge blur, but I do recall Martha saying, "Carolyn is the most beautiful creature I have ever seen," and Sandra saying, "Oh My God, how did you ever not pick her over me?" *Finally, at our next appointment, Dr. Arnaud said, "Ronan, those are some women you have in your life. Good Luck!"*

— — —

Mixing business with pleasure, our honeymoon was to be, in part, a business trip for both of us. My part was essentially London and Carolyn's was to be Paris; however, after the notoriety engendered by the publicity surrounding Carolyn's marriage (a bigger thing by far in France and the UK than the USA!), Sir Richard sent a very nice letter saying his wife would very much like to have him host us for lunch at the Royal College of Physicians & Surgeons. A separate note from Dr. Jean Bignon allowed he would be delighted to host us at La Caravelle in Paris.

In *Vogue*, all of the female wedding party was in one photo from the garden behind our Mill Valley house. The spread was 10 pages, plus the cover where Carolyn looked as angelic as I shall always remember her next to me at the altar in Saint Anselm's Church in Ross. Kate, as the Matron of Honor, was shown in two outfits, her high-fashion suit for the wedding itself and her dress for the reception. Maeve and Meaghan were shown with Carolyn and her Patrick in one photo and my two sons were shown with those two in another photo. Carolyn was in every photo, She wore three outfits: in addition to the wedding gown, there was a simpler gown for the reception, and lastly, a going -away outfit. The other two outfits were equally glamorous, and all of them promoted her "All-American Girl" image.

The reception itself was a six-hour marathon for the wedding party; Tinker and the boys stayed in their tuxedoes, while I eventually changed to a blazer and slacks to "depart." But in addition to Carolyn and Kate, there were outfit changes for Ingrid and my daughters. Then there were the guests: everyone I invited wanted to meet Carolyn. So, I spent a great deal of time introducing her, but eventually, she just started to meet people on her own as she fit into the crowd. Thankfully, no one seemed pushy. Martha was charmed, telling me in a brief aside, "She's so nice, reminds me quite a bit of a youngish Mollie!"

Manny's wife was beside herself what with meeting Carolyn and being photographed by *Vogue* and others. All of the activity notwithstanding, we did have a one hour lunch, complete with speeches and the cutting of the wedding cake (no smashing it in anyone's face!). Also, there was some dancing, but mostly a great deal of talking and generally a level of noise indicative of celebration. Amazingly, many people knew the photographers were present, but they were so incredibly unobtrusive in their work that they simply went unnoticed. (*Vogue* presented us with a 108-page wedding album that must weigh 20 pounds. I pulled it off the shelf behind my desk while I write this.) in all, a most memorable event and a seeming shift in mood from the prevailing grief following Mollie's death. (I often wondered if she looked down on her evolved family, especially Carolyn and me, that day as she had orchestrated our wedding!)

That wedding day was the first time I was to meet Vera, Carolyn's Patrick's "Other Mother," she was quite pretty and at least fifteen years older than Carolyn. When we spoke, it was as if she had rehearsed what she was saying about their relationship, but after a few sentences, she paused, then seemed to ad lib, "You have no way of knowing this, but I always had the feeling that even in our most intimate moments, I never had all of Carolyn's attention. In the last few years, I have come to know: even if she did not admit it to herself, Carolyn always, possibly from the time you first met her, and before she met me, was in love with you; and more so, yet in a different way, than any of her women, even Lisette. So, going forward, I shall be Aunt Vera, and so very grateful for your continuing to involve me in the lives of the two people I love the most. Now, please go back to your party and your many friends. We'll have time to talk in the years ahead."

Lisette was present as well, dressing to her high fashion best, but with somewhat less make-up. She was another favorite with many of the women who recognized her as well as Carolyn. She was very pleasant and good-natured. When we talked, she barely mentioned our Paris meeting and instead focused on her future with Carolyn, saying something like, "I hope you don't mind if I do not give up Carolyn. After all, she is my very best friend, my little sister, and perhaps, my creation: and, she is utterly delightful and incredibly nice. You are so lucky!" Then she thanked me for inviting her, including a European buss on each cheek.

At some point, Carolyn had changed outfits for the first time to an elegantly simple gown of light periwinkle blue. At around 7:00, an hour before the celebration was scheduled to end, Carolyn beckoned to me to follow her. We wound our way back

through the kitchen and food prep areas to the offices. The far-
thest one contained the bridal gown and what appeared to be a
woman's suit. My "departure clothes" were there as well. Carolyn asked me to unhook the back of her gown and pull down
the zipper. With that it fell to the floor. She bent over and picked
it up and with seemingly a single motion, put it on an appropriate hanger. Then, she turned and faced me, saying, "What do
you think? Now, I'm all yours."

When I made a move, she said, "No, no. Not now. Later. Our
guests have to see us off. Kate and the girls will see to all of our
things. Hurry up and dress. Don't keep Mrs. O'Neill waiting!"

11

OFF AGAIN TO PHILADELPHIA
AND CHARLESTON

Both Carolyn and I had many tasks to complete before we could actually undertake our European honeymoon, four plus weeks after the wedding. Immediately afterward, we did take a few nights in Bodega Bay, up the Coast in Sonoma County, but that was all.

I needed to get back to working on a more regular basis. The Mollie crisis followed so closely by the wedding had taken a great deal out of me, both emotionally and physically. My enthusiasm continued to feel diminished after dealing with Mollie and confronting her mortality (and derivatively my own and that of all who were dear to me). Carolyn was just great and I knew we would have a wonderful life. Nonetheless, I continued to have the sense of some kind of void growing inside me.

The NCC meeting at Tinker's office was to have an emphasis on the SCHOOLS and the COLLEGES class actions, which were at vastly different stages. I brought Martha along for SCHOOLS, but was going with only Tinker to Charleston. We left SFO on Sunday morning at 6:30 and we both got upgraded. (Rumor had it that TWA was having financial issues.) At about 12:30 eastern time, Martha and I had our first cocktails. I stopped reading briefs and turned to a *LAUSD* Declaration explaining how its experts were going to pin down which company's products were in what building (they were still on that same issue after more than 18 months!). Martha leaned over toward me, tipped her glass against mine and said, "Congratulations again on your wedding. Carolyn is spectacularly beautiful and seems so young for someone who's been around a fairly long time. Her son is really handsome. He'll be a girl slayer, if he takes after you!"

Me, "Girl slayer? I'm not sure what that means? And why would he take after me?"

Martha, "Well, he looks an awfully lot like you, don't you think? Not that I'm saying you're his father, but could you be?"

I paused, caught unaware, but not wholly unprepared, yet I needed to get this right, "From what Carolyn tells me, his father was a tall, good-looking Irishman, Navy carrier pilot, about eight years older than Carolyn. She fell hard for him from the start, and they spent two weekends and several nights together before he flew out to catch up with his carrier. She never saw him again and only got a few letters. She never got to tell him that she was going to have his baby."

Martha had pulled back from me ever so slightly as I went through the "our Patrick story." When I stopped, she leaned back closer, and said, "Oh My! How sad. So, what does Patrick call you? Uncle Ronan?"

I let the subject die there. As I had told Carolyn when I explained this story, it's benefit was in its simplicity and its difficulty in showing it to be a lie, especially with how Carolyn had handled her pregnancy and delivery, by going into a form of isolation with Vera for six months, including buying her first place in Connecticut.

— — —

When we got to the Mayflower and I was in my usual suite with Martha in her usual adjoining room by 3:20. Tinker was bringing Elaine to dinner at the Dining Room at 6:00 to become better acquainted with Martha, who was also spending so much time in D.C. and the U.K. We had some time. I called home and checked in with Carolyn and Ingrid. Martha knocked and came in when I answered. She was wearing a different outfit than I had seen on the plane, doubtless to impress Elaine. I admired it. She looked at me and said something like, "Would you like to see what's underneath?"

Without waiting for me to respond, she seemed to step right out of that outfit and into my arms. It had been a long time since we made love, and we both did so avidly! So much so, that we had to hurry pulling ourselves together to be in the Dining Room before Tinker and Elaine.

Dinner was excellent, including the food. The conversation was often about children, but Martha knew mine and seemed to delight in hearing about the Tinker children and their great age disparity, one of whom was looking at colleges! That led to a discussion of all types of higher institutions. In all, a peasant evening with little, or no, work accomplished.

I reported on the evening to Carolyn on my return to my room. All of the children were home, and I spoke to the boys as a group of three on a speaker phone, while my daughters needed individual, yet seemingly superficial, attention. Next, I spoke with Lily and finally Manny to keep him apprised of my whereabouts and what we were trying to get accomplished. It was after nine when I finished. I rang Martha's room to see if she wanted a nightcap or 'anything else.' She opted for the 'anything else!'

— — —

Alicia Goines could not stop effusing over being invited to the wedding and the Rehearsal Dinner at the Marines Memorial Club in San Francisco.

The meeting itself was a difficult affair. First, there was the lack of useful responses to written discovery form the SCHOOLS class plaintiffs, that would require two motions as the discovery was different to each plaintiff. But second and conditioned on those discovery reponses was the ability to take meaningful depositions. One group, led by US Gypsum and WR Grace wanted to ask for a total delay in the discovery period to deal with what they termed "bad faith responses." A second group, which included National Gypsum (Alicia) and CAL Board were fine with those motions, but felt the need to move forward by having the class plaintiffs put forward their "persons most knowledgeable (PMKs)" in depositions to be taken by various lead counsel, including Alicia and me, in the near term in order to protect ourselves against the Judge's schedule expiring without getting potentially pivotal, critical evidence "on the record." After much discussion, we all decided to do all of those suggested steps, plus a report to the Court about the "heal-dragging" by plaintiffs' counsel.

Next was the COLLEGES: once again, there were two camps, as evidenced by the last Charleston meeting. I began by asking quite candidly whether or not the local Charleston counsel, especially for US Gypsum and WR Grace, were operating in concert with the NCCs attending this meeting?

That did not go down well! After what came close to an *ad hominem* attack on me, we allowed that neither of those speakers were present in Charleston and what was being said in these NCC meetings was not consistent with what was being said in Charleston. In turn, their steadfast denials called into question whether the lawyers in this NCC meeting were, in fact, acting to coordinate their respective client's defenses in these other large scale class and joinder actions. The problem for those of us who were NCCs was that we could not trust, and therefore depend upon, what was being said in either meeting! Many of them did not like hearing this, and they especially did not like Alicia siding with me!

The rest of this discussion was desultory to say the least. I allowed that we would see how this all played out in Charleston: especially, what would be the level of cooperation amongst the defense counsel actually in attendance. At that point, Alicia

Goines spoke up again, saying, "I had no plan to attend that meeting, but now I think I will. At the Omni?" (At that moment, I was not at all certain whose side Alicia was planning to take.) As we were walking out, I asked Martha if she could switch her schedule to attend that meeting as well in case I needed a "truth-sayer" in Charleston!

Sandra Allen caught up to us in the elevator, thanked me again for the wedding invitation, and said nice things about Carolyn as well as Martha's outfit. When I asked her why she was so quiet in today's meeting, she said, "The client wants to take a lower profile going forward in these PROPERTY matters. I will not be in Charleston for that reason. I assume you are both going, so have a good trip." On the walk back to the Mayflower, I postulated to Martha that WALLBOARD was up to something, either that or its carriers were beginning to be pressed for cash. I explained that their Bodily Injury (BI) Asbestos case volume was probably at least twenty, if not a hundred, times greater than that of CAL Board, ending with perhaps "possible reinsurance problems on a mammoth scale!"

— — —

The meeting next morning at Tinker's firm was relatively brief as Tinker had debriefed his team about the NCC meeting at dinner over drinks and beef. Mace and Tod were amused by the "game" being played by some of the South Carolina counsel. Mace got exceedingly vocal in public and Tinker had to ask him to hold it down!

Martha was unimpressed with the suburban scenery driving into Charleston from the airport. However, the Omni, especially once inside, changed her mind! (I could not figure out how Martha managed a connecting room to mine, but she did. For some reason, I could not bring myself to ask how she did it on such short notice!)

We dropped our things in our rooms and repaired to the bar. Josh Smoulders was there and Tinker, who was on our plane, had stopped and left his order. Josh had a table with five seats. He gestured to it, and sitting there was Alicia Goines whom Josh had met at my wedding. When Tinker arrived, Josh and he came over. We chatted about the trip, the hotel and then dinner, deciding on Josh's favorite near-by second floor walk-up seafood restaurant with the great she-crab soup.

At dinner, we talked at length about how to approach the Central Wesleyan Complaint. The time for a decision was upon us and tomorrow's meeting was to be the last opportunity to try to reason with those who had decided to file an Answer to the Complaint and then attack the class: being a federal case, their position was a Motion to Dismiss could always be brought, as a Rule 12(b)(6) motion was one of the few which was never waived.

At the meeting itself, the Answer proponents had another argument: saying our position that there was no actual injury as of the Complaint filing would be unavailing since that newly created Central Wesleyan Complaint was brought in express reliance on the EPA's Rule requiring the very removals which that plaintiff sought to have litigated (and that Rule said nothing about requiring *actual* removal.). Our rebuttal that this was simple circular reasoning was not, however, persuasive. In the end, the bulk of the defendants decided to join in a single Answer. Seven of us decided to bring the motion. Alicia said they would join us. Tinker and her office divided the duties on the initial drafting. Each of the other Defendant offices were given a distinctly pleaded claim for relief to attack. Everyone had a copy of the *Mullen* decision and that case's briefs.

When I got back to my room, I had a message from Lily; another frequent client, Cary Crawford, General Counsel for Haley Pumps in Upstate New York, had called with a potentially urgent matter, and could I please call him. I did, and suddenly, I was busier than before I made that call!

12

MARK TWAIN'S CAREER-ALTERING TOWN

Drive eastward across the great Central Valley of California on CA Highway 4 (Said as, "C-A 4") and you pass through Lodi, and along the way, through endless fields of grapes and a few vegetables. Eventually, you come to the Sierra Foothills, also known as the Gold Country. Nestled in these quiet hills is the quaint town of San Andreas, smaller population-wise than it was in the latter half of the Nineteenth Century when gold mining was the main occupation of this region. A young Samuel Longhorn Clemens came to town in those early halcyon days, spent some time, made some observations, and watched a frog-jumping contest. He wrote about all of this in *The Jumping Frogs of Calaveras County*. Shortly thereafter, he became famous as Mark Twain after publishing *Life on the Mississippi*.

When I arrived in town on a still, hot summer afternoon, I went, as instructed by my client, Cary Crawford, to the Black Bart Inn and checked in with a seemingly pleasant woman of indeterminate middle age at the front desk. She told me they had poor room air conditioning and asked if I had a room preference. I thought for about five seconds and asked for the east side of the hotel, the corner away from the street. She nodded, turned and pulled a key from its slot, and handed it to me. Smilingly, she said, "My name's Maggie. I'm the owner here. Are you one of those lawyers come to deal with Bo Hobart's accident?"

When I told her that I was, she suggested that I take my cocktails and food here in her hotel as the other two "watering hole places" in town were a "Cowboy hangout" and a "Biker bar," and I might not be welcome in either, to say the least. She also allowed that a phone for my room was an extra two dollars/night! I took her up on that.

— — —

Cary had left a message at the front desk saying he had a flight delay in Chicago and was only going to get the last flight to Sacramento and would drive up to meet me tomorrow. With that, I called home and was surprised when Carolyn answered "our phone." (*I was still getting used to the concept of being married to another woman, and not Mollie. Because of our past relationship, I still got a bit of an erotic thrill on first hearing Carolyn's voice on the other end of the line. When I told Dr. Arnaud about this, she smiled, then laughed silently, saying, "Don't you realize that almost every man at your wedding was beyond enviousness over the fact that you were marrying that beautiful creature; and, strangely, I was perhaps the only one that knew your entire history with her."*) Without Cary showing up timely, I had no one with whom to have dinner, and told Carolyn about that (She did not offer to drive three hours each way to be with me for one night. Ah, now, alas, I knew we were married!). Then I spoke with the three youngest children. The Twins, Patrick and Meaghan, were seemingly transfixed by the Black Bart Inn. So, I told them the story of Mark Twain and the "Jumping Frogs." They loved that. Finally, I called Lily and went through my schedule for the rest of that week and the next as well.

I decided to eat at the bar which was an area immediately adjacent to the dining tables, with a pool table at the far end of that large open room. The bar itself was rustic and looked like it had been in place for a hundred years or more with back mirrors that looked like they were slowly failing the test of time. The bar had a foot rail for those who chose to stand and elevated stools (no backs) for a sitting preference. The door from the Main

Street, open to allow a breath of air, was at the one end of the bar where the stools were grouped. One stool was occupied by a white-haired man of roughly sixty, maybe older, nicely dressed, but no tie, his collar open. He sat nearest the door (perhaps poised to escape!). I left the stool beside him empty and sat on the next one.

I began to study the bottles of spirits behind the bar, arrayed in front of the mirrors: few brands were known to me. The bartender appeared in front of me, saying, "What'll ya' have?" The only Vodka I recognized was Smirnoff, so I ordered a double "on the rocks." He produced a short glass, filled it with ice, then filled it with Smirnoff, and added, "That's our premium Vodka. Two dollars a shot. Cash or credit? When I did not answer right away, he asked, "Are you, by chance, a hotel guest?" When I nodded "yes," while sipping my vodka, the bartender added, "I'm Boots. You can sign your tab, but you cannot add tips."

I responded' "Hello, Boots, nice to meet you! I understand about the tip 'thing.' My name's Ronan O'Neill and here's my room key. Why don't you wait about ten minutes or so, and I'll have another one of these, please."

Boots nodded and moved down the bar to where other patrons were standing, some with their elbows on the bar or their backs against it. I sensed a movement to my right and turned that way. The older gentleman had stood up. He extended his hand, and introduced himself, saying, "I'm Jim Downing of Walkup, Downing, counsel for Bo Hobart. I reckon your new on this case and are here for Haley Pumps. Would you like to sit and chat for a few minutes? Off the record, of course?"

To which, I responded, "Of course," and Jim was off and running. He explained that he had this case because he had gone to the University of California in Berkeley with the injured plaintiff's father, that they had been in the same fraternity and remained friends until Bo's father died a few years ago. Bo, his wife and family lived in the main house on the ranch property

and were responsible for the on-going conversion of that property to vineyard sections. A primary need, particularly here in
the Sierra Foothills, was adequate water during the grape growing season. As a result, submersible pumps and water distribu-
tion systems accounted for virtually all of the water on their
property of about six square miles of arable land.

Downing sounded like he knew what he was talking about.
He allowed that Bo's father, Herb, had spent time educating Jim
in the ways of grape vines and viticulture, right up through the
harvest and blending of grapes and the making of wine. Jim
Downing later mentioned that he had his own property in northern Napa County which he had begun to develop as a vineyard.
I was impressed by all of this, and it provided background well
beyond what was in the Complaint with which my client had
been served, together with the notice of tomorrow's inspection,
and the need for preservation of evidence, all of which was why
I was in San Andreas as that was set to kick off the very next day.

Lastly, as I was on my third Vodka and he was ahead of me,
that plaintiff attorney told me the most remarkable version of
facts of how Bo Hobart was on the top of a huge water pressure
tank, preparing to check the functioning of the water pressure
relief valve, when he shouted to his son, Ephraim, twelve years
old at the time, to turn on the submersible pump to create an increase in water pressure. Ephraim did just that, and within just
a few seconds, the pressure tank exploded, with Bo on top of it,
taking off like a mini-rocket ship, flying up in the air, over the
stone wall nearby, and coming to rest on a lawn on top of Bo.
Only Ephraim saw anything, and he did not necessarily understand what he was seeing, especially why it had happened. Bo's
wife, Ruth, came running. She assessed the situation and called
the Sheriff who got all of the first responders on scene as quickly
as possible.

Turns out Bo had an IQ of 124 before the incident. Afterward,
it was 81. Bo was physically active and healthy before. He be-

came a total right-sided hemiplegic, his dominant, side, and could no longer sustain an erection. With that and in a tone of finality, Jim Downing said, "How about dinner? My treat."

— — —

Jim Downing and I met for breakfast the next a.m., and I bought that meal. I followed him out to the ranch, signage over the main driveway, reading, La Ventura. Jim drove a Mercedes SL two-seater, I followed in my BMW 530i. I waited while he talked to Ruth and Bo. During that time, three more attorneys arrived: all defense types, two from Sacramento and one from Stockton. They seemed to know each other, and were a bit stand-offish toward me, probably because I was from the Bay Area. They each represented component manufacturers on the overall water system. I asked if the installer was represented. They said he had no insurance, "just a 'good old boy' who installed pump systems."

I asked about the tank manufacturer. They claimed no knowledge on that point. It was warming up rapidly for very early in Spring. I took my suit coat off. They stayed the same. Time seemed hardly to pass during this waiting. At last Jim Downing, along with Ruth and Ephraim appeared. We all stipulated that anything said by either Hobart was 'off the record.'

We all walked down the three stone steps in the wall which led away from the house at the ground level. We turned right and walked a good thirty or forty yards to where the wall turned to run parallel to the house. Turning right again, we eventually came to a very large round water pressure tank lying on its rounded side on the ground, with presumably its separated bottom leaning up against its side. One of the lawyers produced a tape and the side of the tank measured eight feet tall. Its attached top was round and rose to a pointy peak from which a device which I took to be the pressure relief valve (according to Mr.

Downing last night) protruded. On the side of the tank was another device which looked like a control of some sort. The Stockton lawyer allowed that it was a pressure control switch which
would cause the pump to turn on and add water to the tank
when the pressure dropped below a certain level and would stay
on to allow the pump to add water until the tank reached a
higher set level causing a pressure increase, and thereby shutting
down the pump. In the event that switch failed to shut down the
pump, the pressure relief valve would go off to keep anything
really bad from happening. CLEARLY, some part of this system
had failed.

All Ruth Hobart knew was that her husband told her the tank
was "not cycling properly" and that he and Ephraim were trying
to find out what was wrong, so Bo could fix it. Ephraim added
that the pump went on and off whenever he threw that switch
at the well site about 50-60 yards from the tank site. He did not
know if the pump started or stopped when he was throwing the
switch on the pump itself, because it was so far underground.
These three system components on the tank were represented
by the three Central Valley lawyers. I asked Jim Downing who
represented the tank company?

He looked at me and smiling ever so slightly, said, "You are."

"But my client does not manufacture tanks," I replied.

"Maybe not," answered Downing, "but it sure looks like
your client sold this one." With that, he rolled the tank about
ninety degrees to expose stenciled words, somewhat faded, on
the side of the tank saying, "FROM HALEY PUMPS, City of Industry, CA" to "ROSS WEATHERBY, Arnold, CA." Jim then
added, "Weatherby installed the system years ago, but he does
not believe in insurance. I'll default him just to get his cooperation. The manufacturer's plate is missing and we have searched
for it repeatedly, with no success. If you try hard, you'll be able
to see where it was affixed once upon a time."

At about that moment, my client, Carey Crawford, pulled up

and quickly came over. While the three Valley lawyers conferred with the professional photographer, hired by the plaintiffs, Downing conferred with his clients, and I tried to bring Carey up to speed. The Central Valley lawyers then left, each in their own car. Upon that departure, I introduced Carey to Jim Downing, stressing that he had flown from Syracuse, New York, for this session.

Jim shook Carey's hand (Carey was 6'4" tall and weighed about 350 pounds and had been an offensive tackle, starting four years for South Dakota State), saying, "Ronan told me of your travel problems. I'm sorry we started without you, but those other attorneys were here and so were my clients. I gave Ronan an outline of what happened as far as we know now. But, of course in California, this will be a case of strict product liability. Please let me run through all of this for you. After all, you've come a very long way, and we'll take that as a sign of your good faith."

Carey replied simply, "Thank you. I might enjoy meeting you under different circumstances. Ronan has represented Haney in a number of matters in California over the years, and we have a great deal of confidence in him. That said, I understand that your firm, and you, enjoy a sterling reputation in the litigation community in California and a few other jurisdictions."

With that, we settled down to understand in more detail than had been provided to the others, in terms of background of the system, its history of operation, and its components. In the course of this discussion, it became clear that Downing had already interrogated installer Weatherby after securing his cooperation in return for not trying to prosecute him. Downing also allowed that he did not know any precise dates for the installation; or, if this was the first system which Weatherby had installed using that same tank. Weatherby claimed he could not remember and was "terrible with paperwork."

Carey and I went back to the Black Bart. Downing went home, but only after asking me if I would like to ride up with him the next time when we both needed to be up here. I agreed to discuss it with him near that time. Carey and I hit some golf balls and caught up. I dropped Carey at Sacramento Airport that next day, went right to the office, spent a few hours catching up there, then home to Mill Valley to my new bride and our family.

That Saturday was to be my retirement from the active U.S. Coast Guard Reserve.

13

FAREWELL TO *SEMPER PARATUS*

For those more than twenty-four years that I had spent in the Coast Guard, it seemed to become an intrinsic part of my adult life: a time during which I never waivered from its path of Duty, Honor, and Country. At times, that path might have begun to fade, but I would find my way, and I remained steadfast. I came to respect every man and woman with whom I served, while developing a special respect for many of them.

But as with all things human, a military career has an end: passed over once for promotion to Captain, and on advice from the Chief, Eleventh District Reserve, that my competition was such that a second non-selection was a certainty, and having sufficient time served to qualify for full Reserve retirement benefits at age 60, I submitted my papers to retire from the Active U.S. Coast Guard Reserve as a full Commander.

While parking my car, I realized this could well be my last trip to Coast Guard Island. My thoughts ran over all of those years of my Reserve duty: the countless forays first made to the active units for legal assistance and to the reserve units for mobilization preparation in the Twelfth District. Then a few years later, the merger of all California units into one district, the Eleventh, sending me even further afield. Finally, under VADM Robbins, to all of the PACAREA units. In between, for a few years, I functioned as XO, then CO, of the District Reserve Personnel Support Unit, out of which I received all of my orders for travel over the years, located here on Coast Guard Island. In my last few years, my unit was reassigned to Yerba Buena Island in the middle of the Bay Bridge!

But then, as I sat in my car waiting, my mind drifted back to the Point Arena in Viet Nam. My life will forever remain intertwined with that 82-foot patrol boat and its crew, all of them, but especially LT Stone and QMC Terwilliger, with whom I spent so much time combing the north coastal waters of South Viet Nam; and in that horrific instant, they were no longer there. The nightmares were almost totally gone, but that deep sadness sometimes still creeps into me. (As I write this, I am now sure it always will!) Those are the men I celebrate most in my living, especially Chief Terwilliger.

So it was that I chose to use most of my two-minute retirement speech time allotment as a testimonial to those who gave their lives on that dreadful night more than two decades ago. The Coast Guard can shift from Treasury (when I entered) to Transportation (most of my career) to Homeland Security (from which I am retired), but whichever its federal department will not matter, because in time of war, it becomes part of the Navy. It was that slice of my time in the Coast Guard that made me who I am, as I told those retiring with me and those assembled for them to celebrate that day.

Carolyn, Kate, my now five children and Ingrid, all got dressed up and came to that retirement ceremony for eight of us on Coast Guard Island that day. The formation, the speeches, the presentation of one last medal, and the small reception for the actual participants, all lasted little more than an hour. I noticed Kate must have cried during the ceremony. Later, she told me that it was my speech, and how it transported her back to those weeks that became months while I recuperated from what today would be called "Post-Traumatic Stress Syndrome." While in the hospital on Oahu, she was present for so many weeks, during which my recovery, both physical, but especially mental, was not a certainty. Outside of Carolyn's hearing, she ended by asking, "Does Carolyn know any of this?"

The Twins came up to me and gave me a hug. Then, they

produced their new cameras from last Christmas and asked to take some photographs. Most of those present had not been to our wedding, and they wandered over in a steady stream to wish me a bright future and to be introduced to my new wife, the famous model, who had done her best not to look too glamorous, but she still looked great. There was small talk, and then we piled into two cars and rode down the Embarcadero, parked in my office lot and went to *Trattoria Pescatore* on the Oakland Marina Pier next to Jack London Square, where we had a delightful luncheon of Sicilian seafood.

At home, when we went upstairs to change, Carolyn had me unhook the back of her dress and she slid right out of it. She turned and looked at me and said, "Please put on your cover one last time, I just want to admire you for one more minute. Even though the uniforms are no longer khakis, remember that was how I saw you for the very first time on that parking deck!"

Carolyn kept looking and she came over to me and helped me out of my uniform. Then, she helped me out of my other clothes. Then, as more than twenty years ago, Carolyn had her way with me. At the end, she began to laugh. Her happiness was contagious, and I started to laugh as well.

When we got down to the kitchen and family room, Ingrid and Kate were there, so a still smiling Carolyn said to them, "In case you don't know, the first time I saw Ronan he was wearing the older version Coast Guard khaki dress uniform and was a few months away from becoming a full Lieutenant. This may well be the day when he has worn his Coast Guard uniform for the last time. Let's have one last bottle of champagne to celebrate the end of that career. A job well done!"

With that, Kate looked at me and smiled. She could tell I had not yet told Carolyn about my PTSD.

14

CHESHIRE & BOOTH'S TEST SEARCH

During the time I was covering all of my various matters stateside, our London Team was finalizing the plan to undertake the first, and what we hoped would be only, test search of Cheshire & Booth's (B&R) Lloyds policy placement filings in their stored condition. Stanley Booth had deputed his second son, Frederick (he had four and they all worked in the firm, learning their trade "hands-on."), as our team's liaison and guide for dealing with those floors of stored policy documents. Although I had been privy to these planning cycles, the actual nuances that would drive the search had, at least to-date, eluded me. What I did understand fully was the general plan, the basic tactics which underpinned it, and how it should work. Furthermore, I understood all of the basics of our *pro forma* budget, based on this plan. The time was approaching to start the task. I conferred with Manny and John O'Sullivan to see whom, if any of us from the United States, should attend for a few days. They asked me, and Martha, if she would be needed on that trip.

I flew down to Phoenix and drove out to the Scottsdale HQ office of Desert Mutual. The entire management staff down through Manny attended that meeting in the executive conference room. Candid discussions about the worsening state of DMIC's finances were laid out on the table. Our written budget for the test search was reviewed.

Charley Sewell, the President, said we needed a result in no more than 18 months; and by "result," he meant a serious seven, if not eight, figure cash transfusion. His bottom line was straight forward: the time for planning was over. DMIC needed action, and it needed a successful outcome quickly! Charley looked at John O'Sullivan, whom Desert Mutual had charged with shepherding this project. John spoke for the first time in many minutes, "Ronan, you are our man on this. I have been there with you, met the people and signed off on the planning. The Board has approved the budget. Now, we need "one voice" with the Brits, and that will be you. Please get over there as soon as you can to get them moving full speed. If this test vindicates the overall search plan, great. If needed, tweak it. Come and go as you need. Keep Manny and me posted. We all wish you success, quick success, if possible. Any questions or comments?"

I suggested that I cancel my hotel for the night, head home, and make all the needed arrangements posthaste (inferred in all of that was I would skip the customary drinks and dinner to expedite matters, as well as to cut some small expense).

I called Carolyn on my cell and asked her if she wanted to come. She asked to defer until my next trip which would hopefully give her more notice. Moreover, our new home was ready for a final walk-through, in which she hoped I would participate before departing. I pulled out my calendar as soon as I got to Sky Harbor, started to plan, got my assistant, Lily, on my cell, and asked her to work with Mary in Oxford on plans for my hotel and my flights. (I would make this trip alone!)

— — —

Arriving two days later at his offices, I was greeted by Bradley Campbell's assistant, Madeline, who escorted me to his office. On the way, she said, "I heard you already remarried. Bradley showed me a photo of the bride and you in the Times. How long had you known Carolyn Tyne?"

I asked her to pause for five minutes and explained how we knew each other and how Mollie had become so fond of Carolyn, including the wedding promise. Madeline looked me right in the eyes, smiled quickly, then turned and pushed the elevator button. The doors opened. We entered. The doors closed. She leaned up against me, saying, "I hope we can still get together while you're here?"

I smiled, nodded affirmatively, the doors opened, and we emerged into the narrow hallway leading to Bradley's office suite on the rear of this top floor. As we entered, Bradley rose, as did Quincy Franden-Jones (Q), and his Chief Clerk of Chambers, Wilfred Smythe (Wil). We all shook hands and exchanged greetings, seemingly aa old friends. Madeline disappeared, returning a moment later with a cup of black French roast/Italian blend press coffee for me. She then retired out of view. Being about 10:30 a.m., Q seemed subdued, but seemed to revive somewhat as Bradley began to speak.

Bradley rose, came around his desk, leaning against the front of its massiveness, he seemed to address only me, "We have some potentially very good news. Please recall Stanley Booth told us that he, and his firm, were committed to our success. We took his delegation of his number two son, Frederick, to this project as a tangible sign of that commitment. Frederick was extremely forthcoming and helpful in formulating the very latest version of our search plan, especially since he was trained in the policy document storage area by an expert in long standing, Grayson Turnbull, Jr., a lifetime employee of Cheshire & Booth as was that man's father. They each spent about thirty years being in charge of the actual storage of those Lloyds placement document filings.

"While you were making the crossing, we had the privilege of interviewing Mr. Turnbull who is now almost seventy-eight years old. Retirement turns out to be mandatory at C&B at age 70.5. Employees can retire earlier, beginning at 60, but their pension is greatly reduced. Mr. Turnbull worked until the very last day allowed by that mandatory age.

"Mr. Turnbull, Jr., allowed that, with the exception of

relatively recent years of coverage where the actual reinsurance documents are all that will be needed, it is the long-tail reinsurance documents that cover all of the years after the expiration of each primary reinsurance, and have no expiration date or 'stop-loss, which are the policy documents that must be found. These are the ones needed to generate the cash flow for each initial casualty reinsurance year.

"Mr. Turnbull, Jr., who will accept a fee as your client's consultant, knows the approximate whereabouts of these groups of documents for about sixty years, as he succeeded his father about two years before he died at age seventy-two, to become in charge of the spaces in the C&B basements. Together with Frederick Booth, they will serve as guides to our searchers when this project begins the morning after next at 10:00 a.m. I believe this latest discovery, attributable to Frederick Booth, makes your chances for quick success, substantially greater. I do consider this a major break-through. But now, we must wait and see what actually comes to pass."

With that, Bradley walked over to the door to the pantry, and Madeline reappeared. They spoke quietly for a few moments, and Madeline left. While I was talking, I asked Quincy, "What do you think this means? I have seen those rooms, there is almost no signage."

Quincy stroked his chin and seemed to be musing, then his head came up and he said what I was hoping he would say, "You are correct. There is very little signage. Please recall that the senior executives knew only the major divisions of coverage: maritime, then the advent of aviation; but property and casualty must make up the bulk of their placed coverage, and one can only suppose reinsurance, retro-coverages, if any, and long-tail coverage for those areas. Of course, there are the specialty coverages, but I very much doubt that Cheshire and Booth would be involved in very much of that. No, I suspect that the map of what coverages for which periods of time live in the memories of key personnel, becoming essentially "institutional knowledge. Mr. Turnbull, Jr. may well be one of those surviving institutions."

I decided to write a short report to Desert Mutual. I asked Bradley about sending it. He responded that he would have Madeline type it and fax it as soon as she could. After all, there was a seven hour time difference. It read:

CONFIDENTIAL/ADDRESSEES EYES ONLY

TO: John O'Sullivan and Emmanuel Garcia:
Potential breakthrough: may have located a retired employee with institutional knowledge of the general whereabouts of different types of coverage which may shorten search time. Process to start in less than 48 hours. Will attend for one or more days.
Will keep you all advised. Ronan

Madeline typed it and sent it after cocktails and a slow, very pleasant luncheon in Bradley's office.

We all broke up at about 3:00. Bradley had business outside his office. Q and Wilfred wanted to get back to their chambers at Twenty King's Bench Walk. Bradley said to me, "Feel free to use my office for your needs now. Madeline will help you. Come by tomorrow, if you have any need. Otherwise, I shall drop in for the start of the search on Thursday morning," Then to Madeline, "Please see to Mr. O'Neill's needs, would you please, Madeline."

With that, the three of them were gone. Madeline turned to me, smiled and said, "I really must clean up. Bradley is quite freakish about any form of disorganization. I simply cannot afford to trust staff to get it right, although they do empty the trash just fine. After that, is there anything you might want?"

Me, smiling back at her, "I'm certain we can think of a thing or two!"

— — —

By that Friday lunch time, the search team had found five reinsurance filings and three of the long-tail coverages for those five. Plus, we now had the sense of the process which would need to be followed to find all of the other Desert Mutual/Lloyds Syndicate filings stored at Cheshire & Booth. Moreover, Bradley's firm was promptly putting the Syndicate Lead Name Underwriter on notice as soon as each policy form was discovered, as well as the formality of advising Cheshire & Booth to close that loop and to begin providing the systematic notice needed to generate payments to Desert Mutual on all pending past claims as well as future claims for reinsurance reimbursement.

At 3:30 ZDT Friday afternoon, I spoke with John O'Sullivan while sitting in Bradley Campbell's office. He was ecstatic with the news, and agreed on the spot with our suggestion that we abandon the "test" designation, and continue to pursue all of the coverages, as arguably available. The projected cost of the search could be reassessed in a month, and I would fly back to London for that. He ended by saying, "Take the key players on this somewhere nice and buy them some double-doubles. WELL DONE!"

— — —

I called Carolyn when I got back to Grosvenor House much later that night and told her I would be home for a nice dinner on Saturday night. She said the weather was great and suggested we bar-b-que. I agreed. Then, she talked dirty for ten seconds and said, "I Love You." Then, she hung right up before I could respond!

15

CAROLYN AND LONDON,
MARTHA AND EXPERTS

The news from London continued to be positive with an average of almost one policy/day being discovered by the search team of four under Quincy's nominal lead and Wilfred Smythe's actual hands-on supervision, but especially attributable to the continuing advice of Grayson Turnbull with the active interaction provided by Frederick Booth. (Bringing those two along with the search team for "Double-Doubles" at the Savoy Hotel's American Bar had assured their continuing loyalty to the Desert Mutual cause as well as continuing to maintain our joint level of productivity.)

— — —

The need to follow up with our experts in the UK and especially in Paris was a need that I was forced to ignore as I undertook other tasks, but Martha reminded me almost weekly. I asked her if I brought Carolyn along for our somewhat delayed honeymoon, would she mind. Of course, she said NO. (I was thinking we could go several days early, perhaps nip up to Oxford for a night or two. Then stay on a few more days in Paris after visiting with Dr. Bignon.) Carolyn bought in, as did Martha. The Desert Mutual people were fine. In fact, John O'-Sullivan offered that he would come over for a day to meet with all of the "Reinsurance Recovery Team" as it had been renamed with a stream of payments being promised by various syndicates.

— — —

The Hobart/Haley Pumps case in San Andreas was getting
all the initial pleadings and opening discovery in place. I was
using a younger associate, Joshua Small. Reggie Black, our local
counsel in New York City, called me quite a few months back to
tell me that he had a nephew who was a second year associate
at a big firm in San Francisco and disliked the work somewhat,
but especially found the people strange. I asked Reggie if it was
racism, but he demurred saying instead that his read was that
they were intellectual snobs. (Knowing something of that firm's
reputation, I tended to agree with Reggie.) Since we were always
looking for skilled diverse lawyers, I asked him to have Joshua
call Lily and set up an appointment for as soon as it was con-
venient. This was all about a year ago, and Joshua had turned
out to be a pleasant addition to my team. Now, he was doing
the draft pleadings and written discovery on the *Hobart* matter.

I reviewed his work, made some suggestions and asked him
to get the pleadings filed and all of those documents served.
Joshua asked if I was going to sign everything? I told him that
he did most of the work and it was time for him to start signing
things with my approval or that of another partner, or Martha.
He looked slightly surprised, so I told him he had proved himself to me and the members of our team and that was all that
mattered. Joshua turned to go, but stopped and said, "I thought
you hired me as a favor to my uncle?"

I looked squarely at him for a full second before responding,
"Your uncle got you into our interview process, but you got
yourself hired. After a year, you've proved yourself. Anything
else?" Joshua 's smile widened, he turned and left my office.
From that day forward, he was a confident, reliable lawyer who
knew his bounds were based on his performance.

Checking-in with Carey Crawford, he determined that the

subject tank had been sold, not just shipped, by their City of Industry Branch in Southern California. He was following-up with
them to get the sales invoice itself and the purchase document
for the tank as Haley did not manufacture water storage tanks.
He would get back to me when he knew more. In response to
his inquiry about what was next, I told him the single Superior
Court Judge in Calaveras County was going to set an Initial Status Conference in a month or so, and I would do my best to attend personally. I also told him about Joshua Small, the associate
helping me on his matter.

— — —

Martha told me that *LAUSD* was once again bogged down
and the judge was becoming impatient waiting for something
that would pass as an arguably viable plan to identify the manufacturers of the offending products in that school district's
buildings. We were a continuing thorn in the side of plaintiff's
counsel as Martha repeatedly rallied the defense counsel group
to sign on to our exposing the defects in LAUSD's lawyers' plans
to prove any sort of product identification (product ID).

— — —

SCHOOLS and COLLEGES were both in briefing phases
which made the weeks ahead an ideal time to head over to London and Paris. I called Mary, Sir Richard Doll's assistant to ask
him if this would be an appropriate trip when he would like to
see me and perhaps have his wife meet my new wife. Mary responded that our picture was buried in the Society section of the
Times, and she had shown it to him.

The next day, Mary called back and said that Sir Richard's
wife insisted that he invite us to lunch at the Royal College of
Physicians & Surgeons, and to bring along that other lovely

young woman he had told her about almost two years ago. He also offered to invite Corbett and Alison, as well, even Julian Peto, hoping they would be able and willing to come! She gave me a couple of dates. Once I had cleared it with Carolyn, I turned potential arrangements over to Martha to coordinate. (She and Sir Richard's Mary were "thick as thieves" by then! Plus, she had spent more time with our experts than I had in the last year; and finally, Carolyn liked her.)

Next thing I knew, Carolyn was getting Martha fitted in one of her "extra" cocktail dresses for that luncheon, meaning that they would be wearing outfits that did not "clash" as Carolyn explained. (Who would serve as Martha's escort? I decided not to raise that as a point.)

— — —

The day finally came for our deferred Honeymoon to get underway with First Class seats on one of TWA's last direct SFO to Heathrow flights (Our return was to be its next to last day!). Kate was staying at our Mill Valley home with Ingrid (who signed on for one more year) and the children. They were busying themselves with affirming their friendships in anticipation of our forthcoming move to the Ross house. (The first time Carolyn took them to see it, they went "GA-GA" over its size, and their bedrooms. Kate was pleased with her in-law unit. I thought Ingrid stayed that extra year to enjoy her new quarters, and perhaps hoping to find her "Mr. Right.") We talked about all of this, and more, during cocktails and dinner. I suggested we try to get 4-5 hours of sleep to allow us to enjoy most of our first day in London (Check-in was set for Noon.).

— — —

A driver was holding up a sign for Mr. & Mrs. Ronan O'Neill

when we cleared Immigration. He explained that The Grosvenor House wished to show this special service to their "Honored Guests." (Carolyn never stayed there and I was uncertain how this occurred.) Their car was a Bentley sedan (a second vehicle took our luggage). Of course, this was not Carolyn's "first Rodeo;" so, she stepped right into the passenger compartment and patted the seat next to her for me to sit alongside her. The driver was extremely professional, and since it was a Sunday morning, the traffic going into London's West End was quite light. He discretely offered a few thoughts and stopped talking after mentioning coffee, tea and some French pastries in the storage alongside our seats. Realizing this was my first international trip with Carolyn (the obvious reason for this proffer of "grandeur," or possibly something engineered by Martha and Sir Richard's Mary!) gave me a sense of excitement which I had not felt for years, and thinking back, it reminded me of that random, yet fascinating, first day that the two of us had spent touring Paris several years before. Looking at Carolyn, I was smiling. She saw that and asked me why. So, I said, "This is our first real international trip together, and I sensed it reminded me of something. On quick reflection, 'twas that marvelous tour you gave me on my very first day ever in Paris. I smiled because I am only realizing now just how much I really do love you, and what a truly lucky man I have been to have had Mollie, and now to have you."

I leaned over to kiss Carolyn, only to realize that she was starting to cry in spite of her beaming smile.

— — —

Upon pulling up to the main entrance to the Grosvenor House, there was a small contingent to greet us. Heading up that group was Mr. Phillip Carlsen, the General Manager of the hotel. I had met him once for a handshake, in passing, during an earlier stay.

That day, he shook my hand as I alighted first from their Bentley. But then, he moved ever so quickly to take Carolyn's hand as she began to alight, held it in a polite grip, and bent to kiss the back of that left hand, saying, "Welcome to the Grosvenor House, Mrs. O'Neill, we are so incredibly pleased that you have chosen to join your new husband, a seasoned guest of our establishment, and hope you will find everything to your liking. Would you both please join us for a few moments while our people convey all of your things to your rooms?"

With that, Mr. Carlsen and several others, lead the way to a private room, heretofore unnoticed by me, next to the Red Room Bar. He offered us plush seats, and attentively asked our choice of beverage. We both chose water and French Chardonnay. The only other lady present, Ms. Lambden, was introduced as the Rooms Manager who would see to any need which might arise. She deftly passed a plate of cheese, fruit and crackers. A gentleman called Jean Marc, the Food & Beverage Manager, poured the same Chardonnay for everyone, including their last member, Mr. Dalrymple, the Front Office Manager, who offered, "Anything we can do to make your stay more comfortable, please call on any of the four of us. A pleasure to have you join us." Turning to face Carolyn straight on, he asked in an obliging voice, "May I also call you Ms. Tyne as that is how all of our staff knows you. So many of the women workers are beside themselves that you are staying with us. If any of them prove at all difficult, please do let any of us know. Ms. Lambden has already sent a message to all of them. We just want you both to know what a privilege it is for us to host you both."

Carolyn looked at me. I responded for us both, "Believe me, I understand that Carolyn, my wife, has a face that is recognized very widely. She does not mind being recognized, nor do I. But as I am certain you have advised your staff, we would appreciate their observing our privacy under most circumstances. On the other hand, stopping here and there, and chatting briefly can be acceptable. I wonder if I can leave a tip for our driver and his helpers?"

As they looked at each other, and before any could answer, I handed a 50 pound note to Mr. Carlsen, and asked him to please express our thanks. Then, turning to face the four of them, I said, "Perhaps you have a question or two for Carolyn, or even me?" They did and we spoke for about ten minutes, mostly about our wedding, and how the Church and its setting which appeared in a few of the photos in the *Times* looked so English. A woman in uniform appeared and whispered something to Ms. Lambden, who spoke pleasantly, "Your rooms await and we do hope you find everything to your liking. May I show you the way?"

We crossed the great lobby and all of those present stopped whatever they were doing to watch Carolyn (and I supposed me too) as we followed the ever-friendly Ms. Lambden with her staff looking on. We entered the elevator and our guide inserted a key which stayed in place as we rode to the top floor (I had never stayed there). We followed our guide to the end of a short-ish corridor and she used the same key to open that door, which somehow appeared a bit overwide. She moved aside just inside the door so Carolyn could enter first followed by me. Carolyn was drawn across this splendid room, devoid of beds to the middle of five overlarge windows which looked down and out across on the vast expanse of Hyde Park. Other taller buildings were visible against the cloudless sky and above the park's foliage. "What an utterly magnificent view!" exclaimed Carolyn. Ms. Lambden allowed that the master bedroom was just to the left, and shared a similar view of the park as did the lady's bath, accessed through her dressing room. The gentleman's bath looked out over other rooftops which was fine with me.

After a few more instructions, Ms. Lambden handed both keys to me, and said in parting, "We wanted Ms. Tyne to know how much we appreciate her staying here. Ms. Walsh will be

upgraded to your usual room when she arrives. Thank you for
your continued business, Mr. O'Neill. It's a pleasure to serve
you, and we hope we have the pleasure of seeing your children
again one day." I mumbled our thanks and with that, she was
gone.

I turned to see Carolyn pulling her suit top over her head,
saying as she did so, "I always wanted to stand naked at windows like these, looking out on all those people and knowing
they cannot see me. Will you join me?   "

— — —

We bent a rule and almost went right to bed upon arriving
in our rooms. At 5:00, having dressed in crisp casual attire, we
went directly to the Red Room for cocktails. Other tables were
occupied and apparently some of the high-end clientele were
aware of my wife, our recent wedding, and even me. We were
unable to buy our own drinks, and this precipitated some pleasant, albeit superficial, conversations. At 6:30, we excused ourselves, exited into the lobby, turned right away from the main
door where a few people appeared to hover, went a few paces
and out the original front door onto the Park Lane sidewalk.
Once there, we were quite alone. We turned left and walked a
few blocks, passed Curzon Street, turned left again, and meandered to the edge of Shepherd's Market. Then, we circled to go
back up Curzon where, with the shadow of MI-6 hanging over
it, sat our favorite Wheeler's front door. Albert was present as
was Paul, the owner. Both doubtless alerted by the Grosvenor
Concierge. Condolences were offered by Paul, as I had seen Albert briefly on my last trip. After a few moments, the fuss was
over and Albert turned to serving us, beginning by asking for
our drink order. Carolyn asked for a glass of French Chardonnay and I intervened by asking for a wine list.

Voila! It appeared in moments, and with Carolyn's acquiescence, I selected a bottle of French Chardonnay. I had a double Grey Goose, and then Albert subtly told us what we should order, which included two Dover soles as the main course. After inquiring briefly about Carolyn to learn her profession and that she was the mother of one, Albert had served drinks and taken our order.

The evening passed pleasantly. Only when we began to depart, did a slightly aging American woman approach us and ask, "You look amazingly like the couple who were the featured in this year's Wedding issue of *Vogue*. My husband says I'm silly, but I just have to ask. Are you?"

Carolyn looked at me, and flashed a smile. I thought the woman was going to faint. Carolyn responded, "How very perceptive of you. Where are you all from?"

With that, the woman stammered out, "Philadelphia. You know, Pennsylvania."

Carolyn responded, "Perhaps you know of my new mother-in-law, Mary Katherine O'Neill?"

The woman, with an astonished face, managed to utter, "Would that be Kate O'Neill? My parents thought the world of her. We are from Chestnut Hill."

I smiled, took Carolyn's arm, and said in a neutral voice, "Please tell me your names. I'll relay them to my mother. But now, we really must go."

The couple did that. Looking back, Albert and Paul were looking after us, seemingly bemused, as we went to exit their restaurant. Once outside, Carolyn laughed, "You really will need to work on this. It would seem some fame has rubbed off on you as a result of your *Vogue* exposure." We made love that night and the next two and a half days floated quickly past until Martha arrived.

The McDonalds and Julian Peto had accepted Sir Richard's invitation, so our Introductory luncheon at the Royal College of Physicians & Surgeons was to take place that next day, and

would obviate the need for three special instances to introduce
Carolyn. That Club's Bentley arrived timely to pick up the three
of us. Carolyn looked fantastic in a muted turquoise cocktail
gown that was just on the conservative side of demure. Martha
was striking in a subtle light lime green dress which somewhat
understated her marvelous physique. Seeing them together, I realized how close they must be in age and how somewhat similar
in appearance in these Parisian creations!

We were the last to arrive at the Royal College. A footman in
dark green livery assisted the women from the car. A doorman
held the outer door open, as did a man in uniform for the inner
door. Standing just inside the Club's doors dressed in his afternoon tux was Sir Richard, and next to him, an elegant, extremely
well cared-for, somewhat elderly woman who was his wife, Eugenia, also attired in a subdued blue cocktail dress. Next came
Corbett and Alison McDonald. She wore a less formal dress of
tan with an embossed pattern on the skirt. Corbett and Julian
were less formally attired and I felt more comfortable upon seeing them. Introductions ensued upon our entrance, and Sir
Richard escorted us to a slightly secluded section of the Dining
Room.

The older ladies were extraordinarily generous in their praise
of Carolyn's and Martha's dresses, even more so when Martha
explained that Carolyn had intervened and assisted in the creation of her dress in Paris. During our entrance, I could have
sworn I saw a photographer recording our arrival. Sir Richard
allowed that Ms. Tyne had quite a following in London, so the
Club President and its manager allowed that one newspaper,
The Times, should be given access to take some discrete photos.
He hoped we did not mind.

The luncheon was hugely successful. Some legal business,
some medical as well, was mentioned, but a great deal of chatting took place as Carolyn and Eugenia became slightly more
informed about our various undertakings. For coffee afterward,

the men and women separated for twenty minutes or so. Almost three hours after our arrival, it was time for our departure. Sir Richard invited us up to Oxford (next trip hopefully), the McDonalds for cocktails at the end of a working session and Julian for a gastropub lunch.

In the Bentley on the return drive to Grosvenor House, Martha opined what a shame it was that Mary, Sir Richard's assistant who was so unfailingly helpful to us, went uninvited to the luncheon.

Carolyn allowed that here in the UK, class distinctions still endured. So, that type of thing was not untypical, and she doubted anyone thought much about it. Martha seemed not satisfied with that response, looked at me, and refrained from revisiting her comment.

— — —

Parts of each day were taken up by some form of work, including the needs of Carolyn to make visits to clients. In one case, I came along to an earlyish dinner, so her key contact could take a train home more than an hour away. Not so apparently, much of this had to do with Carolyn working exclusively for a certain company in a precise business area (only later, did I learn that the fee for that exclusivity was a mid-six figures per year).

One social engagement which I had not really expected to encounter was with those involved in the DMIC reinsurance recovery project. When Bradley Campbell learned that Carolyn was in town, he felt compelled to meet her, but also to include his wife, Gabrielle. Neither Quincey Franden-Jones nor Wilfred Smythe lived anywhere near the City, each having a small *pied de terre* in London. Bradley suggested some cocktails at his office and a nice dinner at Simpson's on the Strand. I felt obligated to accept.

Carolyn was being a very good sport, very understanding

about all of my business contacts. Bradley hosted the cocktail hour, but Madeline did all of the work. Gabrielle, Bradley's wife who appeared somewhat older than Carolyn or Martha acted as if she was a bit uncomfortable in the company of so many strangers, without much regard to their being English, Welsh or American. Twice, at least, she asked me about my Irish background. (The second time, I asked her about hers, presumably English? "Heavens, yes!")

How interesting that she warmed to this inquiry: seems that Bradley and she were the union of two families who had mutual interests in lands in the country sides of England, Normandy and other sections in the west of France. They were introduced a few times and then simply told that they were to be married (later she was to learn that Bradley approved beforehand, but she had no actual say in the decision). This all occurring at some point in the latter half of the twentieth century!

Having told her story, overheard by Carolyn and Martha, her manner improved somewhat. I went to go to the gentlemen's. Once outside Bradley's office, another door opened and Madeline was standing there, "Your new wife is more gorgeous in person than her photographs, Congratulations! Would you ask Bradley to invite me to dinner "to balance out the sexes, please? I just want to see more of you, and her, for that matter."

With that Madeline went back to her pantry. When I returned, I mentioned the "balancing" to Bradley and pointed out that Madeline was "part of the team." He quickly agreed without seemingly a second thought. (Then he came back to tell me that Gabrielle was quite cool to that idea, but because I asked, she acquiesced.)

At dinner, Carolyn sat between Bradley and Quincey, while I was between Gabrielle and Madeline. That left Martha and Wilfred who made the best of it throughout dinner. Madeline often deferred to Gabrielle in our on-going three-way discourse, but her knee frequently found mine. (Surely, she must realize that nothing at all untoward was going to occur that evening.) With that seating arrangement, very little business was discussed, but a great deal of wine was being consumed by the other three men and my two immediate dinner companions. Bradley had laid out a four-course meal. By the time I had my pre-main course (poached salmon), followed by a small salad, I was feeling a bit tired. I looked over at Carolyn and she caught my eye with a signal that she was ready to go. With that, I raised the remains of my third glass of white, struck it once with my knife, somewhat softly, and when all at our table looked my way, said, "I am afraid that Carolyn and I are a bit overtired as we have been keeping relatively early hours since our arrival in town. We have had a marvelous evening and I will be pleased to advise the client that all is going very well. For that reason, I feel we must apologize and leave a bit early. I shall see three of you tomorrow at Cheshire & Booth at 10:00. Gabrielle, it was a pleasure meeting you. Wilfred, I may see you. Madeline, I hope to say farewell tomorrow, but that might not happen. Bradley, thank you for all of this and we hope the rest of you will carry on!"

— — —

Carolyn and I salvaged what was left of a splendid night. I saw Martha for breakfast the next morning. She did not look well and spared me most of the details of the large part of that evening that we missed when our group seemingly closed Simpson's (apparently, Gabrielle used our exit to turn pedantic in her treatment of Madeline)!

That day's meeting goal was a current assessment and projection of what was left to be found, and what was needed as a follow-on by each side. Drafts of charts and graphs were passed out covering the status of the overall project, and what was left to complete it. Agreement on those, as best as could be done at this stage was completed. That left the follow-on: what comes next?

I rose to speak, heretofore not done at these meetings. I began with, "I trust that our NDA remains in full effect?" Our team nodded YES. After Stanley Booth said, "Yes. Of course." I sat.

Then I began, "Desert Mutual has a proposition for all of those involved in this project." I went on for the better part of an hour. When I finished, all heads turned to Stanley Booth who said with a straight face, "I think I see why none of this is written down. We have notes as I am certain you all do as well. This is more than we had expected, so let us have some time to digest what you have said and we'll let you know when we are ready to meet again."

With that, we left as a group, but outside, I said to Bradley and Quincey that I needed to get back to my bride and would go directly back to Grosvenor House. Martha joined me. In the black taxi, I asked her to transcribe her notes, if possible that day so I could have them whilst in Paris. She agreed, but allowed she needed a nap first. Carolyn was delightfully surprised when she walked out of her bath and found me sitting across from our un-made bed taking off my shoes. She smiled, saying, "Are you going to keep going, (her bath robe dropped open) or shall I get dressed now?"

— — —

Much of that day and the next, before we flew to Paris, was spent looking out our rooms' windows at rooftops across London, or at the ceiling in our room. We had one last Dover sole dinner at Wheeler's, and made love after that, too.

16

PARIS: DOCTOR BIGNON AND MORE!

F lying to Paris with Carolyn as my new wife was somehow
even more bittersweet than flying into Heathrow and
staying at the Grosvenor House. All of my firsts in London had been with Mollie, or I was alone. But in Paris, that very
first night, I had encountered Carolyn, and those days had
proved magical in their own way.

*But then, with Mollie gone and flying back with Carolyn, I had a
sense of melancholia that made me feel emotionally flat. Later, following
that return, I told Dr. Arnaud about those feelings, or sensations, or
whatever they were. But I also added, Carolyn was so excited to have
me back in Paris that her ebullient feelings became contagious. Still,
later that first night, and several others, once Carolyn had fallen asleep,
those same melancholy feelings intruded again just as I was falling
asleep.*

*Dr. Arnaud listened, shook her head, asked a few questions, one of
which was how I felt the next morning. When I said that sensation had
passed, she answered, "Maybe you should not dwell on that particular
phenomenon lest it become a fixation and you give it a significance
which might not otherwise occur.*

— — —

We flew from the City Airport in London into *Orly* in Paris.
We had decided to stay at *Le Meurice*, not so much for its loca-
tion, but because it was the site of our chance meeting those several years ago. When Carolyn called her agent in Paris to tell her
when we would be arriving, that agent, Celestine, who had not

made it to our wedding, insisted that she take us to dinner. Moreover, since she had participated in producing the *Vogue* wedding coverage, Celestine insisted that she invite Robert, the driving force editor and chief of photography/executive producer of that feature in Paris, as well. (We had four nights in Paris: one was already dedicated to Lisette, and another to Dr. Bignon. This Celestine night left us only one night to ourselves.)

Arriving just before the afternoon rush, we soon were in our accommodations (booked by Carolyn under her working name), well above the *Rue de Rivoli* with a view that overlooked the *Louvre*. We stood, side-by-side, our arms around each other's waist, in front of one of the floor to ceiling French doors and looked out over the grand museums, a huge park with a Ferris Wheel to our immediate right, *Notre Dame* to our left, and a few small glimpses of the River *Seine* as it meandered through the heart of Paris. I heard Carolyn slowly take a deep breath. She turned to face me still held in my arms, adjusted her face slightly upward, looked into my eyes, and said, "I remember what I told you on the top deck of the Eiffel Tower that day of our Parisian walkabout. Now that daydream has come true. I want you to know that I will always love you more than anyone else, except Patrick, and he is both of us." With that she lowered her face and placed her head on my shoulder and we went back to our looking at rooftops as I squeezed her waist bringing Carolyn ever slightly closer to me.

— — —

Lisette was hosting dinner that first night in Paris. She had a companion, Mathilde, who came only for a cocktail. As the weather was pleasant, we four sat at a table by an open window that would be closed when the onset of evening brought its first chill. Lisette was doing a shoot the next morning, so we started the dinner process earlier than is usual in Paris. Our goal for that evening was to reassure Lisette that she was always welcome to stay at our home, or if she preferred at the Cote d'Azur, whenever she was in our greater neighborhood. (I had a similar "reassuring talk" with Vera at our wedding, but had no such opportunity to do so with Lisette who was constantly surrounded by admirers that day.) The other woman, who was lovely and older, rose to leave and we all got to our feet. Lisette was thanked, and Carolyn said she would walk Mathilde out.

We two sank back into our chairs, and as Lisette was about to speak, I started, "Lisette. I am so fully aware what a great friend and mentor you have been to Carolyn. I want you to know that our marriage is not meant in any way to undermine your relationship with Carolyn. Please feel free to talk about this with her, but please be aware that we shall have a room in our new home for you whenever you wish to stay. I want you to know that you will always be welcome." At that moment, Carolyn returned to the table.

As she sat, Carolyn asked, "What have you two been talking about?"

Lisette looked at me, and said, "Carolyn, Ronan here, has just made the most interesting statement. Did you know he was going to do such a thing?"

Carolyn then took a couple of minutes, and literally built on what I had said. When she finished, Lisette said, "I am so grateful that you are both so willing to accommodate me. It sounds like Ronan would remain willing, or perhaps only tolerant, if you and I were to be together in the future. But please allow me to tell you a little bit about why I so much wanted to have this dinner with you both. This is not my springing a trap, but it is about me moving on with my life, much as you have moved on with your lives, both of you, and especially you, Carolyn."

"Since I found you almost twenty years ago, came to love you, and guided you into your career where, I am certain, you are now more successful than me. What did *Sports illustrated* say about you when you returned after a few years hiatus. I think it was, 'The All-American Girl has Become the All-American Woman, who can wear any bathing suit and look great in it!' To me, that describes your career and, with my help in the beginning, you have launched yourself into a major success. Your Wedding Feature in *VOGUE* was a *coup d'etat* on our whole profession."

"But enough about you. I wanted you both to meet Mathilde because in a few years, I plan to be more like her. I do not really want my life to change. I, especially, do not wish to go backward." So, Lisette slid her chair back, stood, and made a beckoning gesture. I glimpsed a tall, somewhat tan young woman with beautiful facial features and eyes that were a dark, seemingly purple, highlighted by very dark reddish-brown hair almost shoulder length with body and flowing waves, rise from her bar chair and start toward us. I rose as she approached the table. So did Carolyn. Linette gestured to Mathilde's vacated seat, a waiter appeared and cleared that place, quickly resetting it. The young woman, perhaps very young as I saw her more closely, seated herself directly across from me. "Carolyn, please meet DonaViva. She is my new protégé, actually the first since you. Ronan, this is DonaViva. Sha has a great many things to ask you both. I hope you will indulge her. You see, we have become a couple, of sorts, as I had been for all those years with you, Carolyn. Of course, as always, there were others."

"One just left."

"The timing of our first meeting was not dissimilar from when I met you the first time, Carolyn. The details, however, are unimportant as we only have tonight, since I have a 6:00 a.m. call tomorrow. DonaViva, please tell them about your name."

Her first words, as her greeting was more gesture and so French, came as a bit of a surprise, "I am the only daughter of two Swiss people: an older mother from a Swiss-French family, and a somewhat younger Swiss-Italian father. I am what you might call their "Love Child," as my mother died giving birth to me before they could marry. My father stayed by her bedside the whole week while she fought for her life. He feared her family, who held him in reproach for their relationship, would deny him as my father. When she passed, they say he wept inconsolably for almost a week, his only needs being light sustenance and the continued presence of his child. My mother's parents were quite old and had raised five children. Only one of them had turned out wrong, and that was my mother. But when they saw how my father behaved, they rethought my parents' whole adventure. After all, my mother and he were both musicians; he wrote and played, she sang. That was how they met, and they lived for five blissful years together. My mother's parents suggested my name for my Baptism, DonaViva Anna, made my father sole godparent and signed over all of my custody to him. They all, the three of them, became fast friends, a family of sorts, and I became a Swiss child of two cultures.

"I was going to interview with a potential agent when Lisette saw me through an open door as she was passing down the hall toward another office. I looked up, and she suddenly stopped, staring at me. I found myself quickly staring back at her. She nodded at me and I rose and went to her in the corridor. She asked if I was there to interview. When I said YES, she told me to come with her. Almost fifty steps down that hallway, my world changed. We walked into Lisette's agent's office. I followed her. She nodded to a secretary and walked into an office otherwise unannounced. She said, "Phillippe, you have been looking to replicate Carolyn for some years now. This young lady may be the one. Turning to me, she asked, 'What's your name?'"

"When I said, 'DonaViva Anna.' The man rose from his desk smiling. As he came around the desk, he was assessing me. I could tell. My eyes were on him. I could not clearly see that Lisette was assessing me as well. Phillippe looked at Lisette, and said, 'I think DonaViva. We drop the Anna.'"

"When I turned to look at Lisette, she smiled at Phillippe, and then radiantly at me. That was almost eighteen months ago. My life has not been the same since I met Lisette."

I ordered another round of drinks, thinking. "What a story," but then what must it have been like for Carolyn all those years ago; and then, what was this like for her now. Not long to wait. Carolyn smiling widely, got up, walked up to Lisette and gave her a great hug, then turning to DonaViva, opened her arms and the young girl just wilted into them. Hugging DonaViva, Carolyn looked over her shoulder to Lisette and said, "I am so happy for you both. So incredibly happy!"

The rest of the evening was most convivial, and not what either of us expected. It seems that both of the new couple wanted to know how I ultimately became Carolyn's very first, and perhaps only, part-time heterosexual partner, and about our hidden life over all of those many years. Turns out the story was so much better coming from Carolyn; and her introduction of Mollie into the conversation was nothing, if not artistry. Her Patrick, however, was not a point on which she was at all willing to divulge anything. Finally, Carolyn started a reiteration of our chance meeting in that bar at *Le Meurice*.

That night at Lisette's Parisian flat was described by Carolyn, who blushed a few times, but ended by saying, "Much as I thought I might want it, that night I realized that my life as a Lesbian was not going to work with a heterosexual partner in that mix. In fact, when the invitation was extended to Ronan, I suddenly became afraid that he was going to join us. My relief at his saying he would watch a bit, caused me to fluster; and, as Lisette will tell you, I never wanted to miss an opportunity with her until that night."

"When I returned from walking Ronan back to his hotel that night, Lisette was still awake on her side of the bed. She looked up at me, smiled, and said, 'Take off all of those clothes and come into my bed. I want to make you forget, at least for tonight, that you are in love with that man.' Oh, but I will say this, 'You have an excellent eye for what looks like very choice male talent.'"

Carolyn smiled at me over the rim of her wine glass, we were down to our last sips.

Up in our room, after our host and her new significant other departed, I inquired of Carolyn about how she felt about this night. Her reply stayed with me as fascinating over our future years, "Ronan, at one point, you and Lisette both asked to be excused and I was left alone with our new friend. Before I could say anything, she asked me why I decided to seduce you that very first night we met. I actually thought for a second and answered, 'He seemed to be nothing like the men that I had run away from almost three years before: tall, clean, elegant in his uniform, polite, pleasant, even friendly, and open to meeting me without trying to make a pass. When he was in the No-Name Bar waiting for me to have that drink, he was more of the same, and kind of humble too. I decided at the Bar on my second drink that I would actually make a run at him if he needed a ride up the hill. When he gratefully accepted my offer, we were back on the roof deck in no time. On the way, I thought for a second that if I kissed him in my car, he would think that was enough and go straight back to Tinker's. So, I decided to wait until we went inside the building, and asked him if he would like a nightcap, and saying he was early for his time due back at Tinker's. He came into Lisette's apartment with me and she was gone. He was so easy once I sat down next to him, and asked him what he would like, kind man that he is."

I was a kind man that night as well. Carolyn had seduced me once again.

— — —

We had a light brunch late the next morning, a few doors down the *Rue de Rivoli*. Then, crossed over the *Seine* to the *Musee d'Orsay* to ponder the world's greatest collection of Impressionistic Art. Dinner that evening was to be with Dr. Bignon and his wife, aptly named Camille, whom I had yet to meet, at *La Caravelle*. Carolyn knew neither, but did know of INSERM, and was very impressed with our putative dinner companions. I also told Carolyn about the dinner Mollie, Martha and I had with Dr. Bignon at that same restaurant on Mollie's first trip to Paris before she began to take ill. She chuckled at some of my comments on that retelling.

We walked back to our hotel across the *Ile de la Cite*. Carolyn allowed that this was the very best place to live in all of Paris: in the center of everything as she put it. I asked her if she was going to miss Lisette when she returned to Paris. That made her smile. She said, "If she invites me, I'll probably stay, but there definitely will be no DonaViva for me, and probably no Lisette. After all, I have my hands full now with you, My Love!"

Carolyn dressed for *La Caravelle*, advising me it was much more of a "see and be seen" dining spot than *Tour d'Argent* .

Her dress was a heavenly blue, a few inches off the floor, flowing in simple lines from her bodice, and it did not emphasize, or disguise, her breasts. She wore simple jewelry, and her hair was up without outside assistance. Upon arrival at the restaurant, I said to the Front Desk Greeter, "Mr. & Mrs. O'Neill for Dr. Bignon and his wife, please."

The Greeter at *La Caravelle* wore a full tuxedo and bowed to me, then to Carolyn, nodding to her, and saying, "A pleasure to have you with us again, Ms. Tyne. You look radiant. May I congratulate you both on your nuptials and our house will be pleased to pour you a bottle of our prize Champagne." He then nodded to a table captain who escorted us to our table in the center of the restaurant. As we moved behind him, almost every head turned toward Carolyn, and some toward me. Photographs were taken. Dr. Bignon was standing, and as we approached their table, so did the woman I took to be Camille, the Chief Doctor of France's wife. She was younger than I expected and her face was quite attractive. She took my hand in greeting and I kissed hers, brushing it ever so lightly with my lips, as instructed by Carolyn. Dr. Bignon bowed and performed the same ritual formality with Carolyn. Four men in full livery stood behind our chairs and we were all seated. Bignon turned to me, and said, for consumption by our table, and perhaps for those very nearby, "Camille suggested to me that your entrance might set off some excitement, and I must admit the two of you appear to be first rate celebrities here in Paris, especially for Americans." While saying most of this Bignon was studying Carolyn's face, but her glances included her three companions and a number of those nearby. I suddenly realized that Carolyn was an expert at dealing with attention by seeming to largely ignore the looks or stares of others.

Camille and Carolyn seemed to enjoy each other's company, and they spent some of their time gossiping about Parisian society and things which they might have in common. Dr. Bignon was a most gracious host and engaged in making merry over our recent nuptials. Right before we began our seafood course, the Doctor talked about meeting Mollie almost two years before at this very restaurant. He seemed somewhat uncomfortable. Carolyn reached over and patted his hand twice, very lightly, saying, "Mollie and I became very good friends. Her illness was so sad. She was so concerned for Ronan and her four children, that she talked to me about marrying Ronan on several occasions before she passed." Carolyn looked at Bignon's face at that moment, and added, "Often, like now, I feel Mollie is with Ronan and me. I feel that way now." I looked over from Carolyn to Camille, and she had tears coming down her cheeks. Carolyn adroitly shifted to a topic suitable for seafood and the rest of the evening worked out just fine!

While the women excused themselves, Dr. Bignon and I did all of the business which was needed between us on this trip. As we departed, Camille and Carolyn exchanged the dual Euro-buss. I could swear I heard one or two cameras.

— — —

The next morning at breakfast in the hotel salon, the *Maitre d'* asked if we would like to see all of our photographs from the morning newspapers. Of, my! I really was married to a celebrity. Carolyn commented that many of them mention that I was with the man from her "Wedding Shoot" for *Vogue*, a few issues ago. I wonder what the French edition did say about our wedding? (Or, if it even did! I thought.) But then Carolyn focused on the day to come, a characteristic which required her to seem to know ahead of time, precisely how she was planning to spend her day. She said, "How about we do just the *Louvre*? Then dinner tonight with Celestine, who in the end is a very real and darling woman, not gay I believe; and Robert (Ro-BEAR), the feature editor from *Vogue* who was at the wedding. He was so inconspicuous, as to seem a photographer. Actually, he directed the entire shoot. Did you meet him at all? Carolyn paused while I nodded YES with a slight head shake (I remember my mouth being full so often when she would ask me something; and if I spoke with food in my mouth, she would make the worst faces to mock me!). Continuing, "Well, Celestine left a message for me while we were at dinner last night. We are to meet those two at the bar in the *George V* at 7:30, with dinner in the Main Salon at 8:30. That will mean my last evening dress. So, how does that sound for today in Paris?"

Me: "What about some time for just us?"

Carolyn, "Sex will take place after our afternoon cocktail, at about 5:00. Will that be OK?"

Me: "I'm sorry I was so tired last night. I didn't think I drank that much."

Carolyn: "Quite alright. After all, you are so much older than me!"

We had a fabulous four hours in the *Louvre*. Only a few people seemed to recognize Carolyn. She seemed quietly happy the entire time! A cocktail at an outside table brought just the right feeling to close that part of the day. We retreated to our suite enjoying an hour together before Carolyn needed to start the process of readying herself.

— — —

Carolyn wore a soft rose, close fitting evening dress with a matching wrap. The *George V* Doorman at the curb and a Concierge appeared to be waiting for us. They stood on either side of her door from the car which had fetched us, which I quickly realized was to obscure, as much as feasible, Carolyn from the *paparazzi's* ready cameras. No avail at first, but when I took Carolyn's arm and lead her up the five stairs, they gave us space on my side. My look across to my wife's unescorted side may have had some distancing effect as well. But, when we got to the top step, Carolyn paused, turned, struck a pose with a diffident waive, and then spun on my arm, entering that hotel. (All in much less than 20 seconds!)

The other guests in the Lobby and much of the staff noticed the fuss just outside. A gentleman in tuxedo came forward and greeted us by our married names. Carolyn and I both smiled acknowledging that fact. Many of the guests not recognizing those names began to go back to their ways when one woman, obviously an American, said in a too loud voice, "Oh, they are the fashion model, Carolyn Tyne, and her husband. They were in all the Paris papers this morning. I just do not understand all of that fuss!"

Another woman turned to the man on her arm and said,

"What an utterly delightful couple." The manager swept us into the Bar and there, apparently stood Celestine, smiling happily, and while hugging Carolyn asked *sotto voce*, "How did you enjoy that greeting?!" Introductions were had, and we settled down for a drink. Celestine appeared to enjoy bantering. I tried not to encourage her, but she was amusing, and tireless. Robert had trouble getting a sentence or two into the conversation. Finally, I asked him how we had almost completely avoided meeting each other at the wedding. He responded that we actually met informally when his whole team was being introduced, but we had almost no meaningful interaction thereafter. Now, he was looking forward to hearing more about me over dinner. I asked him about himself, but he seemed extremely reluctant to talk about anything of a personal nature, and I felt uncomfortable addressing his work. But with Celestine present, there was no opportunity for a vacuum of silence lasting more than a split second.

After picking two wines for our appetizers, Celestine launched into the unexpected: "Carolyn. I know your wedding feature was a major hit in the U.S., but you have no idea about over here! In the UK and Italy, it was huge as well. Here in France, it was a trend-setter. Robert and I have been conferring and we would like to do a follow-up feature on both of you. Ronan, we know you are not a professional model, but we both believe you are so natural that you could bring this off. (Robert was nodding in agreement.)

"Carolyn tells me you two have bought an older home, and it is almost finished being remodeled. We would like to do three features: the Remodel, the Move-In, and the First Party in your new home. Also, you have five children between you, all of whom are very photogenic. Carolyn has shown me some pictures and it looks like a dream home. And it's so close to that charming church where you were married. Our people in the U.S. have done some research on that town, Ross, I believe. It is inordinately wealthy, but not obviously so. Of course, Vogue would not mention that in any way in any of its features.

Robert, "*Vogue* does see this as an incredibly unique opportunity. Celestine, please explain our offer."

Carolyn was smiling, but not with a total confidence. When I looked in her eyes, they went down, Celestine was just preparing to speak when I held up a hand to stop her. I looked at Carolyn, saying, "Carolyn, My Love, do you really want this?" She grinned shyly and nodded affirmatively.

I turned to Celestine, and said, "Tell me the deal for which I am signing up."

The offer was much greater than generous. The *George V* Champagne arrived, and we drank a toast to the deal as we ate our first course. The balance of the evening became a party, and even Robert opened up a bit.

That night, we made special love. Carolyn was so happy with the way I had responded and my calling her. "My Love!" She said, "I thought that would always be reserved for Mollie." I smiled, making no reply.

For our final day in Paris, we did the cruise on the Seine, and went to a near-by bistro for a simple three course Parisian meal. It was a perfect way to end that trip.

— — —

On returning to the hotel, I had a fax from Martha waiting for me. In essence, it said that LAUSD and its attorneys proposed dismissing KK Small Enterprises in return for our client waiving its rights to any recoverable costs against that plaintiff. I smiled. Martha had done an excellent job maintaining the pressure on both that plaintiff, its attorneys, and the Court itself. I wondered if LAUSD had dismissed any others (its second wave defendants had proven troublesome, being more than willing to follow CAL Board's lead).

Yet, in the middle of the night, I had a thought, "What happens to my practice when all of this ends?" I lay awake for an hour or more mulling those prospects!

17

THE BLACK BART INN

Judge Hiram Forestall, the only Superior Court judge in San Andreas County, set a Status/Initial Settlement Conference for 10:00 a.m. on a Wednesday in early April. Carey wanted to be there and he planned to bring the senior Cayuga Mutual adjuster from Pasadena with him. They would spend the night in Burbank and arrive by 9:00 flying a charter into the San Andreas Airfield! I met them, and we drove into town. Strom Nordquist, whom I had met several years before was the Cayuga Mutual adjuster, located in Pasadena. We went into the coffee shop at the Black Bart Inn for a quick light snack as they had nothing to eat or drink on their flight (relatively inexpensive according to Strom). Carey told me, at a later date, it was one of his most scary adventures ever.

The Court House, in the County Administration Building was no more than a half mile from the Black Bart on Highway 49, the main road running through town, and connecting many towns in what was referred to as The Gold Country of the Sierra Foothills. There were two court rooms, one for the Superior Court and one for Municipal Court, which handled traffic matters, misdemeanors, Small Claims matters, and other civil actions not pleading the jurisdictional dollar amount of damages exceeding the Superior Court's statutory minimum limit. Thus, all of the "serious matters" were in the Superior Court, including criminal procedure and trials, bail hearings, family law, probate, and civil litigation having a dollar value greater than the Municipal Court's top jurisdiction. Judge Forestall was not only the Superior Court Judge for that county, he sometimes served as a circuit-riding Superior Court Judge for Alpine County, having the smallest population in California.

The Sacramento Valley lawyers were present with their three clients, but they brought no insurance company claims people to this initial Settlement Conference.

Attorney Downing was present with Ruth Hobart. A man looking uncomfortable in a sport coat with a tie was alone. I took him to be Ross Weatherbee, the pump installer. We filed into the next to last row of seats on the defense side of the court. Promptly, at ten o'clock, a bailiff called the Court to order. A door behind the bench opened, and a white-haired man in flowing robes appeared. There were two other matters on that Court's docket and each was dealt with summarily, neither taking as much as five minutes. Then, the clerk called *Bosley Hobart, Jr., et al versus Haley Pumps, Incorporated (Hobart v. Haley Pumps)*. Attorney Downing stood at his seat and made an appearance for all plaintiffs, Bo's entire immediate family. I went next and introduced Carey Crawford, Vice President & General Counsel for Haley Pumps, Inc., and Strom Nordquist, Senior Adjuster for Cayuga Mutual Insurance Company. The others made their appearances.

The judge asked if any more parties were to be added. Mr. Downing and the other counsel said NO, but I allowed that Haley Pumps was undertaking a painstaking search of its records to find the purchase or shipping documents for the subject "exploding water pressure tank." After some discussion, the judge told us we would have 150 days to complete that search and to file a motion, if need be, to add that company. As adding a party would forestall any other key dates, the status conference would be renewed in six months, or sooner if that putative entity appeared at a time making that feasible.

Judge Forestall then went about having an initial settlement discussion with each party to develop a "feel for the value of this case." He spoke with the Plaintiffs' side first, in his chambers.

Then he spoke with each of the other three defendants, each separately, but only after noting at the outset of the "settlement
talks" that Haley Pumps had one person from New York state
and one from Southern California. Therefore, it would behoove
each defendant to have a client rep and a claims person for any
future settlement talks. He saw our group last, and he kept
everyone else waiting. I began by stressing that no party had
found our client's pump had malfunctioned in any manner.
Therefore, any source of liability would have to be attributable
to the tank which we clearly did not create, but apparently did
sell to the uninsured installer. Furthermore, I stressed that the
company was doing an "all-hands" search to try to find the purchase documents for the tank. Carey had gotten the sales invoice
to Ross Weatherbee, but it did not name the tank manufacturer,
only describing it generally, including its size. The transaction
had been six years before the accident. We were hopeful of finding the missing documents related to Haley's purchase of that
tank.

Judge Forestall looked at Carey and Strom, saying, "Mr.
Downing sees you all as the "deep pocket" here. I'm not at all
certain your company is the most culpable, or even culpable at
all. But I will tell you this much: no jury in this county will let
Bo and his family go uncompensated for an accident like this,
especially one with such devastating injuries. Bo grew up here.
He's known as a good guy, a real straight-shooter."

Me: "Did you tell this to the other defendants?"

The Judge: "Most all of it. Mr. Downing likes you, Mr.
O'Neill. He thinks you are very smart and you will build a case
against your fellow defendants. At least that's what he told me.
Please know he did NOT tell me NOT to pass that along to you!
Do you all have an offer today?"

Everyone looked around for a few seconds. When no one
spoke, the Judge rose and headed for the door to his courtroom.
The others all rose as he entered. "Sorry, fellas!" said Judge

Forestall, "try as I might, I could not get this case to settle, but the next time we are together, I will expect some real offers from the defense, no excuses, and claims people present."

When no one spoke, the judge said, "You all are excused. Please let my clerk know, if you need anything. Thank you all for coming. Ross, you do not have to attend unless I order you to be here."

— — —

We drove back to the Black Bart for a late lunch. Carey was clear on the point that now was the time for an all-out document search, or we would lose the right to sue that potential target defendant. Strom was nervous, saying, "I understand there's no manufacturer's plate on that tank. Without that, how will you ever prove what company made that tank? How will anyone be able to prove up a purchase document as specifically applicable to that precise tank?"

Carey's reaction was calm and assured, saying, "Haley has never been in the tank business. We build and sell pumps. Occasionally, as an accommodation, we will buy other components for a special customer. Also, sometimes, we buy OEM (other equipment manufacturer) components and we get stuck with them, if, for example, an order gets cancelled after our purchase. If that's the case, this might prove more difficult. But since the recipient was in California, the tank must have come from our City of Industry Regional Sales & Supply Center. I have been in touch. They claim to have not found anything, but I do not know what they have actually done by way of their search."

I looked at both of them, and decided to change the subject to a settlement strategy, "Just for a few minutes, please consider that everyone, the plaintiffs' attorney, the judge, the co-defendants, all think that Haley Pumps is *the* Deep Pocket defendant in this case. My guess is that even if we find the tank manufacturer, they'll want to blame you all as well. So, what I'm going to suggest is we come up with a number that's big enough that it sounds reasonable, that we make that offer at the next settlement conference, and we tell the judge that amount is our final offer. Then, we will stand on it through a trial, if need be, proving others liable, if not more liable."

Carey, "How much?"

Me: "Cannot be as low as $100,000, not with these injuries."

Strom, "$200,000 is real money. What do you think, Carey?"

Carey looked at me quizzically, "Ronan?"

Me: "A little more might go a long way: How about a quarter of a million dollars?"

Strom, "That certainly has the ring of very real money, even in L.A.; and up here, I'm guessing those are big bucks!"

Strom looked at Carey, then me, then back to Carey, who said, "Can you get it?"

Strom said, "I sure will try. I have no great desire to keep flying into this death trap of an airport!"

— — —

A couple of weeks later, I got a call from Carey. He was down in the City of Industry at their regional office. He had been through about five years of purchases before the accident. But one problem was that none of the discovery responses to date had established when the system that failed had been installed. That regional office had quite a few sales to Ross Weatherbee and they all included pumps, but none included a tank! Moreover, the historical invoice filings were reverse chronological, but not always. Carey was pressing his people as to the rest of their files. Could I send help if he needed it?

I thought about his issues. I called Jim Downing. Surprisingly, he was in his office and took my call. I was frank as to the search issues. He asked me to hold, and was back in less than five minutes. He said that the best evidence so far from Installer

Weatherbee was the system was installed between six and eight years before the accident. Based on this info, we will not get it any closer than that range of time.

I called Carey back at the City of Industry office. He had found a room full of dust, dirt and worse, containing hundreds of boxes. I asked if he would like to have Joshua Small, the associate on the case for a few days. He agreed (but I think he wanted me). Then I told him what I had gotten from Downing and he was delighted. Joshua flew into Ontario and was at Carey's hotel in time for dinner.

Late the next day, I got a call from Carey and Joshua. Once they organized the boxes by date, they started on those six years out. In less than twenty boxes, they had found an invoice with "the pump" from the Hobart property accident, a 450-gallon water storage tank, and various components. The manufacturer of the tank was identified as Sterling Pressure Tanks in a suburb of Kansas City, Missouri, including a serial number. In two more hours, they found the Haley Pumps Purchase Order for two water pressure tanks, including the subject tank. They were second-hand tanks. That gave us two new targets: their tank seller and the manufacturer. They had the manager of the office go through the search process with them, so that he could be used to authenticate all of those documents.

In less than a week, Joshua had filed and was in the process of serving those two new Cross-Defendants. (For his assistance, I gave Jim Downing a heads-up if he wanted to sue them. He thanked me, but said he would leave them to Haley Pumps to prosecute.) A few more months went by with our sending and answering written discovery, producing documents, and our re-taining an expert on pumping systems. We were ready for the deposition phase of discovery.

Oh! We also did hear from Strom Nordquist at Cayuga Mutual that he had $250,000 in authority to settle, but also that their claims committee told him that was all that they were ever going to put up. So, they were all crystal clear this was not a starting point for negotiations against Haley Pump Company, but rather a good faith contribution by Haley's insurer "to prime the pump" with a view toward settlement by all of the other parties defendant.

I told Joshua to keep me up to date on any discovery developments and to write a report when our two cross-defendants were served. I gave him instructions to start getting our expert prepared. Back to the big asbestos property matters for me, but I also had to come to terms with our move, the new house, and with the potentially protracted "*Vogue* shoot!"

18

SCHOOLS CLASS: THE LEIBNITZ INSTITUTE

Some months before anything major happened, Martha came to me and said that she had read about a big asbestos symposium being put on in Boston by a scientific association calling itself the Leibnitz Institute. She had the proposed agenda and it sounded like it would play directly into her expertise. Moreover, a number of the speakers were known to be among the Asbestos Plaintiff Attorneys' experts. Should we ask Desert Mutual to pay for her to attend? If not, would our firm? I suggested we call Manny in Scottsdale and see what he had to say. I asked her if she would please make the case to Manny that she had just made to me. Martha initially appeared reluctant; yet, when I told her I would be on the call to support her, she agreed.

Much to her surprise, Manny said YES, and also allowed that Desert Mutual was getting a steady stream of reinsurance payments from London. I allowed that the search at Cheshire & Booth might be closer to its end than the beginning, and its cost would come in well below any of the estimates which we had provided while being conservatively cautious. Manny asked if this would provide an opportunity for him to start to get up to speed on the science, especially from the plaintiffs' perspective. Before I could agree, Martha stepped up and said YES. (Not much longer in those days until she became a full-blown partner candidate!)

Three weeks before that Institute program in Boston and the week before our "ROSS Move-In Shoot" was the next Status Conference in the SCHOOLS Class. That was combined with a

National Coordinating Counsel Meeting in Philadelphia the day before. I asked Mary if she thought Martha should go. She agreed. Mary had worked with Tinker's office in renewing our Motion to have one of the CAL Board entities dismissed for lack of venue, twice previously denied as premature because plaintiffs' counsel had not completed their discovery (we had confirmed that failure to complete in writing the second time!). She would argue that motion, if need be. Martha would be there for the Science issues. (I asked Martha how she wanted to handle Mary being there for the hearing and she pointed out that Mary could fly straight to Philadelphia while we went to D.C. for the pre-meetings. Once in Philly, Martha thought it prudent that her room be next to Mary.)

— — —

In this particularly hectic period of my life, I still managed to keep in contact with Dr. Arnaud who was seemingly impressed by the capacity for goodwill inspired by Carolyn (whom I had advised of my visits to my psychiatrist and many of the underlying reasons, especially Viet Nam). Yet, Dr. Arnaud remained steadfast about Martha whom she regarded as a potential source of trouble with Carolyn in my future. Many of our sessions were by telephone (which she recorded) and often occurred when I found myself troubled. Then, there were the "Vogue Shoots." Somehow Carolyn just included those details in her ongoing life's work. I had a problem doing that, especially as Robert, the Vogue editor, had rented a two-bedroom apartment in Corte Madera from which to stage the shoot and coordinate his crew. Dr. Arnaud basically told me that I was not ready for how highly competent Carolyn had turned out to be! In retrospect, over a relatively short time, I came to agree with the good Doctor: Carolyn was amazing! I was a twice-over lucky man!

— — —

Although it upset the children, I put the Mill Valley house up for sale. In consultation with Carolyn, and her choice of real estate agent (who had helped her find and buy the Ross house with help from a friend), we settled on an asking price which I thought way too high. But I was in no real hurry to sell (unlike Carolyn who was committed to the various components of the "*Vogue* Shoots."), especially as I wanted all of the children to finish their school year without the trauma of the move occurring before that was accomplished.

What a surprise when we got two offers for the asking price within 48 hours. Our agent advised that we counter with terms about when we would vacate and ask for $25,000 over the asking price. Both accepted those terms. We then went just to price and asked them to bid (one of our terms was 'all cash'). After six more days, we got $150,000 more than our initial asking price. Even with all of this, our new place in Ross would cost much more, especially because of Carolyn's many improvements. She did not seem to care as she had me set aside serious money for a trust for each of my children (Divided four ways: half of the net sales price which Carolyn said was Mollie's share under California's Community Property laws, and even though Mollie had left her entire estate to me!). Carolyn said to recall that this Ross house was her wedding present to me. She had reluctantly allowed me to help to pay for it.

— — —

Martha and I took our final TWA flight to Dulles on Sunday morning. (TWA was merging into American and we would henceforth fly United as it had taken over so many of TWA's gates in key airports.) The flight attendants, many of whom we had come to know over all of these years were nostalgic. A few were transferring to United, but that airline appeared not anxious to take on many older women. One of them hugged Martha and me when we got off that afternoon. Our return flight was to be United.

Carlton greeted us at the front door of the Mayflower and Robert whisked us up to our usual rooms on the eighth floor. After twenty minutes or so, Martha knocked on our connecting door which I had forgotten to unlock. I quickly admitted her to the living room of my suite. She smiled as I apologized for my oversight, saying, "I'm guessing you're a bit out of practice. We don't get many opportunities like this anymore. What would you like to do about dinner?"

Me: "I was thinking we could put it off for an hour or so. But only if you want to?"

Martha turned her back to me and asked me to undo a button or two. In seconds she was out of her outfit and in my arms. We made love for more than an hour, ending with her, "I have missed you. For the longest while, you've been my only man. Do you think I should change that?"

She turned, picked up her clothes and went to her room to get ready for dinner without waiting for me to answer. I thought: was this all premeditated? I thought some more: ask her if something is bothering her? Or, ask if there is something she wants? I thought: get her to open up!

We went down to dinner in relative silence. The Dining Room, as usual, was more than half empty, so our table was somewhat isolated. We ordered cocktails and I did not wait once the waiter left, "Back in my bedroom, was anything bothering you? Or, did I just imagine something?"

Martha, in a seemingly irritated voice, "Yes and No. Do you take me for granted?"

Me: "No. Why do you ask?"

Martha, "When Mollie died, you went straight to Carolyn. You just seemed not to give me a moment's thought as your next wife. But you seem quite happy to make love with me just as we always did before. That's why."

Me: "I explained about Mollie and Carolyn while it was happening, and even more after Mollie died. You were then, and you are now, wonderful. My feelings for you remain unchanged. If that's taking you for granted, then perhaps I am somewhat guilty. But I do not love you any less and I continue to care just as much about you." I looked at Martha, and held her eyes for that last sentence or two.

Martha; "Enough for now. I need to think more. Can we make love again tonight?

— — —

The next morning at breakfast, Martha was all smiles. She was "on her game" at Tinker's office as we readied for the NCC Meeting. We spent part of the afternoon on very lengthy call with Josh Smoulders in Greenville, SC, about the finalization of our briefing on CAL Board's Motion to Dismiss in the COL-LEGES Class before Judge Blatt in Charleston. We finished early and left ahead of Tinker and his partners for dinner at Georgia Brown's.

Later, when we were alone, Martha said, "I'm not sure what got into me last night. I'm sorry. Can we just put all of that behind ourselves?" We made love very intensely twice that night.

— — —

We stopped briefly to confer with Alicia Goines in her office before the formal meeting itself. We wanted to ask her if the Leibnitz Institute Symposium on Asbestos in Boston in a few weeks was on today's agenda, and if not, was it worth discussing?

From her expression, somehow, I sensed that Alicia had missed this potential development. We explained that Martha would attend and that was, at least in part, because so many speakers appeared to be Asbestos Plaintiff BI Experts. She appeared surprised by this. In the NCC Meeting itself, many of the topics seemed a rehash of issues discussed on prior occasions and the reasons for a lack of consensus were too frequently restated. But in the Expert area, USG allowed that perhaps Dr. Bignon would make an excellent witness for the Defense in the SCHOOLS Class. But that was a springboard to criticism of Corbett McDonald and Julian Peto, both of whom had written extensively about the "Dangers of Asbestos." Of course, this was little more than a reiteration of their company's outmoded position that using these experts was an admission that asbestos was dangerous. To which I responded rather brusquely: that the very point in this Defense offering was to differentiate between when it was dangerous, and when it was not!

Then to change the discussion, I raised the Leibnitz Institute Symposium which Martha discussed and to which Alicia added that National Gypsum, her client, wanted one of her attorneys to attend as well (quick work on her part). Nay-sayers sprang to the fore with examples of how the Plaintiff attorneys could distort any defense attorney's attendance. At the end of that discussion, I was confident that more discussion would be had on that topic next month.

After the meeting, Martha and I pulled our bags to the Rittenhouse Sheraton on the city square of that same name, a few blocks from Abbott & Tweed's office. Mary Smith, one of the other younger partners on our team was waiting for our arrival. She came over to us as we waited in line to check-in and shook my hand while giving Martha a peck on the cheek. We decided to go to our rooms, make our calls, and meet in the lobby bar for a drink before proceeding to a nearby bistro of their choice. I started by calling Tinker, then Lily, my assistant, and Reggie Fox, my most senior partner at Klein & Kelly who was in charge of all of the CAL Board NorCAL BI cases. Then, I got through to Carolyn who spent twenty minutes telling me about our move

CHAPTER 18   165

that was now ready, more or less, to go fully forward, the day after school ended. She concluded by reminding me that the first phase of the *"Vogue* Shoot" of our actual move would have its first session this coming Sunday.

I responded by saying, "My feet are getting very cold."

Martha and Mary arrived together at the bar downstairs, looking a bit tired. I put that down to a lawyer's perpetual lack of a good night's sleep (knowing how little Martha must have gotten last night). But it wasn't long until I concluded that they had doubtless found some time to "fool around" in addition to making their phone calls. We had a very pleasant night of a few cocktails and some very good seafood which we all shared graciously. Back at the hotel, the two of them declined my offer of a nightcap, and when I reminded them of breakfast, they started to giggle – not sure why?

— — —

The Status Conference with Judge Kelly went on for a while. Part of it was the thinly disguised antipathy between Co-Lead Counsel for the Class representatives making veiled claims about each other, but they both focused most of their time on pressing the judge to move ahead with setting a trial date. In turn, the Defense spent ample time condemning the trip, stumble and delaying tactics of Plaintiff counsel in being ever so frequently non-compliant with all of their discovery responses, while concurrently failing to respond at all in writing, failing to produce (or in some cases identify) or object to producing documents, and blatantly failing to produce any number of lay witnesses for their depositions. As such, the Defense was not in the least yet ready to begin taking any expert discovery. The Judge gave the Plaintiffs another six months to cease those tactics and to cure those deficiencies. In other words, they must complete all of their fact discovery obligations before again asking him to set a firm trial date.

Next, Judge Kelly heard motion practice and we finally got him to hear CAL Board's Motion to Dismiss for Failure of Proper Venue, among others. Of course, he took all motions under submission. Scott Kelly allowed that we should win our motion, but warned us not to be too surprised, if the judge found a way to deny it.

We all had a nice evening at Scott's club. Ted Darrow was delighted with the stories about the experts, and I praised him for his role in recruiting them. I had gotten Manny to invite Ted to the Leibnitz Symposium.

— — —

I caught the 6:30 AMTRAK Metro Liner to D.C, on Friday morning, then met Tinker, Mace Snow and Tod Clifford for an early working lunch meeting. Mace graciously agreed to drive me out to Dulles Airport where I rolled into Seat 1B on United to SFO. I was home for our final Friday Evening Cocktails in Mill Valley with Carolyn, Kate, Ingrid and the children. The final phase of the move would be completed tomorrow. Robert and his *Vogue* crew took photos of all of us all during the weekend, having started before I got home from D.C. The women always looked "working glamorous!"

That weekend was a blur of sorts. I felt I spent more time changing clothes than I did in most weeks. Carolyn wanted new bedroom furniture for us, and used the set from Mollie's room in Mill Valley for her sleeping alone/make-up room (she sometimes kept some very strange hours with her shoots and flights.). Clearly, she felt more comfortable having us not using Mollie's personal things going forward. She caused vast amounts of furnishings to be donated, and much of the furniture to be sold by a second-hand shop (big in Marin County). She was mostly silent about dealing with Mollie's other things, which my daughters did not want.

The move was softened by the bedroom arrangements: each daughter got her own room, both adjoining a common bath, The three boys were in a large bedroom with a large bath and a second room, ready to be converted to a bedroom when, and if, needed. Ingrid's rooms were between the boys and the girls. Kate's rooms were down two floors. Carolyn and I had the top floor which was smaller than the very large second floor. Carolyn thought of everything, at least it seemed so. All of the women were delighted with their areas, especially Kate. (My mother was proceeding nicely through her seventies, still played golf twice a week and at least two afternoons of bridge; nevertheless, her favorite past time was her grandchildren, and she even came to treat Patrick Tyne as my fifth child. My sisters' children were older, and Kate would see them once or twice during the year when she visited each daughter.)

Some of the furniture was "new," although the pedigree of much of it also may have been second-hand shop. (I came to realize in our first year together that Carolyn was very careful with money: not cheap. Rather, she wanted, and appeared to get, value for what she paid.) I was shocked at how little there was for me actually to do in connection with our move: a good thing too, with all of those outfit changes. The kids had a great time with the whole thing, and Robert made certain that Kate would be in some shots. Even Ingrid, who became more attractive in her early 20's, was included.

I had no role except to pose in a few photos of Carolyn showing me rooms following reconstruction for the first shoot, which took only parts of two of my days to complete. This whole "Move-In process" had proven very time consuming, but not a real problem. Seems, however, I had forgotten about that third phase: our "House-Warming Party" shoot. Carolyn allowed that Robert needed to be gone for a couple of months and could we do something at the end of the Summer. I suggested an inside/outside party on one of the last two Saturdays in September. Both Carolyn and Robert agreed. Kate said she would re-book her Fall trip to see my sisters and their families (for what was now her annual trip "Back East!") as she loved being around Robert and his crew. Ingrid asked if she could stay another year (if she could get her visa extended. Carolyn said she would help, if needed.). I had taken Monday off for the move: so, I told Lily about the party and the dates.

Martha came into my office that Tuesday to discuss her trip to the Leibnitz Institute Symposium, particularly how to interact with Manny from Desert Mutual and Ted Darrow from Scott Kelly's firm in Philadelphia. Things like who should pay for what, and other potential protocols. She was planning to depart that Thursday, attend some meetings in Los Angeles, and week-end in Boston with a number of friends. She would not see me for almost two weeks. As she was leaving my office and I was about to give her a small kiss, there was a knock on my door and Lily came in. In that split second, I put out my hand to Martha, and said, "Have a great trip, and let me know if anything is going on in L.A. or at the Symposium."

Fifteen minutes later, Martha called and said, "Great save!"

— — —

A week to the day later, I got a call at few minutes before 8:00 a.m. from Martha in Boston on my work line at home, "You'll never guess who's attending this conference?" I was silent for about two seconds, and she blurted out *sotto voce*, "Judge James McGirr Kelly!"

I was momentarily dumbstruck, then, "Are you certain?"

Martha: "Yes! Tod agreed. Moreover, I think there are other judges hearing asbestos matters from around the country here as well. Tod says he knows one from the Court of Common Pleas in Philadelphia who presides over nothing but asbestos BI cases!"

Me: "WOW! This could be huge!"

I thought for a few seconds, considering judges' ethical considerations and codes of conduct, and about evidence that might be needed for any future practice on this issue, then added, "Do not throw any materials on this meeting away. Keep everything you can lay your hands on. Is there an Attendees List? A Final Syllabus? Any other materials or handouts? Are there any networking events sponsored by the Institute? Please, Tod and you go to everything you can get into. If there are events from which you are excluded, please make whatever observations you can about what's going on inside. And, by all means, Tod, you and Manny make contemporaneous notes about all of your observations. I suggest none of you talk to any judge unless you are directly addressed by one first. Please ask Manny to call me as soon as he can. Great job!"

I hung up to await Manny's call, and thought, "What has this Institute wrought!"

Turns out: Only time, and the United States Court of Appeals for the Third Circuit would tell!

19

CENTRAL WESLEYAN: JUDGE BLATT IN ACTION

October in Charleston, South Carolina, is delightful: warm, but not muggy, with crisp, starry nights. The local Charleston defense counsel were due to meet tomorrow morning. Tinker and I were staying at the Mills House. Josh, who told us about it, could not get a reservation and was a couple of blocks away. The Lobby, its dining room and its bar, as well as the display cases of Confederate uniforms, gear and weapons, all seemed an attempt to capture, if not an ante-bellum atmosphere, the sense of a war not forgotten. Moreover, it succeeded: "The War of Northern Aggression" was its Deep South appellation!

Tinker and I looked at the Mills House dinner menu and persuaded Josh to give it a try. Both of us agreed to make calls and to meet in the bar at 6:00. I called Mary. Then Martha when I found she was in the office, then Lily. Reggie had not left word for me, so I did not bother him. Then I called Kate, only to leave her a message. Too late to call Ingrid who was doubtless gathering the four younger children at their new schools: Maeve, a first year, at Katherine Branson School, a few uphill blocks from our house and an arch-rival of San Francisco University High School in Pacific Heights, where Patrick Tyne was a sophomore. "Tyne," as his half-siblings referred to him, was already a star athlete and his mother had a car and driver fetch him every day at the close of his school activities. (Carolyn had armed Patrick and herself with the smaller "cell phone" which had come into fashion among those who could get them. Carolyn wanted

Maeve to have one now that she was in ninth grade! I was un-
decided for the moment, but my daughter had a birthday coming up in a few weeks. I decided to wait and see if Carolyn
would get her one.) Robert, eighth grade, and the Twins in fifth,
were all, much against their will, at St. Anselm's, again a relatively short walk from our house. (St. Anselm's Church, Rectory
and Meeting Hall were all on, or just off of, Shady Lane at its
very west end where Ross itself ended. Its school and convent
were in the charming town of San Anselmo, only a few blocks
west of the church.) Because of their newness in the area and the
absence of sidewalks in Ross, Ingrid was kept busy. That left
Carolyn for me to call, and she answered promptly on my second ring.

"Celestine and Robert were delighted with the photographic
product of the house redo, but they were more enamored with
the move itself, especially two pictures of the final product. That
silly one of me laughing happily on your lap in your chair as the
last piece is placed in our family room is being seriously considered for next month's American and Northern European covers!
What do you think of that?" Carolyn's voice was full of joy! I
was so delighted that this project had worked out so well for
her.

"I could not be happier for you! Will the magazine pay you
a bonus?" I chortled into the hotel phone.

Carolyn, almost giggling: "Yes, of course. You sound merce-
nary, but I think you are joking and probably surprised. An unspecified cover shot always gets a $10,000 bonus. You know
what? You are just giving your image away. Maybe I should talk
to Celestine about getting you compensated too? Would that be
OK?"

Me: "Of course. it's OK if that's what you want to do. But just
remember I would continue to do all of these things solely to
please you. After all you are the professional, not me. I'm just
window dressing to your youth and healthful-looking beauty!"

I knew this was one phone call that would not be discussed over drinks tonight, especially after Carolyn's sexy rejoinder to my last comment.

— — —

The dinner and drinks were good and, without Martha in town, I had a great night's rest.

The defense counsel meeting at the Omni Hotel was similar to those earlier Charleston meetings: lots of lawyers, but not very much creative thinking. In opposing our motion to dismiss, the attorneys for the COLLEGES tried to explain how there were ongoing injuries being incurred by the class members as represented by Central Wesleyan. Both the representative injuries and the overarching claim that future removal at unspecified places and times as required by the US EPA Rules seemed to be a weak basis for finding actual injury to support moving forward. How would the class plaintiff provide evidence against any, or especially all, of the named defendants? Also, we had added a footnote (with a Request for Judicial Notice) which pointed out the relatively unlimited nature of these EPA-claimed damages; and, in the text of our motion had argued that the result of this over-reaching litigation could well undermine the ability of the remaining solvent defendants to compensate the very real injured human victims of actual airborne exposure to workplace asbestos fiber dust; thus, highlighting this potential to add to that human suffering as a by-product of this unneeded ACM removal process.

The bulk of the Southerners thought that whatever merit these arguments held would be best utilized in defeating the motion for class certification. We debated the viability of delay in utilizing this tactic, but the majority remained unshakable in their position! In the end, we turned to getting organized for a Case Management Motion and the desired contents of that order which, in turn, would frame the needs of the case management argument.

— — —

Judge Blatt was in one of the new courtrooms in the expanded federal court complex in downtown Charleston. He looked every inch a federal judge and conducted himself accordingly (Josh was clear that our judge did not like Northerners, and perhaps the only group he cared for less were Californians. Accordingly, I had no plan to speak that day.). *Central Wesleyan* was last up on the docket that morning, and the seats in the courtroom remained full waiting for that hearing. When that class matter was called, the lawyers moving around in the court needed several pedestrian traffic controllers. Finally, all of the counsel scheduled to speak were settled and the Judge started through his agenda: first was CAL Board's Motion to Dismiss. Ron Motley rose to argue for the Plaintiff and a few others followed him up to the plaintiff table. Josh and two lawyers for parties which joined in our motion went to the defense table. The Judge allowed that he was inclined to deny the motion, but first he needed to deal with the matter of a number of the Motley partners, who were once his partners before his being called to the federal bench. (Josh had pointed out that no local counsel would challenge this judge since he was fighting with his former partners over his entitled compensation as a firm founder for leaving his firm ["No love lost," per Josh.]. We acquiesced in Josh's advice to do nothing.).

Having paused for more than a few seconds after his announcement, Judge Blatt inclined his head toward Josh, saying, "Mr. Smoulders, please let your partners up in Greenville know that we would like to see more of them down here in Charleston. I have read all of the papers on this matter and those filed in the *Clemson* matter to which both sides refer repeatedly. The cases are different and the matter of class certification is not presently pending before this court. Please explain to me why the named plaintiff is not entitled to seek damages for any removal of asbestos from its buildings when that process appears required by the Rules promulgated by the United States Environmental Protection Agency?"

Josh went through all of the verbal argument that we had prepared for this line of logic as it was the main argument advanced by the plaintiff. Moreover, *Central Wesleyan* had claimed that it had removed asbestos containing products from several of its buildings following the guidelines provided by the US EPA. Our rebuttal to the removal was that if it was necessitated because it was damaged and releasing fibers into the air, then that itself, if proven, would sustain some level of damages. Ron Motley tried to build on this point, but Josh was able to undercut that position with encapsulation arguments. In the end, Motley always came back to the "Required by EPA" argument as "his clincher." Finally, Judge Blatt had heard enough and he took the matter under submission.

Surprisingly, Judge Blatt then advised all counsel that he would hold off on a scheduling order until he had decided the CAL Board motion. That ended the day. Co- Lead Defense Counsel quickly advised that the Omni Conference room would be available at 1:30. As Josh was packing up, Ron Motley came up to him and asked for a word with "his team." Josh came over and told us of Motley's request. We agreed. Josh waived and Motley came over. He shook hands with Josh, then turned to me and put out his hand which I shook while Josh introduced Ron to Tinker. He undertook about five minutes of small talk, then said, "Ronan, your team is very good. I was very unhappy when you took us down on that *Clemson* motion, but you really did us a favor. We could have gone along, got the class certified and been deep in discovery and you could have blown up *Clemson* then. We would have lost millions. Instead, we took a much harder look at this class. It may be smaller, but that might make it more lethal. Anyway, you all appear to be 'straight shooters,' so if you need to talk, feel free to get in touch. By the way, as far as the other Defense-types are concerned, this conversation never happened." He did not wait for a reply, just turned and walked back to his people.

We stopped at a small restaurant and had sandwiches for lunch. "What do you think that was about?" asked Josh. I looked from him to Tinker, then back, before answering.

"I think he wants us to take the very best motion steps along the way. He's hedging his bets. If he's going to lose, do it before he wastes a pile of cash. That's what he just told us." I looked at Tinker, who nodded affirmatively. Josh thought for a few seconds, and he too began to nod.

— — —

For the Defense Counsel Meeting, Tinker went home, while Josh and I remained, but were silent for several hours. When one of the leaders looked at us, he put up his hand and asked why we were silent. I told him that it didn't make a lot of sense to plan if we did not know what comes next. That leader countered that it was highly probable that the Judge would uphold the Plaintiff. I said, "What if he grants the motion with Leave to Amend?"

That meeting ended minutes later with serious mumbling on the way to the elevator!

20

GROWING LITIGATION:
ANY END IN SIGHT?

Just before the final *Vogue* shoot on the last weekend in September, I got a fax from Josh Smoulders with an Opinion and Order from Judge Blatt in South Carolina, denying our motion to dismiss and setting a status conference in ten weeks. His Opinion was not at all fact intensive and, boiled down to its essence, allowed that the EPA Rule on abatement of asbestos containing products (ACP) was sufficient to support this suit in the face of the CAL Board Motion. Furthermore, he denied our Request for Judicial Notice of a great many facts which supported our motion. CAL Board might have another day: class certification would require the judge to confront many of those same facts which, under his discretion, he had chosen to ignore. I called Manny and advised him. He did not seem upset, saying, "Ronan, even you cannot win them all!" We went on to talk further about the Leibnitz Institute, and then he suggested that since we had so many more lawyers, and needed to do planning on a larger level, that it was time to have another CAL Board Attorney Conference in Scottsdale. We talked some dates, and he said he would call CAL Board's General Counsel, Austin Smith, and get his thoughts. I called in all the partners on my team and Martha to tell them about the Central Wesleyan decision and the attorney meeting with the tentative dates. Finally, I asked Martha and Mary to stay behind. I told them that I wanted them for briefing in the *Central Wesleyan* case. Deep breathes followed. I asked if we needed more help. They said YES.

When they left, I went in to see our two senior partners: both

Mr. Klein and Mr. Kelly were delighted to have been invited to our house warming, but especially their wives when they got the invitation containing a note from Carolyn pointing out that photographers from *Vogue* would be present and asking them to sign a release for themselves and their spouses, and to return it in the "acceptance envelope" included in that mailing. They were both in a good mood. I started in on three points: the developments in the CAL Board litigation, the need to raise Martha to partner lest we lose her to a San Francisco firm, and the need for two more lawyers with at least two years of the right experience. With a minimal amount of protest, they agreed to all of those requests.

I left them and went right to Martha's office. Mary was there and they were talking about moving forward. I told them about the two new hires, and then said that I felt the more junior partners should do those interviews, and run the final selections by me, Mary asked if that meant Phil was going to do interviewing down south. I nodded my head NO, and said, "I rather think, Mary, that you and Martha should do that all here. Martha, you will be a partner effective October first. That should help." Both let out suppressed shrieks! I shook their hands and set off to find Reggie, the team's second most senior partner, to tell him the news. Lastly, I called Phil in Pasadena to tell him. He said he would like to have part of one of those hires, and I told him that was part of the plan, asking him to confer with the ladies for his input.

— — —

Our *Vogue*-sponsored Housewarming Party turned out to be attended by almost as many people as our wedding. We, particularly Carolyn, had made friends with several new neighbors on Northwood in Ross, inviting them and a few from Mill Valley. Some relatives and other connections a bit more tenuous were omitted from this gathering as were some of our business contacts. Still, it was an event lasting six hours, with food, drink, music and fun: not nearly as structured as our wedding party. The people from my office had a marvelous time, especially the spouses. Not surprisingly, Robert and his *Vogue* photographers moved seamlessly throughout the day and into the evening recording whatever they thought of as potentially glamorous, interesting or newsworthy.

That night, after the clean-up crew had departed and everyone was in bed, Carolyn and I sat out in our backyard, warm in our sweaters and with my arm around her shoulders. I nestled my nose in her hair, which as always smelled of lavender, and said in a low, but hopefully loving, voice, "I just want you to know that you are so much more than I expected. I am so in love with you. How are you feeling right now?"

Carolyn moved, so her head, still staying on my shoulder, came more around and our faces were almost touching, softly whispering, "When I saw you get out of that car on the deck that very first time in the fading light of Sausalito, as you put on your uniform jacket and cap, I saw what I thought was the most handsome man I had ever seen. That's why I asked you to have that drink at No-Name. When we talked for less than an hour at their bar, I thought you were the nicest man I had ever met. When I decided to seduce you and succeeded, I thought that if I ever began to really like men, I would want someone just like you. Almost seven months later when you appeared again on that same deck and I was desperately trying to find the right person to pick up Lisa's share of the lease, and, without any hemming and hawing, you just calmly said YES, I decided that you were my man, the one I wanted whenever I wanted one. Now that I actually have you. I don't ever want anyone else." Then she leaned into my face and we kissed for a very long time.

In those moments, I realized that Carolyn was replacing Mollie in my heart. It was a very strange feeling. *(When I told*

Dr. Arnaud about that night [she had earlier been at that party], she smiled and said, "You never really realized that you loved Carolyn, or perhaps how much, before Mollie. It was just differently. Now, not so differently.")

— — —

I got a call from Manny a few days later with suggested dates for the CAL Board Defense Attorney Meeting which would again be at the Biltmore behind Fashion Plaza in Phoenix. He asked me for a list of proposed attendees. I mentioned that the number would be seriously more than a few years ago and that we should have every partner with a significant role in each jurisdiction. He agreed in principle. Then he broached a related subject: "Our upper management is extremely pleased with everything you have done for us over these last years, the novel defense concepts you have evolved and your extraordinary handling of the Lloyds Coverage matter, the latter in the face of your losing Mollie. Toward that end, we are hoping you can persuade your Carolyn to join you for a few extra days and nights here in Scottsdale, following that meeting, so that we all may fete you on Saturday night and then you two would have a few days to yourselves to rest in luxury.

I called Lily and told her to put all of our Partners and Deirdre on notice of the exact dates and place of the meeting, and I asked her for a list of all of the local counsel with an active case in the last two years, and finally asked her if she would like to be there to help out on the meeting itself. Her YES was given without a moment's hesitation. Then, I called Tinker and told him all about the meeting, even mentioning the celebratory weekend (which got me to thinking that without Tinker, much, if not all, of this would not have happened). He sounded ready for another trip to Phoenix.

Finally, I called Carolyn on her cell, hoping to get her in New

York City where she was working. She was part of a meeting, but was able to get excused briefly. I told her about the main attorney meeting, and then about the special weekend to honor me, but to include her. I asked her to come for that. She had to check her calendar but would do everything she could to arrange her schedule. She rang off!

An hour or so later, she called me back, to say she was good with it all. Then I asked her about Tinker and Elaine, explaining that his relationship with me predated ours, and that he was causative in ours, and a massive help on the strategy and tactics in this litigation. She thought for a few seconds and said YES. (I hoped I had not made a mistake!)

I called Manny and asked him about Tinker and Elaine. He said he would get back to me, then we talked a bit about the Attorney Meeting agenda. Martha and I headed south to Los Angeles and the Desert for meetings with Phil on Science and Medicine for his BI cases and a possible trial in a few weeks, and then for Co-Defense meetings on the San Bernardino, Riverside, Orange and San Diego Counties' four mass-joinder cases. We had gotten wind that those four suits were being actively considered for Coordination by California's Judicial Council. We had spent some time with Tinker and Mary thinking about the merits of doing just that: first, we believed that the bigger the case, the more it was susceptible to "dynamic gridlock," like *LAUSD*; second, there would be three sets of Plaintiff's counsel (San Bernardino and San Diego Counties had the same firm) who might not always agree; and third, Coordination might save on defense fees. All four of those courts had motions pending to dismiss those suits under the "*Mullen* no injury theory," each included a Motion for Judicial Notice of slightly different facts for each county, and all motions were being delayed in rulings (one case for more than six months), all without explanation. Our team, with DMIC and CAL Board's blessings, had agreed to support a Coordination, if proposed. We intended to present this proposal to the largely local counsel defense committee meeting in San Bernardino on Wednesday.

On Monday, we arrived in time to check into a new Marriott Residence Inn just off of California Street in Pasadena. Phil had us go to a Japanese-Mexican fusion restaurant a few blocks walk from the hotel. He wanted us to start with a Mojito in a crazy-looking leaning "upright glass." He and Martha each had one and loved it (also the hot bean dip). I happily abstained as I could not handle Tequila in any form nor could I do Mexican style beans. Phil was like a new man after almost two years in the "LA Area." He was thinner, more assertive, and much more confident. (I would need to discuss this with Klein and Kelly.) We talked about the area, his caseload, his associate and his need for more help.

We also talked about the Rams departure to St. Louis, USC and UCLA football and basketball, and the Dodgers. I chided him about going over to the "Dark Side of the Force" by switching his allegiance away from the Giants; but, 'lo and behold, Martha came to his rescue as another "Dodger fan." (I was going to call Martha a "Closet Dodger fan," but knowing about Mary, I quickly rethought that one.)

That night was the first time in a long time since Martha and I had been together. Afterward, before sleeping, I wondered how much I still missed her. The next day, we spent five and a half hours getting Phil ready on the science for his trial on a cancer patient who was a sixty-pack year smoker (if you smoke two packs of cigarettes/day for six months, that equals one-pack year). We had our Oxford friend, Dr. Doll, on the smoking causation side and we had Dr. Doll with Julian Peto saying no certainty for causal connection without smoking. The defense argument was that the overriding medical logic supports smoking as the causation factor. My concern was simple: Mary knew this Science without hesitation, but Phil, as the "partner on scene" wanted to be the only lawyer to try this first SoCAL case.

Austin Smith, CAL Board's General Counsel, was alright with Phil. With that recommendation, Manny went along. So, here we were trying to get Phil ready. I really wanted Martha to do that part of the trial, but I understood Phil's position.

We drove to Palm Springs planning to spend two nights at an older tennis resort hotel where the meeting was scheduled to take place. Checking-in, we found ourselves to be not nearly alone as we encountered any number of other defense counsel who were spending the night. As we were about to head to the elevator, who should appear but Alicia Goines, National Counsel for National Gypsum. We chatted briefly and agreed to have dinner with her and several others (with whom she had already made arrangements).

Our rooms, not surprisingly, were connected. (I sometimes wondered if Lily knew, or even suspected, about Martha and me.) There was ample time before dinner, so we decided to make calls because we were in our home time zone. Most of my children were in post-school activities, Ingrid was out and Carolyn was on a plane on her way to Paris to work for some ten days. Lily had little, and no one left me a message. As I hung up from my last call, there was a familiar knock on the connecting door. When I opened my door, there stood Martha in a full length, very sexy, black lingerie outfit. It took her one short step to be in my arms. We passed a most pleasant hour or so!

— — —

At dinner, I decided to float the coordination concept, which rumor had it was the ostensible reason for this meeting. Turns out that Alicia's guests all had the same concept in mind, but none of them had any details. That caused me to say, jokingly, "Why don't we just discuss it in a knowledge-free environment?"

Alicia picked up on that with a few questions like: would

LAUSD be part of that coordination, or what if the different county joinders have different defendants that do not overlap, or what happens if some counties want it and others don't, or what if new counties with mass joinders want to be added?

Talking about those topics took up much of dinner, and avoided the key potentially disruptive topic: to support or oppose the coordination? As soon as the dessert orders were taken, I asked Martha to raise our question. She did, very precisely. The silence that followed was broken by Alicia, "Our initial reaction was to oppose, but considering the issues we discussed among ourselves which were fewer than those covered here tonight, we began to think that a coordination might well bog the plaintiffs down and perhaps cause any number to abandon their cases as the cost of administration alone for some of them would probably prove too great. I mean look what's happening in *LAUSD*. That district is mired in its own quicksand on how to come up with product identification. Imagine the exponential impact of that issue on a coordination. We think the best tactic, short-term, is to abstain; but support, if need be."

The silence that followed was deafening for thirty seconds. I kneed Martha gently. She spoke up, "We essentially agree with Alicia. Plus, an added selling point to the clients is that the cost of defense will almost certainly be much less than defending each of the joinders separately."

Dessert was eaten largely in silence which led us to believe that shock had set in for those others who came to Palm Springs ready to oppose coordination, some vigorously. Fortunately, the meeting the next day was at 10:30, 1:30 p.m. on the East Coast, which created time for any willing counsel to get potential revisionism sanctioned.

— — —

I had a call from Carolyn in Paris that night while Martha

and I were entangled (A first time!). I feigned waking, and carried on reasonably well. Martha did tickle me at one point. I told Carolyn that I had checked at home and all was fine there. We exchanged small talk for a few minutes and she let me "go back to sleep."

The next day was almost a repeat of dinner, but with more players and more options. Virtually nothing was decided. Afterwards, Martha and I had a drink with Alicia and her local counsel wherein I discussed that these local defense counsel meetings were of little assistance in doing big picture case management. Her local disagreed, mouthing the usual platitude: each jurisdiction may be different, certainly each state! I looked at Alicia. She rolled her eyes. I wondered if that was what her client's in-house people really believed. No wonder we had such a splintered defense effort in many jurisdictions. After the meeting, Martha and I discussed this more. Certainly, this raised a topic for DMIC's CAL Board Defense Counsel Meeting coming up in a few weeks.

— — —

Martha and I also spent time going over the materials gathered at the Leibnitz Symposium. The Attendee List was forthright, naming more than forty state and federal judges who had elected to attend. Also in attendance were the lead counsel from almost every major asbestos plaintiff's firm in the entire country, numbering more than one hundred lawyers (we knew seven firms from California and six judges). Other populous states were highly represented, although none more so than California.

I called Manny and asked if he, Ted and Martha would do a presentation on that Symposium at our upcoming nationwide counsel meeting, having more than forty lawyers scheduled to attend. We also began working on an agenda for the meeting and quickly realized that an extra half-day would be essential if we were to cover all of the needed topics (more for BI cases with this Science and Medicine than for the property classes, which were in far fewer jurisdictions). Manny responded that he would be pleased to work with Ted and Martha; and having learned that we were in Palm Springs, asked if we could fly over to Phoenix tomorrow for a half a day's meetings. A call to United indicated that the flight schedules were unhelpful, so we decided to drive. Manny's assistant took care of rebooking our flights that next afternoon at 4:15, Sky Harbor to SFO.

— — —

Manny had us at a new Westin Hotel, The Princess, in North Scottsdale (somewhat isolated, then). It was on his way home and he stopped for a drink to give us a quick view of tomorrow's agenda, primarily about London and the sudden slowing of payments and the Broker policy search beginning to drag, the increasing number of BI suits, especially in a few states where the client had no real presence, and planning for the upcoming attorney meeting at the Biltmore. I leaned over to Martha who got up, went inside and came back in five minutes with her laptop computer and six sheets of paper. After handing four of the sheets to me, I glanced at the top two, and handed the other two to Manny, telling him that this was a rough draft agenda which we were creating on these travels.

Manny was pleased after glancing at it. We were to meet at 9:30 which would give the Desert Mutual people time to come up with input. The two top executives would only stay long enough to talk about London.

Martha and I stayed at the bar, had another drink, then burgers and a glass of wine. Back in my room, I called home and spoke with Kate, then Ingrid and three of the five children (the Patricks were still at their respective basketball practices). It was the middle of the night in Paris, so I did not try Carolyn. I knocked on Martha's door. She opened it and looked tired. "Do you want to take a pass tonight?" I asked,

She looked at me and gestured for me to enter her room. In twenty minutes or so, I was headed back on my way to my own bed!

— — —

The Desert Mutual meeting started poorly. Both Charlie Sewell, the CEO, and John O'Sullivan, the COO, were unhappy because the checks they had been receiving from the various Lloyds syndicates were slowing in number and, more importantly, dollar amount. Also, the document recovery search at Cheshire & Booth was dragging, and there were still about 20% of the Desert Mutual placements to be located. John had asked both Bradley, the lead solicitor, and Quincy, their lead barrister, but neither seemed to give a satisfactory response. So, I asked who was running the cash receipts from the syndicates on the Desert Mutual end? How did they know what to pay? It seemed to me that the issues might be largely internal to DMIC, and they would need to come up with a system which would perform credibly to all participants. When the payments started, how did the syndicates know what to do? Who was directing them?

As to the search, Thornton, Campbell had cut the number of staff in half to save costs at DMIC's request. I told them that halving the workforce, might well double the search time. Thus, the seeming slow down. Moreover, Jayson Turnbull was only committed for a year. He had been the primary driver of success and was not getting any younger. I told them I should meet with Bradley, Quincy and Stanley Booth to sort all of this out. I could probably do all of that in three days in London, if I flew over from Philadelphia at the end of the next NCC meeting in a little more than a week.

They seemed satisfied, but I pointed out that DMIC probably

still needed to put a person in charge and come up with a system to bill the syndicates and not wait on them to act on some unedited spread sheets which might be supplied by Cheshire & Booth or Bradley Campbell's people. They might go through Bradley's office, assuming that group was not too expensive, if they preferred. All of that seemed to satisfy the highest-ups who departed with courteous thanks.

Manny had passed out our outline for our attorney meeting, and they were ready with comments and input. The next two hours brought us to a point of satisfactory consensus and we decided to run it past Tinker and our Reggie for further input and to go from there.

I would not be home much at all that final week leading up to the CAL Board Counsel Meeting. Carolyn got home from Paris the day before I had to leave for almost two weeks, with a brief Ross respite of less than three days before the Scottsdale meetings.

— — —

21

THE PATH TOWARD RESOLUTION
BEGINS TO BECOME CLEAR

The Friday before our flight to Dulles, we received a copy of Judge Kelly's Order in the SCHOOLS class action denying our motion to dismiss the CAL Board subsidiary for a lack of venue, specifically stating that our motion was not timely filed. Rarely, did I lose my temper, but I went out on our office's deck (I had my own door for that) and ranted for a good two or three minutes.

When I called Manny to tell him, his reaction was like mine: Twice Judge Kelly had denied that same motion as premature, now it was somehow too late, all of which he failed to discuss any detail except for the 'late timing' of our current motion. I suggested a motion to reconsider to that judge. Manny did not sound enthusiastic. I told him I thought we should do that to protect the client's appellate rights, or perhaps even better, to set up a writ petition. He finally agreed. On the flight, I went through some of this with Martha and asked her to have an associate write that motion to reconsider and send it to me in London, so I could read it on the way home.

That NCC meeting took place at Abbott & Tweed in Philadelphia on Wednesday, with hearings beginning at 10:30 on Thursday before Judge Kelly. I was taking the "Red Eye" to Heathrow on Thursday night, and persuaded Quincy and Bradley to have our first get together on Sunday at three in the afternoon. Martha and I spent time on our travels making notes and trying to put together an interface plan for DMIC to interact with its reinsurers. However, we lacked Bradley's advice on whether or not that would be acceptable in the UK market. Somehow, I began to think not, and to have an American and a British interfacing on behalf of DMIC made more sense. I called Manny and discussed this with him. I asked for the DMIC initial feedback, if I could get it before their next weekend, for when I arrived in London on Friday.

— — —

Much of Tuesday in Tinker's office in D.C. was spent on how do we approach the issue of the judges' attendance at the Leibnitz Symposium, and especially Judge Kelly. Since our upcoming meeting had the nominal lead outside attorneys for all of the major player defendants attending, tomorrow seemed to be the day to get this ball rolling. We included our two lead Philadelphia counsel on this call. We broke the process into parts: first, any dealings with the judge should probably come from Philadelphia area counsel, being best known to him, but who? Second, what should the defense ask for in light of his attendance at that conference; and third, how far should the defense go with this issue? (Understanding that an Article III judge is appointed for life and has extremely broad powers, and there are all of the other judges who sit in all the other courthouses around the country: careful, prudent planning was needed.) A little after 3:00, Martha and I went back to the Mayflower for our luggage. Tinker would come up tomorrow so that at dinner, Scott Kelly and Ted Darrow of the Philadelphia firm and we three could discuss the day's meeting and its impact on Thursday's hearing.

During that train ride north, Martha asked if we should have connecting rooms. I decided why not and asked her if I could leave my bags in her room on the way to my "Red Eye."

The rest of the trip, we worked on the Scottsdale Meeting and the UK experts whom I would see if I had the chance. We were starting to stay at the Four Seasons, getting a very favorable rate thanks to some business friends. (But no special rate on their dinner prices!)

— — —

Following a pre-meeting with Alicia and Sandra, her first time attending in some months, and agreeing on generalized objectives, we attended what turned out to be the most contentious NCC meeting-to-date! About half of those present were utterly clueless about the mass attendance by asbestos judges at the Leibnitz Institute Symposium, and many of them just wanted to brush it aside. It wasn't until several senior and very influential Philadelphia-types, not usually given to speaking at any length, made damning arguments about the taint on the reputations of those attending judges, one called their behavior, "Well outside the bounds of innocent impropriety...;" while another said, "Such attendance clearly went beyond the mere appearance of impropriety...." By the end of the first round of debate, most of those present came to realize that the only way for the SCHOOLS CLASS matter to proceed was with a new judge presiding. A Suggestion of Recusal would have to be forthcoming tomorrow from one of the lawyers in this room from the Philadelphia federal bar. Finally, Brad Eustace, a senior partner at a large Philadelphia firm, Williams, Spence & Wright, rose, stated that he was a Third Circuit Liaison for the lawyers in this area, and he felt that he should be the one to ask Judge Kelly to step down. Hearing no objections, we proceeded to discuss an implementation strategies, finally settling on a request to be heard before any substantive matters were discussed; any client opposed to recusal should openly separate itself from the defense group so that will demonstrate an outlier status; and, Mr. Eustace would be the "One Voice" for the Defense at this hearing.

The rest of the meeting seemed far less stressful than those hours just passed. As we prepared to leave and head to Scott Kelly's office, Tinker having joined us, Alicia asked if we three could stay for a drink. Her concern was twofold; what if the judge were to refuse or want time to evaluate his options, but then begin to proceed with other tasks from his agenda for the day?

We do not want to turn this into a series of contempt hearings," I began, "For example, I was going to raise his denial of one of my client's motions to dismiss as untimely, following its filing close on the heels of his twice denying essentially that same motion as prematurely brought. But I can defer that until we file a formal Motion to Reconsider, especially in light of his bringing his neutrality into question!"

Alicia looked at me and said, "I think that is such a perfect argument to cut Judge Kelly short from proceeding with any merits business tomorrow. What if he flatly refuses, should we ask for discovery of the Institute files on the meeting, and particularly its Invitation List and its originating funding sources for the meeting and the judges' attendance expenses as well? Enjoy your dinner!"

— — —

We had a great dinner at a "Pub-type" restaurant. Mary had flown in to pitch reconsideration (not going to happen tomorrow). She, along with Scott Kelly and Ted Darrow, were laughing "in stitches" as we described the goings-on at our recently concluded meeting, and then the far less funny debriefing with Alicia afterward. Mary was staying at the Sheraton for the night. Martha and she were off to New York tomorrow before I left for my "Red Eye." We would meet at the Four Seasons after the hearing with Judge Kelly.

— — —

The hearing in Judge Kelly's courtroom was tumultuous even before it got started. Brad Eustace arrived very early and sought out Judge Kelly's Clerk right away, apparently informing that Clerk of his need to address the Court forthwith before the Judge took up his scheduled agenda. Not only that but Attorney Eustace apparently told that Clerk that he would be speaking in a dual capacity, the role of attorney to his client, International Asbestos Brokers (IAB) but also as an Attorney Liaison for the Third Circuit Bar to the Judiciary of that Circuit. When the Clerk asked if Mr. Eustace had advised the other side of his Request, he replied that "they should be well-aware of it as they were present," or words to that effect.

Our group arrived at about the point where Eustace was withdrawing from interacting with the Judge's Clerk. Any number of attorneys were arriving and that Clerk began to look anxious as none of them were approaching her to sign up as a speaker on any of the Judge's Agenda Items. Promptly at 10:29, the Chief Bailiff appeared through the Judge's doorway from his chambers. As he did, the Clerk slid through that open door into the Judge's chambers. She returned in moments and beckoned to Mr. Eustace who quickly approached her. They conferred and she shook her head negatively, then returned to those Chambers. The many attorneys in the high-ceilinged courtroom set it abuzz with their speculation as to what was transpiring. But in seconds that sound receded, the Chief Bailiff appeared, called the Court Room to Order and Judge John McGirr Kelly mounted the steps to his high-backed chair, banged his gavel on his bench, turned toward Mr. Eustace seated at the Defense Counsel's Table, and Ordered, "Mr. Eustace, since you would not disclose your reason to speak in open court before I called my Agenda, I will Order that your Request is Denied."

Attorney Eustace rose, and as he stood, his demeanor seemed to change, and I thought of great men, like Patrick Henry and Abraham Lincoln at that moment, when he spoke, "If it Please

this Court, I appear in the Dual Capacity which I have disclosed
to your Clerk to Request that Your Honor Recuse Himself from
Any Further Proceedings in these Matters forthwith. I ask that
the Court hear me out in open court at this time; otherwise I ask
this Court to Stay All Proceedings in These Matters Pending a
full judicial investigation following a written motion, any opposition as might be filed, any needed discovery, and a hearing before an disinterested trier of fact. With all due respect, I herewith
request Your Honor to choose my first option,"

Judge Kelly, appearing highly perturbed, "Tell me this moment of what you accuse me!"

Mr. Eustace, "That just a few weeks ago, as a sitting federal
judge with this currently pending asbestos litigation before him,
you attended a Symposium put on by the Leibnitz Institute
which focused almost entirely on the Plaintiff view of that type
of litigation, including many presentations in the fields of Science and Medicine put on by scientific and medical experts who
regularly testify for only clients of the Plaintiff Bar, that you did
not pay to attend this symposium, and that the Asbestos Plaintiff
Bar underwrote the symposium itself and your attendance. A
clear and incontrovertible instance of a major conflict of interest.
Thus, your Recusal is Formally Requested."

What followed was borderline chaos: Judge Kelly rose and
in a loud voice to be heard over the din in his Courtroom, said,
"I paid my own transportation to and from Boston!"

At the same time, several Plaintiff counsel were pushing each
other to see who would counter Attorney Eustace's assertions.
Finally, David Berger, as the most senior of the Philadelphia
lawyers present addressed the Court, first calling Mr. Eustace
an "Assassin of the First Order" and describing Eustace's denun-
ciation as an "Ambush" utilizing. hearsay and innuendo (Martha
leaned over and whispered, "Mr. Berger was not in Boston.").
So, it continued for minutes while others added to the chaos. At
last, the Judge's gavel could be heard banging for order above

the chaos.

Judge Kelly's voice had more restraint, now that he spoke again, "I shall order that all of these proceedings are off the record and, Madam Court Reporter, you are to stop typing now."

She looked at the Judge, her fingers moving and said, "Your Honor, I follow the Rules of the Third Circuit for which I work. This is not a matter that can be 'Off the record.' I am sorry."

The Judge, "All counsel present, those of you who would have me recuse myself, please rise." There was a shuffling of feet, and I realized the count was hopelessly against the Judge, unless all defense counsel did not rise. So, I rose as did Tinker, Mary, Martha and Scott. When other defense lead counsel saw our whole team on their feet, they too had their entire teams standing. So, it was that within little more than a minute, the vote for Recusal was overwhelmingly in favor.

Again, the gavel spoke first, "I should have realized a straw poll would be one-sided with so many more defense counsel present. That poll has no meaning. This is all ludicrous! What we will do is as follows: Mr. Eustace, you and whomsoever may join you may file a Motion seeking My Recusal, accompanied by Declarations and Documentation within 45 days, those parties or interested persons who Oppose your Motion shall make such filings as they deem appropriate 30 days thereafter, and 91 days from today, we will meet here again to argue that motion, if I feel it requires argument. Thereafter, I will decide whether or not my attendance at that Leipzig Institute's Symposium requires my Recusal. All other matters are stayed and continued until my decision. Court is Adjourned!" It was 10:50!

We spent considerable time talking with other defense counsel. I saw Alicia and we spoke for but a minute about discovery. Martha came over and she gave Alicia a list of Symposium documents she had obtained. I suggested we subpoena the Institute's documents on creating and executing that meeting, including its agenda, funding and invitees, and all associated correspondence on those topics. She said she would work with Brad Eustace and that when motivated, which he now appeared fully, was not a lawyer with whom to mess around. Then, she said he liked me and our team. Our team walked back to the Four Seasons for lunch. On the way, I told Mary, Scott and Tinker that they should all be as involved on that motion, as needed.

22

LIME STREET SOLUTIONS

My TWA flight touched down at 0745 on Friday morning at Gatwick (United having purchased TWA's Heathrow gates), almost the same time as the flight from SFO. I felt pretty good considering I had less than five hours of sleep, but well-rested from no Martha. Making my way through Immigration, then Baggage to fetch my suitcase, then Customs (waived through, perhaps for my wearing of a sport coat), I emerged into a sea of faces, many of whom were holding signs. Not expecting one for me, I was shocked to see Ronan O'Neill in large, bold, well-shaped printing. I did a bit of a doubletake, while looking through that crowd for the face below the sign. It turned out to be my friend, Madeline Myles, Bradley's assistant. I caught her attention and signaled to meet further down the cordoned path where the crowding ended. We did. No public display of affection, but a Euro-style buss on each cheek, then a big smile from Madeline.

Not expecting anyone, and with the time-change and a new airport, I was put ever so slightly off-balance. Madeline sprang to my rescue telling me that Barry was sorry to miss me, but had "a thing with his wife" about one of their children over in Margate. Barry also had been busy with Quincy the last few days digging around to find the sources, and hopefully begin to find the solutions, to the Desert Mutual Insurance Company's (DMIC) reinsurance policy slow-down in locating the last 20 - 25% of the missing coverages. Madeline had a briefcase and a document tube with her. It was 9:15 by the time we had gotten into a taxi and were underway.

I decided I needed a quick shower to become more functional for four or five hours. My plan was to rest for a day or so. I had been so busy, but Madeline was insistent in trying to explain the new materials in her possession, but I was more than just a little foggy. Finally, she said, "We should have gotten some coffee in you before this taxi. (Touching my arm.) But let me show you this. (She opened the tube and pulled out a long sheet of paper, handing one end to me.) This is all of the coverages which have been found so far, arrayed under each year of coverage placed for DMIC. You can see the holes. They seem random, but · Grayson thinks we'll find most of them soon. What Bradley wanted you to think about more between now and Sunday is what to do about that potential deal for DMIC with Cheshire & Booth to market this search scheme. He thinks DMIC's delayed response to that proposition is perhaps what may be slowing things. He's convinced himself that Stanley Booth wants a means to fend with the other U.S. carriers when they start to press for what DMIC has helped to develop."

"Madeline, you certainly are informed on all of this. I shall call John O'Sullivan as soon as I get to my room. What about you?"

"Oh! I guess that's part of what I was trying to say: Bradley wants me to help you get up to speed today whilst he's off dealing with his wife and son. If we can work at Grosvenor House, fine. I'll wait in the lobby whilst you refresh yourself. I'll try to find a work area or another arrangement."

So, I continued to try to look at the huge chart, but my eyes kept wanting to close. Oh! How I hated jetlag!! Finally, the Grosvenor House. I checked in. They gave me a nice suite on an upper floor with less traffic noise. I asked Madeline if she wanted to see it. She agreed. On entering, there was a pleasant living area with a sofa, a table with two chairs, a desk and its own chair, television and a wet-bar. The two windows looked out on Hyde Park. Her only words were "Very Nice!" Then, she added, "Where are the bed and 'loo?"

I told her and that I was going to call John O'Sullivan and she went into the bedroom area while I did that. John was receptive to my call and I mentioned the potential deal with Cheshire & Booth, He said they had talked about it and, at a minimum, they would have to have someone in London who could act as a go-between. They decided it was too much cost with no real basis to ascertain if a profit would ever occur. I suggested that Cheshire & Booth might be concerned that DMIC might have a right of participation in the intellectual property (IP) of the evolving system to locate documents which DMIC was funding. How about an agreement to allow DMIC to recover its costs advanced, perhaps at nominal interest, and Cheshire & Both would end up as the sole owner of the IP? That would not require anything more than some interface with Bradley from time-to-time. John thought for a minute and agreed in principle, saying, "See how far you can get. Stay in touch. Call any time. I mean at any time!"

Madeline came back out to the living room and spread her chart on the coffee table. Next, she put her files on the desk. She asked if I wanted to get cleaned up. I agreed and hung up my clothes and jumped in the shower, followed by a shave. Feeling much better, I opened the door to the bedroom and there was Madeline, on the bed, in her bra and panties. "Thought I'd rest here, while you cleaned up. Seems we're both clean. A shame not to use that condition?" As I was wearing only a towel myself, I could not very well refuse Madeline's invitation.

— — —

By far the most interesting item that Madeline had brought with her was a computerized ledger of the payments being made by the reinsuring Lloyds syndicates that were run through Cheshire & Booth, which details were shared with Bradley on behalf of DMIC as its London Counsel of Record, but the payments themselves were forwarded directly to DMIC. The opening date for each syndicate was when it was placed on notice of the claim, with payments listed thereunder. This ledger was apparently not reproduced for DMIC, or they failed to show it to me. I asked if this copy was for me. Madeline allowed that Bradley said "to share it with you." (This conversation led me to ask myself: what is the story here?)

We had a nice remainder of the day on Friday and Madeline went home that night as I began to fall asleep relatively early. She sat patiently in the bedroom later that afternoon while I spent about an hour talking with Lily (at her home), then Carolyn and four of the five children; and, then Kate. Carolyn mentioned that Ingrid was going to get a work visa extension of two years, but only if one of us would sign off on it. She asked me to do it. (I wondered why, but then thought about how she had re-created herself as a run-away.) Of course, I agreed.

Madeline and I failed to make love again before she departed; but instead, we talked at some length. She seemed to want to open up to someone, and as her history unwound in a non-chronological spate of small stories, and an occasional vignette, I came to see that like Carolyn, Madeline was her own self-made woman, lifting herself to new heights in each of her business endeavors. Now, she was the right arm of one of the most powerful solicitors in the City of London. In turn, this gave her power in her own right. As she came to say: that power included being able to seduce me. When said, I sucked in my breath just a bit. Clearly, Madeline was a very self-confident person to say something like that so soon in a relationship (even one not destined to end in a long-term bond of any sort). Yet by the time my relatively short stay was ended, I had come to wonder if Madeline would somehow remain in my life going forward when this matter ended.

Before she left that Friday night, Madeline persuaded me that we should go for a bit of exercise in Hyde Park before breakfast. She arrived in the lobby at 6:45, as promised and a bit to my surprise, I was waiting for her, but only had exercise shoes meant for walking, not running. She had a hefty bag with her and I asked one of the bell staff to put it in my suite. (A 5-pound note did the trick!) Whereupon we set out through the front doors on Park Lane, through an undercrossing beneath that bustling boulevard, emerging in the cool, fresh breeze through the great oaks that form Hyde Park's natural interior barrier against the vehicular traffic on the other side of that park's high stone walls. Horses and riders were out in numbers on the bridle path, parallel to Park Lane. The activity in the park was vastly different than at tourist time, with all sorts of athletic activities underway. Madeline turned right, the opposite of heading toward the Serpentine which had always been my direction of travel to date. We ran for about two miles at a modest pace, slowing as we came to a breach in the stone wall with a gate opening out to what I assumed to be Oxford Street. Madeline stopped. This is where the north end of London starts was her explanation. In turn, as we walked back in the direction we had run, not a very busy thoroughfare, I explained about my several forays to the Royal College of Physicians & Surgeons. As I was discussing this, she signaled that we should enter an eatery of sorts, a quaint bakery with a wide variety of choices and a dining area on the left of the bustling commercial segment with its queuing customers. The smells were sensational. I told Madeline that I loved the place. She seemed pleased, but not surprised. We had fresh fruit compote, pastries and press coffee. She insisted on paying. I did not object. We walked indirectly back to the hotel and she pointed out small sites and places of interest as we walked. Once or twice, we seemed to hold hands, rather naturally. Once in my room, we both headed to the bath (which I had asked be fully stocked) and we both began taking off our athletic-ware. I suggested that Madeline shower first, but she had a very different idea. "You know, I love the smell of good sweat created by exercise. I think it's sexy. It's the same as when you have vigorous sex."

We spent an hour more getting a different form of exercise. Then, we worked and had a light lunch. I really wanted to take her to Wheeler's for dinner, but too many people there knew me, and my famous wife. She came up with a great suggestion, "Since we'll be going to the Prime Rib at the Park Lane Hotel tomorrow night, why don't we go to the Dining Room at Brown's Hotel?" I looked askance at Madeline when she said this.

"Bradley wants me there because I have a marvelous memory, and the four of us will be talking business. Don't worry, he knows I am going to help get you situated this weekend. Nothing more, at all. He has a wife and at least one mistress. That's enough for most men. Don't you think so?" I took that question as rhetorical, although it might not have been meant that way. I certainly was not going to get into any disclosure-fest on lovemaking outside marriage with Madeline!

Brown's Dining Room was something out of an early Twentieth Century British film depicting what a gentlemen's London restaurant should look like: a somewhat low ceiling, much lighting, but all very indirect, dark-stained wood paneling – some carved, some engraved, and rich leather covered arm-chairs. All creating an understated, but posh, atmosphere. We were given a discrete table. (I never got around to asking Madeline if she had requested that. Roosevelt and Truman were both fond of staying at Brown's, very much in the heart of the West Side, but located mid-block, on a side-street, making it relatively easy to secure and not at all conspicuous.)

Our conversation was eclectic, and the seafood was delicious. We split a saute of prawns in a cheese, butter and brandy sauce. Then, we each had a baked Dover sole: mine with only lemon on the side. Madeline had a sublime white wine and butter sauce, which I tried, but found that it somewhat overwhelmed the delicate taste of the fish itself. Oh well! Each to his or her own device. It was a pleasant walk between Brown's and Grosvenor House, and Madeline showed me a different route each way. (As we entered the Lobby, I had a premonition that Carolyn was waiting upstairs in my rooms. I felt so strongly that I bid Madeline wait while I strode over to the Front Desk and made an inquiry if anyone had sought me out whilst I was at dinner. There was a telephone message from Carolyn asking me to call her on her cell, right away. I told Madeline that it appeared urgent. She understood and used my bathroom while I called Carolyn from the living area. We talked for at least 15 minutes; *Vogue* was in touch again with Celestine. They wanted to know if the two of us would do a layout in Paris with her showing me its most famous sites. Of course, I said YES, knowing that scheduling might be a nightmare. Carolyn ended with, "I cannot wait to get my hands on you when you return a few nights from now!" (*When I told Dr. Arnaud about that night, she smiled a great deal, but said she needed to think about all of it.*)

Madeline was still in the lovely dress outfit she had worn to Brown's. She asked if I would like to help her to undress. That lasted about ten seconds as she took the initiative straight away, and before I knew all that was happening, she was leading me into a choreography like nothing I had experienced before, or since –scintillating!

When I awoke the next morning, Madeline was gone. She left a note and said that she would call on me in a taxi at 6:00 to go to dinner this evening. She did not answer her telephone all day. In the taxi, she said, "You missed me all day, didn't you?"

We were at the Hyde Park Hotel in a flash. I was still formulating an answer to her question. Perhaps, I should have just uttered a simple YES, and then all would have moved on. As it turned out, much of what I thought when my mind wandered was, with whom would Madeline spend this night?

Dinner with Quincy and Bradley was social for about twenty

minutes. If Quincy had a social life besides drinking, he hid it well. Bradley had been to Margate, a seaside town, with his wife and three children. He spoke lovingly for a minute or so, then cooled to that topic quickly. Madeline allowed she had met me at the airport with all of the materials Bradley had wanted me to review. She met me in the taxi to come here to be sure all went well, and made sure I understood them. In turn, I had bought her dinner. I mentioned that Carolyn wished them all well and that she had enjoyed her trip with me to London and Paris immensely. Then I told them about the *Vogue* modeling assignment. Madeline feigned surprise. Quincy and Bradly seemed unphased, with the latter moving, instead, to begin our business discussion.

We all agreed that the search needed to be concluded in a forthwith manner. I explained that DMIC would allow spending more if it would move things along expeditiously. But they wanted an understanding of what was happening with the syndicate payments which were not keeping up a steady pace or growing to parallel the discovery of new policies in the Cheshire & Booth file room. Bradley allowed the ledger told the story. Some syndicates were timely, while others were falling behind, and no one had the job of follow-up. Quincy shrugged his shoulders implying he did not do that sort of thing. Bradley's reaction was much the same. So, I inquired if Cheshire & Booth would undertake such a task. Madeline broke the growing silence, "Bradley, I do believe that this type of task would be excellent training for a few of your junior solicitors. It could teach them perseverance, patience and tact. Ronan, if your client is preparing to enter a relationship with Stanley Booth, then they might be the best source for that task as they would have some skin in the game, so to speak. Perhaps, you might share those thoughts with us, if you are prepared to do so?"

The food literally began to arrive, with carts full of tasty appetizers, followed in good order by the meat trolleys. A grand time was had by all. I told them that we would see what we could come up with. However, part of the issue for DMIC was the expense of an agent in London and might be leading them to think any kind of open-ended arrangement would not be worth the time, effort, or expense. The meal was a bit overlong after the meat course, and I begged off after one glass of port. Madeline, whom Bradley had asked to be in the office by 8:00, asked if she might leave as well since my taxi could drop her off by going a few blocks out of its way. The two of us left as they ordered their second, and probably not last, port.

Madeline did not go straight home. Instead, after some mind-blowing sex, Madeline had some very thoughtful concepts on how to proceed, if Bradley did not want to undertake the task. (She thought that Cheshire & Booth would not step up as the chances of causing offense to many of their prospective clients would be too real a potential conflict.)

— — —

After all of our preparation, the meeting with Stanley Booth, his solicitor, Pierce Fields, and three of Stanley's people, one of whom spent a good deal of time "on the search," was ever-so-slightly anti-climactic. Everyone appeared chipper, and I conveyed John O'Sullivan's greetings. Much of what I had learned over the weekend was re-hashed, but one thing became clear as the morning pressed onward: Stanley Booth had no real stomach for doing collections from the syndicate leads themselves (mostly his clients, or their member names). However, he was interested in Desert Mutual's willingness to work with his firm to come up with a plan to allow the DMIC-funded Search Experience to be used as a model for future searches under the Cheshire & Booth auspices. (We made an initial offer verbally and Mr. Fields asked for it in writing.) But the fact that a potential deal was in the offing was very promising. My thought was that all four of us should return to Bradley's office. Quincy allowed he would have a short stay as he had a pressing writ matter that needed his attention badly. We all agreed that a deal for a search/collections partnership of sorts could get done. I said I would work on terms on the flight home, run them by John, and then get that to Bradley and Quincy for a final draft. We had decided to add an interest term for the time value of DMIC's cash investment in creating the search, including its expenses for our trips to London. We settled on the going rate of ten percent in London at that time, but I knew DMIC would accept less, perhaps as low as five percent. They wanted to recoup their expenses and were anxious to get on with wrapping-up the search part of this business. Quincy left.

Bradley asked if I would like a Vodka, and Madeline appeared with a Grey Goose in seconds. She asked if she could join us at the table, and I realized as a certainty, then, that Bradley saw her as more than an assistant. I said, "I guess that leaves the issue of a London agent and collections as the last matter. Do either of you have thoughts?"

I turned ever so slightly to face toward Bradley; but as I did so, he nodded toward Madeline, who said, "I have been here since before seven and met with Bradley about your concerns. Solicitors are not well-positioned to run a collection business, but are well-positioned to assist in enforcing that process. So, what is needed is a small third-party enterprise to accommodate the needed communication with the American clients, and the solicitors on collections and to facilitate routine communications and paperwork with the London broker, as Cheshire & Booth, for example. Bradley is willing to house such an enterprise at the outset, and I should appreciate being the founder if DMIC and you are willing. I shall also remain with Bradley, but in a somewhat reduced capacity as that business might grow. If DMIC wishes to be an investor, or partner, I would entertain either. Your thoughts?"

I turned to Bradley who indicated he was on board and would not be unhappy to have a continuing relationship with DMIC, as needed, and with me. Having "worked with Madeline" at some length over that weekend, I was quite convinced that she was bright and knew her way around finance and numbers in general. If Bradley was convinced, perhaps it was a "win" for all involved. As I sat there, I could see no real downside except failure, and Madeline did not seem that type. So, I asked her, "Madeline, if I am to pitch this concept, because of the money involved, you would have to be bonded. Would you foresee an issue with that?"

She looked at me, smiled demurely, and said, "In my current position I am already bonded. The amount of the bond might have to be higher at some point."

Me: "Rather than do a fancy lunch now, perhaps I should go back to my rooms and make some plans and do some calling. How about an early dinner tonight?"

They both agreed, at Brown's at 6:30. Bradley mentioned, "My wife, Gabrielle, was quite taken with Carolyn and you. Would you mind if I bring her along?"

— — —

I started with the East Coast, Tinker, and ran almost everything by him. His thoughts mostly coincided with mine. I spoke with Lily, then Reggie who both arrived very early every day. Then I tried John O'Sullivan. I provided a report in some detail. I told him about the ledgers and the work done at Thornton, Campbell, and how it turned out that Bradley had caused Madeline to do almost all of it. As I was going on, John interrupted, and said, "That might be the solution?"

So, I went right to the proposition as I left it a few hours before. John was ecstatic, and when I suggested an ownership interest, or loan, he did not balk, although he said he would have

to confer on ownership; then he said, tell them we'll go some
money on a start-up loan, and figure things out as we go.

— — —

That evening at Brown's Dining Room was the beginning of
several long-running relationships. But first, I must say that
Gabrielle emoted effusively about her evening with Carolyn. She
went on for a good twenty minutes. We other three smiled and
tried to look interested. I knew Carolyn would be pleased once
I told her. But when I got a chance, I introduced my call with
John O'Sullivan to a smile from Bradley and a staid British attempt at unbridled enthusiasm from Madeline. Of course, I
pointed out that there were steps that would need to be taken
to get this new enterprise up and running.

My news made dinner a big success, and it made my last
night in London with Madeline unforgettable as well!

23

DESRT MIUTUAL'S SECOND CAL BOARD ATTORNEY MEETING

Despite Manny's last minute desire to plan for the Westin Princess in North Scottsdale, when he asked for competitive bidding, the Biltmore came in with much more favorable pricing, including free transportation to/from Sky Harbor Airport and to the nearby Fashion Plaza. Made no real difference to me. I was given a suite in the main building, the one originally designed by Frank Lloyd Wright (by that time frame, his home had become a museum, located very near-by.), with excellent access to all of the facilities we would be using. The number of invitees had climbed as had the volume and new venues of our client's BI cases, which employed most of these new lawyers.

I had worked with a committee of Manny from DMIC Home Office, our team's Reggie and Phil, Tinker from D.C. and Ted Darrow from Philadelphia. (By then, Reggie had taken on a role as second-in-command in management of BI cases being defended by local counsel. This included providing his trial team for use in jurisdictions where our local attorney was either new, or did not feel up to speed for trying a case. This was why Phil Hassard, our SoCAL partner, wanted to be the one to go to trial. (He did and settled for a very appropriate amount, before the jury came back. He waited to interview some of those jurors after the verdict was read. Other defendants had not settled. The three jurors with whom he spoke told Phil they felt CAL Board would have to pay between $15-20,000 as its share of a judgment. He settled for $10,000. An excellent result. Both Austin Smith and

Manny were quite satisfied.) Reggie wanted four hours on Coordination with Local Counsel and panels were formed for presentation and discussion topics. Reggie would be Program Chair
for that main segment of the meeting.

Another topic was Science & Medicine: and while Ted Darrow was on the planning committee, Martha and I were the two
most knowledgeable among those present at the meeting. Ted
knew what was going on, so the three of us made up a fifty
minute panel. The BUILDINGS cases, including the class actions, involved a relatively small subset of all of those lawyers
present. Nonetheless, the Science & Medicine argument, supported by our European experts, fit much better in that topic.
Also, it provided our launching point for discussing the Leibnitz
Institute Symposium, as a separate 50 minute panel, potentially
applicable to all of those who attended, especially for those with
counsel from around the country whose judiciary attended the
Symposium. (We had alerted five local counsel that their state
court judges were in attendance, so that they had a chance to formulate their thoughts, as we planned to call on each.) We also
had packets of all of the significant handouts from that Boston
symposium for every attendee.

Of course, there was "networking" to take place, as well. For
first time attendees, we had ice breakers, including a dinner for
early arrivals which began to look like most attendees. It had
been three years since our first meeting. Many of the other prior
attendees wanted to reinvigorate earlier acquaintanceships. Finally, word had leaked out that there was to be a special award
for me on the last night and my Carolyn would be in attendance
for that. This resulted in any number of requests for spouses and
significant others to attend, at the individual attorney's expense.
Manny consulted his superiors and they acquiesced. (I warned
Carolyn, but she told me not to worry, just give her a full attendance list with those she had met in the past highlighted and
she would be fine.) The size of that crowd swelled to triple its

original size. (Klein and Kelly, my two senior partners, decided to fly-in for just that one night (The Biltmore had a two-night minimum on weekend nights. So, they decided to stay over. Of course, their wives insisted on attending).

Martha, Reggie and I flew down to Phoenix on Tuesday for final planning, and last minute meetings and arrangements. About seven or eight others came in as well, like Tinker, Mace and Tod from D.C. and Ted Darrow and Scott from Philadelphia. We met in the bar of the hotel that night, counted noses, and decided to go over to the Capitol Grille at Fashion Plaza, utilizing the hotel's van service. We drank a bit too much, limited what we ate, and all chipped in for the final bill. With Reggie's military background on this type of participation, every person paid the same fair share. Back at the Biltmore, only four of us had a nightcap. Then it was two: Martha and me. She said simply, in a forlorn voice, "This is our only possible night?"

I agreed, but said, "Prudence dictates that we take a pass this time." She smiled demurely, nodding affirmatively!

— — —

I had been thinking about the COLLEGES class action and Judge Blatt's ruling that it could move forward to the Class Certification stage. He entered a Scheduling Order allowing the Defendants 180 days to conduct their discovery on class issues, and 60 days thereafter to file any briefs opposing the class. One early meeting, attended by Tinker and Josh, had resulted in the bulk of the defense counsel being in favor of attacking the suitability of the class representative and the uncertainty of the class definition. Some also wanted to attack the class plaintiff counsel. We saw that as a particular waste of resource with this judge and those attorneys.

Tinker and I played with the issues of causation and damages (we had learned a great deal in the *LAUSD* matter): e.g., what

happened if a plaintiff class member had undertaken no inspections, what were its injuries? Or, if there were inspections, but
nothing was found amiss? Or, if there were inspections and only
encapsulated ACM was found –no danger from that unless disturbed, i.e., removal! Since this was not an issue limited to the
law, we could use one of our UK experts to "get the ball rolling"
on our defense theory. Also, could a class plaintiff claim all of
those inspection costs as a form of damages even though no actual injury was found to support any kind of replacement damages? And, if these costs of inspection were to be considered
damages, which defendants would pay if there was no identification of the product's manufacturer?

After considerable thought, we felt we might put this before
the meeting group as a whole to see if anyone could come up
with a meaningful critique. (Tinker and Josh would co-chair that
panel, while Martha would also be a panel member.) We ran this
plan for an agenda item past Manny. He agreed.

— — —

With a few spouses present, the first scheduled night seemed
almost at full attendance. This was supposed to be the chance
for the more senior attorneys and client-types to get to know
those attorneys who were attending for the first time; and who,
in many instances, had little or no face time with the people actually running the defense of CAL Board as well as those at
Desert Mutual who were deeply involved. But with so many
other returnees being present, caused by the passage of so much
time between meetings, the sense of that night was as much re-
newal of relationships as of first time meetings. For this reason,
we let cocktails go an extra twenty minutes and made some ad-
justments to the next day's scheduled starting time, moving it
up an hour, as well.

The rest of that evening flowed well. I met a great many

lawyers for the first time, most involved solely in BI matters and who were retained through Manny, Reggie or with my getting referrals from members of my special "social group," the Society of Defense Counsel (for short). Also, many of them were starting to seem younger. *(My first inklings of the passage of time was Dr. Arnaud's remark when I told her of that sensation the next week.)* Some of us kept the bar open and got to know new counsel on more of a one-to-one basis. Still, I made time to call and offer good-nights to much of my family in Ross (Kate had finally moved in with us. My sisters back East were jealous, or so said Kate.).

Carolyn was in fine spirits and told me she planned to arrive the next day. Several of the older children were wishing they could be there as well, at least for my award dinner on Saturday evening. Alas! We can only do so much. I slept well (and alone!).

A meeting day for me always started before breakfast. I would arrive early to see that all was in order, then grab some fruit and cereal before others began to show up. Then, I would check on the food lines and move from table to table, making small talk and seeing to anyone's needs. Somewhat surprisingly, Manny's wife, Esmeralda was at breakfast. She called me over to her table, which was full and seemed to include a few other non-meeting participants, saying, "Ronan, Carolyn has been so nice on the phone. She allowed that she did not want to be a distraction during the meeting sessions, so she asked me to get a few spouses together and we are going to shop a bit and spend time at the pool." She looked around and most of the others were nodding in approval. All I could think was how generous of my wonderful wife to spend time with people, most of whom were almost absolute strangers; and, of course, while utterly making Esmeralda's day many times over, as her go-between!

The sessions went as planned, starting with the lengthy new member introductions and a bit about their CAL Board case load. Its General Counsel, Austin Smith, was taking copious

notes. With short speeches from half a dozen senior people, including me, followed by a Q&A session, that was the Thursday
morning. The afternoon was dedicated to Reggie's BI agenda,
with the final panel being Science and Medicine, chaired by Tod,
with Tinker and Martha. Those three had persuaded me to sit
at the end of that table on the dais.

There turned out to be multiple components to this panel;
most of those present wanted to talk about whether or not asbestos fibers could cause lung cancer in the absence of cigarette
smoking. (The defense being that "but for" being a smoker, there
would not have been cancer, only a lesser condition like Asbesto-
sis, or nothing. Thus, the plaintiff caused his own lung cancer.
Not a tidy defense, but known, at the very least, to lower the
value of a typical case by a substantial amount based on the con-
tribution of a significant smoking history.) Martha, Tod and especially our Reggie were the leading voices in explanation.

Then, the other topic came up near the end of that panel. Tod
and Martha explained that this was largely used in the property
cases, and tomorrow we would be exploring the defenses to
raise in one of those in which we sought to oppose class certification. This was the *Mullen* Defense: asbestos containing materials (ACM) left undamaged, and especially if encapsulated,
where their microscopic asbestos fibers could not become airborne not only represented no risk to anyone, but any potentially unnecessary removal of that ACM should be considered a
potential cause of an asbestos disease process. This seemed incredibly controversial despite on-going use of ACM having virtually ceased almost two decades ago. So, the one major
contemporary avenue to encounter airborne fibers was through
removal, much of which was unnecessarily mandated by the
EPA, especially by including fully encapsulated ACM. Then, we
briefly explained our witnesses for this topic, and how we were
planning to use them in the PROPERTY cases. Finally, we explained our efforts to figure out a path to the EPA for the "right

person" to make this compelling presentation. On that note and without discussion, we broke at 4:45. Cocktails started at 6:00. I chatted with many of those present, and was back in our suite by 5:00. Carolyn was just arriving herself, having been to the pool area. She took off her cover-up, leaving only her bikini, and said, "We can talk or ...."

I was kissing her before she could finish. We showered together and it was amazing how she could tell me about her day while doing her hair and make-up in no time at all! She'd had a "very fun day."

We arrived for cocktails at 5:55. I knocked on the door. The assistant Food & Beverage manager opened it. I asked if we could start a few minutes early and he said YES. I located Manny and Esmeralda as well as Reggie and his wife, Ginger; and the three couples formed a greeting line with the earliest arrivals queuing up, and then streaming past. At 6:20, I suggested we join the party. A waiter was already there with our drinks which I had ordered a few minutes before. We spoke briefly among ourselves, then dispersed. Carolyn and I moved no more than a few steps and we were engulfed by other couples who wanted to talk and, especially, to meet my wife.

Deirdre and Lily had worked tirelessly on a seating plan for that dinner. There was no actual head table. Rather, the more senior people, not just the lawyers, were assigned so that at least one, if not two, sat at each table. This resulted in everyone meeting some first time attendees and by separating our Klein Kelly team members, and others from firms with multiple attendees, we got an excellent mix of those present. At our table, having asked Carolyn if it would be OK, we did not sit next to each other so that I could meet two new attendees. With bread and salads already in place, we had only two courses to serve and the hotel staff did an excellent job of clearing and replacing, while attending to beverages. Dudley Chisholm, DMIC's Chief of Claims, gave the welcoming remarks reprising his role from the meeting earlier that morning. I spoke briefly as well: a few sentences about the day behind us, a few about the morrow, and wishing everyone a pleasant evening after the dessert and night cap being served at the cocktail party site next door.

Some of us, including Carolyn and me, stayed for two rounds (the absolute limit), and we chatted in smaller groups. Most of the Klein Kelly team got together briefly, and they greeted Carolyn effusively with hugs and cheek-kissing. That did not last long as others awaited their turns, and the opportunities to have a real chat, albeit sometimes brief, did occur. In all, by 9:30, even the most stalwart, knowing the morning started at 7:00, were drifting off. At that moment, Martha, who had not been visible all night appeared. Carolyn knew her best of all the firm's lawyers and gave her a big hug, which Martha returned. They spoke for a few minutes and then Martha came over to me and wished me, "A very good night!"

(H-m-m-m!)

— — —

Friday was to be the last day of the CAL Board Attorney Meeting itself, ending at 1:00 with a box lunch for those chasing a flight home, and a buffet lunch for those in less of a hurry. A sit-down lunch was set for those running the meeting to undertake a post-meeting evaluation in a private room just off of the Biltmore's main indoor dining room.

Carolyn had asked if she could sit in on a session or two, just to see the kinds of things that were discussed. (I asked Manny and Austin and they both agreed.) I invited her to sit in on the last two Friday morning sessions, about 90 minutes. First, we discussed the status of all the major property cases and where we saw them going over the months ahead, and how we felt we might affect the outcomes and move them to a favorable resolution, if possible. This included a discussion of the potential for a

California Coordination of the four County-based mega-joinder cases in Southern California. Out of this, yet again, came the apparent need to interact somehow with EPA.

Then, we moved onto how to approach the Class Certification issues in the COLLEGES matter before Judge Blatt in Charleston. The *reductio de minimis* argument which we had formulated was, at first, found to be a bit awkward, and led many of the newer attorneys to question its viability (A show of hands did not find a great deal of class action experience, but the level of federal court experience was one hundred per cent.) As that argument became more refined, I said, "What would you all think if we had a world famous asbestos scientist sign an affidavit in support of our motion?"

One first timer blurted out, "That might change everything! But where would you get one?"

Martha said, passively, "We have four." Silence followed. "Just as yesterday, we are not quite ready to disclose any of these people as none are Americans." I nodded affirmatively and began the closing of the meeting right there. We had our answer. Now, there was only one question left: which scientist would we use?

— — —

Our lunch meeting proved fruitful. Manny said that now that the reinsurance money was again flowing fairly well, Dudley thought we should have another of these meetings next year. Everyone agreed. We nominated Martha and Tod to be the Program Co-chairs. We asked Tinker to explore what means might be available to approach the EPA. Even with President Bush the First in office, he was pessimistic about that very liberal agency back-pedaling on its "zero-tolerance" asbestos removal policy.

— — —

That afternoon, Carolyn and I spent an hour or so sunning by our private pool, with complete privacy, she shed her bathing suit for twenty minutes to get some sun, but no more to avoid any trace of a burn. We retreated to our bedroom next for an hour of pleasure, then Carolyn began her careful preparations for the evening. I was ready in less than an hour and called Tinker to see if he wanted to have a quick drink before the event. I told my gorgeous wife that I would return to escort her to the event promptly at six o'clock.

Tinker and I exchanged pleasantries and did some catching up. He said that he and Elaine were increasingly unhappy that they had not had a second child. Laughingly, I told him I would donate one, but he didn't laugh. He was serious. I asked if Elaine wanted to try. He said they were thinking about it. She was almost four years younger than him. I thought for a brief moment: ...and Carolyn is more than eight years younger than me. Then I said, "I know there are more risks, but if you all are really serious and it sounds like you are, then you should talk to a clinic and decide sooner rather than later as time is not your friend on this one." *(When I told Dr. Arnaud about this conversation the next week, her response was not what I expected, "Have you told Carolyn about this and asked her how she feels? And, perhaps, even, what she wants?")*

— — —

That Desert Mutual Award Evening as it came to be known was certainly a high point of my legal career. There were seven couples from Desert Mutual, Austin Smith and his daughter from CAL Board, my seven partners from Klein Kelly, five with spouses (Mary and Martha were unescorted), Tinker and Elaine, Bradley Campbell, his wife, Gabrielle, as well as Madeline, with Quincy and Wilfred from Twenty Kings Bench Walk. (During the CAL Board meeting itself, John O'Sullivan, Bradley and

Madeline had been putting the finishing touches on their relationship for what was then a novel entity in London to interface
with all of the lead syndicate underwriters, names and established relationships created by "Long-Tail Litigation." (To be
known as "LTL, Ltd," with Madeline in charge of day-to-day op-
erations.)

Cocktails lasted just past the customary one hour. Passed appetizers sufficed as an appetizer course for dinner. Then we took
our seats. Four tables of ten left two vacant seats at each table.
Charlie Sewell, CEO of DMIC, opened the dinner with very brief
remarks, "We are all gathered here tonight to honor the one
lawyer who has done more for Desert Mutual Insurance than
any other non-employee of the company." He smiled, adding,
"And some might say, 'more than any employee as well!' But I
am not going to sing his praises more for now, as the time to eat
our dinner is at hand. Salad, main, first dessert, and second. I
would ask Ronan and Carolyn to sit here and have their salad
with us and to rotate to John's table next, then Dudley's, and finally Manny's. Then, please return to us at the end of the meal
for the final speeches. Now, a first toast, Here's to Ronan who
has for well more than a decade worked tirelessly to protect
CAL Board, Desert Mutual's Insured and his client, but also
Desert Mutual itself. And to Carolyn, his beautiful wife; and lest
we not forget, to the memory of the lovable Mollie, the mother
of Ronan's children!"

"HEAR! HEARs!" flooded the room. As the dinner itself
lasted almost two hours, two toasts/table were had, not to mention stories and vignettes at each. Carolyn was exceedingly gracious and I did my very best to minimize my imbibing amidst
some good-natured ribbing. A fine time was had by all, and we
finally returned to Charlie's table which included Austin and
Eloise, Mary and Martha, along with Tinker and Elaine as the
last course concluded.

When everyone was settled in their chairs, Charlie stood and walked over to a lectern in the corner of the room. He beckoned to me and I joined him. Reaching down behind that piece of furniture, he was assisted by John O'Sullivan and they lifted a plaque about two square feet, and Charlie read it to me, "Desert Mutual Insurance Company's INAUGURAL BEYOND THE CALL OF DUTY AWARD, given this day of 1990 to RONAN O'NEILL, who has earned it with the UNANIMOUS CONSENT of the EXECUTIVE Committee of this Company. Signed by John here and me." There was more, much more, and then there were John, Dudley and Mannie. Then Austin, Klein and Kelly. Then, to my surprise, Charlie said, "And one final speaker, Carolyn Tyne, who most of you now know as Mrs. Ronan O'Neill."

Carolyn dabbed her eyes, went to the lectern, and spoke for perhaps ten minutes. I know she spoke of our first meeting and our years as friends, rarely seeing each other. Then she spoke of Patrick, then at some length of Mollie, then she spoke of how our love had blossomed, and how proud she was of me, my family and her life as a model and now as my wife. Finally, she thanked me."

I was too choked up to speak at any length, not so much by all the praise, but more by the depth of feeling in Carolyn's words about Mollie, and me. Instead, I took just a few moments to thank everyone for this award, the event and the evening.

Then it was over!

— — —

The next morning, we had breakfast with Tinker and Elaine who were heading out right afterward to Sedona to visit Arizona's spectacular Red Rock Country. That evening we went to an authentic Mexican restaurant in Scottsdale, down the street from a motorcycle bar, with the UK crew and Manny and Esmeralda (great food, great time, and incredible prices!). We flew home on Sunday at noon. We had a bar-b-que at five with the children, Kate and Ingrid, who had asked beforehand, when we were doing the planning, if she could invite my partner, Phil!

— — —

24

SAN ANDREAS/ COLLEGES/ LONDON

Following Phoenix, I had a few weeks to put things together for the balance of another year. Besides an overdue visit to Dr. Arnaud, I greatly needed to formulate a plan for dealing with Carey Crawford's *Hobart* case in San Andreas. Following up with Tinker on the EPA was also a priority, just as was deciding on which expert to use on the COLLEGES Opposition to Class Certification; not to mention retaining a mechanical engineering expert for *Hobart*.

I took care of my San Andreas needs first. Over the years, I had come to know several engineers with Bechtel, a huge Architect/Engineering company headquartered in San Francisco (early on, it worked on the Hoover Dam, and grew to design and build nuclear and other power plants, while expanding to undertake a wide variety of other highly technical construction projects globally). One of them referred me to Chad Darwin who lived in Corte Madera in Marin County, a few towns south of Ross, and just north of Mill Valley. He was a Naval Academy grad with 12 years at Bechtel, all in mechanical engineering, and very experienced with pumping systems, starting out as an engineer in a nuclear submarine. We met for a beer at the No-Name Bar in Sausalito. He was very bright, a good listener, and had an instant grasp of the water pressure system involved in the case. As we sat there, he allowed it was doubtless some issue with the pressure relief valve and also might involve at least one other control for activating the pump (when the system was repaired by Ross Weatherbee, he left the pump in place as it seemed to be running just fine and responded appropriately to the new "on/off" control which he installed on the new pressure tank).

Chad was just fine and I hired him for a reasonable hourly fee and told him to bill half of our meeting, I explained that Lily would send him the needed paperwork and asked that he return it forthwith. He asked when he could look at the components and I told him we would arrange that and get back to him; and that either Deirdre, Joshua, or I would be in touch.

— — —

In thinking about experts to use in the PROPERTY cases, I concluded that Corbett McDonald would doubtless be the best one with which to lead off. Also, because of his age (mid-'70s), it seemed prudent to take a preservation deposition (just in case, especially since he still insisted on riding his bicycle to work each day through West End London traffic).

Once, we started that whole process, we should probably depose Julian Peto as well. (As to Dr. Bignon: I remained somewhat uncomfortable with him based on Mollie's comments about how potentially Xenophobic the Philadelphia Area jurors might be, not to mention South Carolinians.)

I asked Mary to put together a Notice of Preservation Deposition for all of the federal and state PROPERTY Cases for which we were defending (surely less then all of those on file in all U.S. courts as we were in only a few of those except for the class cases which were nationwide in their putative scope). Accordingly, I called Alicia Goines and asked if her client and three or four others would be interested in adding cases to that deposition notice. I also called Sandra and asked her about Wallboard's willingness (they still hated me!) to participate in the notice process as we attempted to cover all extant PROPERTY cases filed in the U.S.A.

I asked Martha to work with Mary and come up with a Declaration for Corbett to sign in support of our briefing on that class and its issues. (That declaration would give context and meaning to Corbett's Preservation Deposition in mid-January. So, it had to be a clear and concise statement of his position on these "needless removal" issues. Martha, because of her time spent with Corbett and Alison, was doubtless the best lawyer on our team to extract precisely what Corbett would want to say from Corbett himself.)

We planned to file our OPPOSITION TO CLASS CERIFICA-TION MOTION in mid-November. We planned to take Corbett's deposition in the third week of January in Washington, D.C. at Tinker's office (his firm was growing seemingly exponentially!). We would prep him the week before, I would do the prep with Martha, Tod and Ted Darrow at Tinker's office over three days. (We planned to limit his deposition time to a maximum of five hours/day, four days/week because of his age. Corbett resented that.) We thought about having Ted or Tod defend Corbett, but Martha had her own ideas on that. Since she had probably spent more time with Corbett than anyone else (I would be her closest rival.), she made an excellent case. (Either Tinker or I would be moments away by phone, and we would see that one of us was always free!)

— — —

I got to thinking, and I asked Tinker what he thought of having Julian Peto be the expert we would ask to interact with the EPA on the issue of reconsidering its rule-making requiring the mandatory removal of all installed asbestos containing products (ACM), even if many, if not most, extant installations posed no hazard to any building occupant or user. As a mathematician, as opposed to a medical science public health professional, he would seemingly have smaller fish to fry; however, as a highly regarded publisher on a myriad of technical fronts involving mathematics in a variety of applications superimposed on real life, he was arguably not far below Stephen Hawking in areas of scientific world regard, especially when one considers his early, and lengthy, relationship with Sir Richard Doll.

Tinker mulled this over. Politically, his firm was aligned with the Republican Party which was looking for ways to assist businesses in avoiding needless regulation. This EPA unfunded mandate seemed to work a special hardship on all those it affected, with the possible exception of the legal community (which also represented an ever-increasing expense to business!).

We decided, that when we finished Corbett's preservation deposition, that we would ask Julian to fly over and have some initial preparation sessions for his deposition should it be needed. In the course of that time here, we could determine his suitability and willingness for this putative EPA task. Meanwhile, Tinker could put out feelers for an appropriately influential Republican who might serve as the potential jumping off contact for this initiative.

— — —

Meanwhile, Carolyn had been working once again with Robert on their next *Vogue* shoot. This was to involve Paris and show it in its City of Light image as a backdrop for high-end fashion. They came up with doing it while that city was decorated for Christmas (even more Lights!). *Vogue* agreed to bring our whole family over, including Ingrid and Kate. Robert was said to be open to a few shots of the family as well; for example, going to the Opera or visiting one of the museums. Of course, Carolyn and I were to be the focus of that shoot. She went over the possibilities in great detail aa they were evolving. It was so good to be home for several weeks in a stretch.

— — —

My next trip to San Andreas with Jim Downing was a two-day overnighter. Since there was no flying for me, and Jim was driving, this hardly seemed a trip. We had a settlement conference that first day at one p.m., and the judge had excused my insurance claims manager and my client because we were seen by the judge as having posted a "good faith offer to settle" whereas the others were seen to be stalling.

Jim parked out in front of the hotel. We checked into the Black Bart, put our things in our rooms and agreed to meet at the bar for a quick sandwich. Jim was a bit late and the other four defense lawyers were at their own table eating. One of them, Ron, who represented the pressure relief valve manufacturer, got up and motioned for a new person to step up to the bar, saying, "Howard Shein, from San Francisco, meet Ronan O'Neill from Oakland, and friend of the plaintiff's attorney, Jim Downing."

Howard put out his hand and I shook it. He smiled a funny smile, and said, "These three gentlemen don't seem to like you very much. Guess you're not a team player." With that he dropped my hand. I said, "I guess not. That's why you're working on this case, because we went out and found that the subject tank was manufactured by your client, and brought it in on a cross-complaint. As to these gentlemen, I explained in the past: multi-party litigation is often not a team game. I represent my client. That's it. If it's in my client's best interest, I do it. Period. Nice to meet you." I paused as Jim Downing walked up, saying, "Howard, this is Jim Downing, counsel for the plaintiff interests in this matter. Jim, this is Howard Shein...."

Jim put his hand out and said, "Howard and I go back a few cases. Nice to see you, Howard. Saw you have the tank manufacturer. Good luck!"

At 1:00, we all reported to Judge Forestall's court room. He called Jim Downing into his chambers for about 10 minutes, then he called me. He said, "We have a real nice golf course down the road a short piece. I reckon you can get nine holes in, maybe a few more, but be back here at 4:15."

I left. Jim had his T-Bird running. We found the golf course. The manager, named Harry, told us the judge had called and told him we'd be over. For Twenty-five dollars each, we rented shoes and clubs, bought socks and balls, and drove out to see how many holes we could play before 4:00 (those days of low fees and rentals are so long gone!). Turned out to be eleven holes and we had the course to ourselves. When we got back, Harry told us that we were the first non-locals to play the course in more than a year!

Judge Forestall was in his chambers with the three component defense lawyers. Howard Shein was sitting at the defense table reading something, when we walked in. He turned to us and said, "Those three are going to milk this case for all the fees they can get. The pump only does what it's told. The tank only holds water. The controls are the 'whole story.'" We both nodded. The judge's clerk summoned the three of us to join the others in chambers. He allowed that the three component defendants each denied any possibility of fault.

Jim Downing allowed that he would be filing an Offer of Compromise as to each of the three early next week. If any of them failed to settle, and he recovered a judgment more than that Offer, that defendant would be on the hook for all kinds of costs associated with expert witnesses, from both their depositions and as trial witnesses. The three looked non-plussed. Finally, the judge asked Howard and me if he could tell the three hold outs about our outstanding settlement offers. I allowed I would have to clear that with my client's people. Howard did not answer. The judge asked the holdouts to step outside. He wanted to know how much more fact discovery was going to be needed. Also, when would expert discovery get started (that would significantly drive up the cost of defense)?

Then, Judge Forestall asked Jim Downing to elaborate if he

would on how he saw the settlement coming together. He did, with the main focus not being the money, but that he felt the need for a structured settlement, with a significant monthly payout. He knew Bo Hobart would have physical deficits with which to deal, but that a medical insurance trust would care for that component of settlement while an income trust was needed to cover the rest for both Bo & Ruth for their lives. So, enough was more than $1.5 million for that funding and his fees.

After we broke up, I asked Howard what he offered to pay on behalf of Sterling Pressure Tank; and, he said he told the judge his client would pay whatever mine would pay. He thought for a case like this, with unclear liability, mine was a good tactic. He asked about my expert. I told him generally. He asked if we could split him as we did not appear as if we would ever be truly adversarial in this matter. I told him I would get back. Finally, on parting, we both thought the same thing and I said, "I would not want to have that pressure relief valve and be the last defendant standing!" Jim Downing, who had appeared disinterested as Howard and I talked, nodded affirmatively.

— — —

Carolyn said that she and Robert were locking down a shooting schedule, which included interfacing with the sites of the shoots. It would mean our entire Christmas/New Year Holiday in Paris.

I thought we should have time for ourselves, but Carolyn assured me that Robert was aware we would all need that. Plus, DMIC had asked me to go to London to check on Madeline, Bradley and Quincy and on the functioning of the new receivables processing business, LTL Ltd. I needed to see Corbett and Julian for final discussions on their visits to D.C. early next year for deposition preparation and Corbett's deposition. (Martha needed in London?)

We decided Kate and Ingrid might need to take the children back at some point lest they miss too much school. Also, I felt we needed to see Dr. Bignon while in Paris just to touch base. When Carolyn told Robert about that and about Dr. Bignon's position, he was immediately on the telephone. On his return, he said the Editor-in-Chief wonders if we might get some photographs of you four at dinner. Carolyn told him probably at *La Caravelle,* and she described *Robert* as practically swooning.

I was left to call Dr. Bignon the next morning: even with the nine hour time difference, he sounded remarkably fresh and it took me no time to understand his accent. I explained about our forthcoming trip to Paris at Christmas time and that Carolyn, and even me, would be posing for *Vogue,* and that I thought it a good time to catch up with him. He asked about dinner. I mentioned *La Caravelle,* and that *Vogue* would like to buy us dinner, including his wife, Camille. Would they mind a few photographs? He started to laugh, and he got louder, ending with, "I think I shall tell Camille about this, but that I really had to refuse as unprofessional." He paused for a few seconds, "...but then *later* when I tell her we are actually doing this, she will love me for weeks!"

I told him about the details, including *Robert,* and between them and the restaurant, *Robert* would set a date. Carolyn was happy, and she knew Camille would be ecstatic!

— — —

I talked to Carey Crawford, Haley Pumps GC, and Strom Nordquist, Cayuga Mutual's Senior Claims Manager, about Howard Shein's request to share Chad Dawson, my mechanical engineering expert. They were cool to the idea, especially about fearing loss of control or some ensuing, unforeseen conflict of interest. I thought the value lay more in leveraging a settlement. I suggested that if Howard wanted to stay "joined at the hip with us," perhaps the best tack was for him to have no expert, but to pay us an option fee that would allow him access, or have a first option, if we should somehow escape and his client remain behind. That way, we would maintain full control, and there would be no potential competing expert against Chad Dawson (who also would have to agree to this deal).

We talked more with Howard finally agreeing to my option. I talked to Chad who saw the deal as a "win/win" for him. Then, I got back to Howard with Chad's agreement. Howard said he would need to think about it. The next morning, he called to say is client had agreed to our deal.

— — —

Major briefing was taking place in the COLLEGES Class on the issue of Certification. Martha and I spent substantial time crafting a first draft of Corbett McDonald's Affidavit, which we ran by Tinker and Josh. Then, when we all agreed, we had to get Corbett's approval. Each cycle of this process proved extremely time consuming, but every word most certainly would be subject to cross-examination at Corbett's Preservation Deposition in late January. We finally got total agreement on that Affidavit two days before our filing was due in Charleston. We also planned to use that same Affidavit as a Declaration in support of all of our BUILDINGS motion practice in Southern California. Martha was in charge of all of that project. She would run drafts past me. That would be finished while we were in Paris.

— — —

The briefing on Judge Kelly's Recusal Motion was duly completed and filed in early November. The Thanksgiving Holiday Weekend began on a Wednesday. That afternoon, our senior jurist issued his ORDER DENYING DEFENDANTS' MOTION

SEEKING HIS RECUSAL, with PREJUDICE. It arrived in that Friday's mail. Martha and Mary were both in the office as was Lily, who faxed it to me: short and sweat. He found no basis in fact or law to recuse himself as attending an education conference was a function fully within a judge's duty to keep himself current on the evolving law and science. There was no mention of his accepting his hotel stay, meals, and attending the conference itself without charge. Alicia Goines and others put together an overnight fly-in at Chicago's O'Hare late the next week to discuss an action plan on what to do next, and who would do it.

Mary attended for CAL Board which agreed to participate in expedited briefing, with its focus on the judge's failure to go behind the conference itself to consider all of the other evidence with which he was presented in the Defendants' Motion, and thereby seek a Writ of Mandamus from the Third Circuit to Order Judge Kelly to Recuse Himself or, in the Alternative, To Show Cause Why The Third Circuit Should Not Recuse Him. I would oversee the initial phase of that briefing by Mary and Tinker from Paris.

— — —

There was no action on consolidation for the four SoCAL Mass-Joinder SCHOOLS cases, as yet.

— — —

Manny was getting nervous once again. The BI case volume was growing and most of the PROPERTY matters were at critical briefing stages, with several starting into incredibly risky discovery with our first UK expert's deposition. We spoke daily. He wanted feedback from London after I finished in Paris. I asked about the new collection joint venture, LTL Ltd., and he said it appeared to be doing just fine with cash flow somewhat improved.

— — —

I saw more of my mother now that she had moved in with us, but less of the children as they grew older and their interests focused more on school, sports and their contemporaries, as should be expected. We talked over a cocktail as Carolyn was out with some of the parish mothers getting a project underway for St. Anselm's School. Kate was beginning to feel her years; her golf drives did not go as far, and her bridge acumen sometimes seemed to wane. I pointed out that she was in remarkable condition; had buried two husbands and might want to be on the lookout for a third. She pooh-poohed me, but then she said, "Ronan, what about your children? Carolyn, I feel certain, thinks of your four as hers, but they are her step-children, after all. For that matter, the same is technically true of Carolyn's Patrick, who, by now, I recognize has been yours all along. I am sure neither of you will ever tell him that. Even a good lie can go bad if correcting it undermines lifelong relationships. Now, if you will take my advice, ask Carolyn if you can adopt her Patrick, and wait and see what happens." She smiled as she took her last sip, and added, "My glass seems to have leaked its contents. Another, please?"

I got up, went to the ice bucket on the bar, added four fresh cubes to each tumbler and poured three fingers of Johnnie Walker Black in each. Handing her the glass, I said, "You must have been quite the young congresswoman in those War years. Dad was a lucky guy!"

— — —

I saw Dr. Arnaud not long after the advice on parentage from Kate. Many of our visits had become catching up on what was going on in our lives, with subtle questions and occasional observations from the

*good doctor about my mental health and my relationships with the
many people in my life, not the least Martha, and she then knew about
Madeline as well. I still remember her saying during that last visit of
that year as she described the Twentieth Century as just beginning its
fade, "Since the first time I saw you, there was always more than one
woman in your life. At first, I thought one was not enough for you. But
over time, I have come to realize that when you care for a woman after
a certain fashion, you really do want the best for her. Moreover, you
always treat, and speak of the women in your life, with respect. All of
them appear to have been cared for by you, and really do not need you,
and yet they are still there for you. I am certain now that I know why:
you just simply care about them. Now, the same seems true of your
children: you have cared for them all along, but as your mother sees,
you must make certain of their future. I think her plan of action is
sound. You should have an agreement with Carolyn before you return
from Paris. Have a Happy Christmas and send a post card or two."*

25

PARIS IN WINTER

This was to be "Our trip to end all trips" with passports, appointments, schedules, children, and clothes! Oh, so many suitcases! *Vogue,* probably through Celestine or Robert, had doubtless heard of our chance meeting in its bar some years ago, and they were able to make some marvelous arrangements for all of us to stay on an upper floor at *Le Meurice.* Carolyn and I had an elegant suite, the boys had a large connecting bedroom with bath, and on the one side, the girls had the same bedding arrangement as the boys, sharing their space with Ingrid who by then, was much more like an older sister. Kate was directly across the hall from our rooms and had an extra bed in case Ingrid wanted some time without the girls.

We had arrived four days before any shooting was to start and three days before any scheduled meetings, but Celestine wanted to arrange dinner with the whole family our first night, and we agreed so long as it was not a "dress-up event" as we were fairly certain the children would all be tired from their trip. Wrong! The boys wanted to see the river and the girls all wanted to shop, except Kate who would have been happy to start touring the *Louvre,* which she hoped to see in its entirety during this trip. Then, Patrick Tyne asked, "Mom, are we going to see Aunt Lisette while we are here?"

Celestine perked up when she heard this, saying, "Carolyn, I had forgotten that you were a bit of a protégé of Lisette when you were young in California. Would you like me to arrange something?" Carolyn did not look happy, and slowly shook her head NO.

Patrick looked slightly downcast. Carolyn told him, "Patrick, I know this seems like it will be a long, somewhat boring trip for you. Ronan and I will be working so much, and I want the children to see as much of the City as possible. You have been here so many times and now you are old enough to be responsible during the daylight hours. I will talk to Lisette at some point when I know whether we will be able to fit in a visit with her on our respective schedules. Meanwhile, I am hoping that you can assist Ingrid in showing the others around the City and in looking out for Kate. Don't forget we have to celebrate Christmas Eve and Day, as a family. Our last night is scheduled to be January 1. You all go home the next day, then almost right back to school. Ronan and I are off to London for three days, then he has to stay on a few days more and work while I return to Ross, after a quick side-trip to Milan.

She continued with the group, "So for now, let's all split up into groups who have a place or two in mind to visit, and go explore. Two groups! I shall talk to the Concierge and find a pleasant low-key place for dinner, get directions, and we can all gather there by six. By the time you get downstairs, the Concierge will have maps ready for all of you. Be safe!"

Everyone went exploring: Kate and the boys across the street to the *Louvre*, and the others to window watch and shop down the *Rue de Rivoli* to the *Place de la Concorde*, and then back through the gardens of the *Tuileries*. Carolyn and I retreated to our suite and each other.

After almost an hour of love-making and mutual affection, we lay on the huge bed relaxing. Carolyn broke the silence, "Ronan, there is something I have been meaning to talk to you about for quite a while now. Mollie's been gone for what seems a long time now and your children seem to be as fully recovered as they will ever get. My Patrick just loves them all, and adores having his step-brothers and sisters....except they are not. They should be more. That's what I want to ask, 'Would you consider, no hurry, adopting our Patrick and having me adopt your four? I know this could be tricky and runs the risk of opening old wounds, but your four are so receptive to me, and I would be clear that, as always, I am not trying to replace Mollie, I am just serving as her successor. What do you say, will you think about it?"

So that is why I remember that day so very vividly! I rolled over and pulled Carolyn against me so I could feel the length of her skin on mine, and looked intently into her eyes, "You are so extraordinary! My answers are yes, and YES. Please know I did not think I could love you more, but I now know more about the true depths of your feelings and love. I was going to ask you to agree to these very same things while we were here, but you have outdone me. When should we tell them?"

Carolyn continued looking in my eyes, saying, "You decide, but not at Christmas, please. Before, please. I have presents for my children waiting to be given. By the way, it would not surprise me at all if Patrick Tyne knows the truth about us, but I do not believe he will ever tell us, if he does. He cares too much for Aunt Vera, and especially, Uncle Ronan!" Then, she pushed me down using my shoulder.

— — —

We had a fun, light dinner at the same restaurant where Lisette and Carolyn had taken me on my first night in Paris. The chicken was just as good as I remembered. Carolyn had provided Celestine with an agenda of those places and activities which she felt we needed to undertake while in Paris. First and foremost was a boat ride on the Seine. The ever-efficient agent had booked us on a reserved cruise at 9:15 on our first full day. We took two taxis to the tour boat dock across the *Seine* from the *Eiffel* Tower. We had nine seats, five in the first row and four immediately behind, but staggered, to afford an unimpeded view for the entire cruise. We were not the first on board, but close. All too soon, one of the American women recognized Carolyn, and worse, me. She was beside herself with joy. Carolyn quickly leaned over and whispered to me, "These noisy ones are the worst kind of fans. Soon, everyone on the boat will know."

Carolyn was correct. Near mayhem ensued for about fifteen minutes. So, only before we shoved off, did Carolyn agree to be photographed; and at the perfect moment, in perfect French, followed by English, she politely warned all on board that she would not cooperate with anyone who upset, in any manner, the tour itself, including no photos of her, or her family, once underway and cruising!

Everyone on that tour boat was quickly in awe of what happened next, the woman tour guide said, "We have a very famous fashion model and her family on board today, Carolyn Tyne O'Neill. Carolyn is sometimes a resident of Paris and while I will describe the sights in French, she will provide an English version." Carolyn then had the privilege of describing the embankments, the various boats and barges, often nested, the bridges, the palaces, the towers, and even the *Tour d'Argent*. But her favorites were the two central islands, the *Ile de la Cite* and the *Ile de Ste. Louis*, with the Cathedral of *Notre Dame* towering above the river. Olde Paris drew the most emotion from the boat full of tourists, including all four of my children, not to mention Ingrid and even Kate. On the return to its moorings, Carolyn and the tour guide took a turn at the other's first language to the amusement of all on the boat. We waited until last to disembark. Amazingly, many of our shipmates were waiting. They all wanted to thank us, and especially Carolyn, for being so generous. No one asked for any more photographs. A tour guide awaited our group and then he took us to the *Eiffel* Tower for a very complete and comprehensive viewing of Paris on a crystalline day!

— — —

That night, we had dinner in a different bistro with three of Carolyn's model friends who lived in Paris, but had not come to our wedding. They were delighted to meet all of Carolyn's "new family," as Carolyn was wont to refer to all of us. Afterward, I began to consider how little time we really would have for ourselves on this "vacation;" also, I had a correlative thought: this must be how Carolyn had lived all those years when on a shoot—not exactly a party atmosphere!

— — —

The next day, we did what we considered a "Must See," the *Louvre* with all of its many famous works: Venus de Milo, Winged Victory of Samothrace, the Mona Lisa, and Jacques-Louis David's monumental Coronation of Napoleon and Consecration of Josephine! We walked the galleries until our feet ached. The children began to mumble "no more museums." So, after a latish light lunch, we broke off the tour and walked around to *Notre Dame*, did a brief self-guided tour and walked down the Left Bank crossing back over the *Seine* at the *Place de la Concorde*, before returning to *Le Meurice*.

That next night, Celestine and Robert joined us for dinner, as they had requested. (Carolyn had met with them for two hours before cocktails and I joined that threesome with an hour to go. We were having a very French dinner in a private room just off *Le Meurice's* main dining room. Lisette was to be a surprise attendee which would please Carolyn's Patrick (but this was where I began to wonder how to broach the subject of Carolyn's past life and her long-time lovers, Vera in Connecticut and Lisette in Paris). This meeting was the first of many, but provided the overview for the entire shoot and the scheduling of various sites and the participants at each. The Boat Tour of the *Seine*, the exterior of *Notre Dame* and the Louvre would use everyone (interiors were in work-up). *La Caravelle,* would include only Dr. and Mrs. Bignon and us. *Tour d'Argent* would be just Carolyn and me. *Musee d'Orsay* would include Kate, Ingrid and the girls. The three boys would go to a soccer pitch for a staged shoot with us. We would all spend a very long day doing the full tour of *Versailles.* (In between this, I had to keep up on my litigation and consultation workload both in London and the USA.)

Only a few minutes into the cocktail hour, Lisette appeared, looking as glamorous as ever. She went straight to Carolyn, both hugged and exchanged long kisses on each cheek, then, at arms' length, stared at each other for a few moments. Just before becoming uncomfortable, Carolyn began, "Of course, you know Celestine and Robert (nods exchanged). Here is Ronan (Hold both hands, kiss both cheeks.). And, *this* is my Patrick."

Lisette looked stunned at the tall, slender young man standing in front of her. Patrick took both of Lisette's hands and bends, as much as I had to bend, to kiss each of her cheeks, "Aunt Lisette, it is so good to see you again. It has been all together too long. I do so miss our walks along the Embankment and your stories of the adventures of those who lived on all of those marvelous boats. It has been some time since the wedding, so please allow me to reacquaint you with my new siblings, Maeve, the oldest, Robert, her older brother, and the Twins, Patrick and Meaghan (Each child did a single hand shake and Lisette kissed each on a cheek.). This is Kate, Ronan's mother, whom I am certain you remember (shaking hands) and this is Ingrid who used to care for us, who has become largely our driver when we are at home, but is now mostly our friend and adult in residence. All of you know my Aunt Lisette who cared for my mother when she was young and continues to love her as such a special person in all of our lives."

With a final hug, Patrick Tyne had transported us all past perhaps many clumsy moments.

Maeve said to me, during cocktails as she sipped on a small glass of sherry, "You do know that Mother told us, right before we met her, that Carolyn was a bit different and liked women more than men. In school, they call that being a Lesbian. But the whole time we have known Carolyn, she has always been extremely nice and apparently normal. We all know that since Mom died, she came to love you deeply, and us too."

Me: "Your brothers and sister know all this?"

Maeve: "Yes."

Me: "How is it you have never mentioned this to me before?"

Maeve: "Oh well, her Patrick explained it all to us some time before your wedding. He told us about Lisette, you as a law student, his father who died in a war, and Vera, his "other Mother," whom he was to call "Aunt Vera" at the wedding and forever after. Mostly, he cares about his Mom. He is so happy to have you. He wants to be adopted by you. (<pause>) There, now, I've said too much. Please do not say anything about that 'adoption thing'."

At dinner, Ingrid sat between my boys and girls. I sat alongside both Patricks and Carolyn sat next to Meaghan, and Lisette was on her other side. Kate sat next to Patrick Tyne and between Celestine and Robert who was next to Lisette around a great oval table. The service is not slow, and the pace pleasant. The food was described before each course by our table captain. The wines appropriate for each course were poured seamlessly. An inconspicuous photographer moved about with no fuss taking what could only be candid shots of the dinner, and perhaps the diners. Voices were low and the chats convivial. Before the first dessert course, Lisette stood, "I should like to propose a toast to the woman whom I once thought of as only my protégé. Carolyn, you have in a short span of years come so full circle as to almost defy description. Not surprisingly, through hard work, long hours, and caring for all with whom you interact, you have risen to the very top of our profession. But that has not been enough. You have raised an elegant son in the quietude of Connecticut, and he now makes his way into the glamour of San Francisco, where we both got our start. Moreover, you are married to a successful lawyer who is a handsome, charming man with four delightful children, all of them coming of age, with you there to act for their mother. Yours is a life to be envied by any woman, and I am surely one of them. To our Carolyn, whom I like to think I helped to create herself!"

A brief moment of silence, then many cheers, and even a huzzah, of sorts, from Ingrid.

As the evening wound down, Celestine and Robert offered Lisette a trip home and, after especially fond farewells for Lisette, they all left together. That made it just the greater family, plus Ingrid (like family, by now). I turned to Carolyn, who was a bit giddy, and asked, "Now?" She seemed to mouth YES.

"Carolyn and I had a chat a few days ago while you all went exploring on that first afternoon. She asked me if she could adopt you four, not to act as a replacement for your Mom, whom she loved, but for you all to have the sense of another woman being there for you for the rest of her life and much of yours. We also discussed my adopting her Patrick. I had also been thinking these relationships needed to be formalized, and I feel that is all we would be doing. If you listened tonight, we all talk and behave like we are already one family. There seems to me to be no reason not to do this, but each of you is old enough to have a say in this. So, if you want some time to think, or want to talk to one of us or Grandmom Kate, or Ingrid, you do not have to answer now. You can, if you wish; or, would you rather wait until breakfast tomorrow?"

Maeve said, "I've had two glasses of wine tonight, so I'm afraid to wait. I might be so hungover I might miss something. I think this is all a great idea!"

My other three looked at each other. Robert spoke next, "I guess that means giving up being the oldest boy. But I really have come to think of Patrick as my other brother, so it really wouldn't change anything for me."

Meaghan looked at Patrick who nodded YES, and she said, "Like Robert, we already think of Patrick as a brother. As for Carolyn, I love her. I think we all do. She doesn't ever try to be Mom, but she is a mom. So, it's all fine with Patrick and me."

When we all looked at Patrick Tyne, his eyes had started to water and his speech did not come easily, or clearly, "Since I was a little boy, I realized I did not have a father. My Mom told me about my Dad, but not much. I know they were not married. I know he died a war hero. When it came to men, the only one she mentioned over the years was Uncle Ronan. When I was small, he sent me presents on my birthday and at Christmas. As I got older, he sent some photos too, some of all of you when you were younger. When I finally saw him a few years ago, standing there at the Baggage Claim at SFO, I thought to myself, 'I wish that man could be my father.' Now, he will be. I am so thankful." He got up, stopped to kiss his mother, then came over and threw his arms around me. I had to fight hard to keep from breaking down!

Kate said, "Quite the evening, this one!"

— — —

It was quite an evening, but for Carolyn and me, it was not only not over, but some of it lives with me every day of my life. As I helped Carolyn out of her dress, I noted her absence of a bra and the tiniest of panties. She quickly donned a make -up robe and tied it. I was not certain if that was some kind of signal, but then she spoke, "Lisette got me alone for just a few minutes. As I feared, she still wants me. The intensity of her desire,... of our long relationship, is so very hard to verbalize for you. You heard her words. They are all true, yet too shallow. They hardly describe she and me."

Carolyn sat on the edge of the bed and pushed me, so I was sitting upright except my legs were on soft giant pillows. "Let me go back in time. GOD! I hate this! From shortly after I started puberty my two older brothers began to look at me differently. I was a bit later in maturing than some girls at school. Our house had only two bedrooms, all three of us children shared the same room. As time went on, my brothers not only became more curious about my body, but they began to act on their curiosity. I went to my mother, but her response was, 'They're just boys. They don't mean nuthin.' They were more than just boys and they began to do things. They especially liked to touch me. After a time, my father became aware. Not only did he not help me, he seemed to encourage the boys. I went to my mother again. She said, "Your father says you enjoy your brothers' attention and you seem to want more of it from them.

"After that, things got so much worse. I had turned fifteen and really began to mature. And they began to force me to have intercourse. I had no money, so I could not run. I took small jobs and saved all I could. After almost a year of things becoming worse, a girl friend who was an only child had to go to Bend with her parents. She asked me to come as a friend for that Saturday night. My mother agreed. When I looked out the back window of that car, it was the last time I saw that God awful farm and those demented people who were my family. I snuck out of the hotel about four in the morning. Then, I found the bus -station which opened at five. The first bus to a big city went to San Francisco. It cost me eighteen dollars. I only had forty-six. I arrived later that day and walked around. Got a hot dog from a street vendor and found my way to Fisherman's Wharf. It was a Sunday afternoon, but all the businesses were open. I applied for jobs and got the third one. They asked my name and I told them the one I had made-up, Carolyn Tyne. From that moment on, I had no family. I finagled my way into getting a social security card, and I began to feel more free from my fear of my family.

"I found another girl who was looking to share a room. All I had was the small suitcase I had carefully packed before leaving. We switched jobs over time and I began to live better. I was working as a waitress in a nice Italian restaurant just off the Wharf. This beautiful woman came in with a man one day and I served them. She was nice and asked me a few questions about myself. Of course, almost everything I said, I made up on the spot. The next day that same lady came back near the end of my lunch shift. She introduced herself as, "Lisa." She said she was a model. Looking at her, I had no reason to think she was lying. She said I had the face and the body to be a model, too. I was shocked. She said she had an agent and she asked him to speak with me. I had an appointment in two days. She went with me to my room and watched me pack my few things and took me to her apartment on California Street. She cleaned me up and did things to my face. She bought me good underwear, including a bra with wire in it, so my somewhat smallish breasts had some real shape and a bit more size.

"Her agent signed me up that very first day, and he placed me at a boat show starting the next day for four days. I had to wear a bathing suit: two-piece, not a bikini. I wanted to do it, but I had no bathing suit. 'No problem' was Lisa's attitude as she had plenty of outfits. We went back to her place where I had slept on her living room couch the night before. She brought me into her bedroom, and opened a drawer containing swimwear, She told me to get naked and I did. She held several suits up to me and said, "We'll have to see what size fits you. So come on over here."

"I stood right in front of Lisa with nothing on. I will never know exactly what followed, but I remember a series of sensations unlike anything I had ever experienced. From that moment on, I was Lisa's lover, 'her beloved,' as she came to say to me so many times. We eventually moved to Sausalito as we both became more successful, especially Lisa. She had one favorite theme for success in our profession: become someone who is recognized as the face for 'a very specific look.' For me, I have spent my career working on becoming 'THAT American Girl,' as in 'the girl next door.'

"One day, I met a tall, handsome Coast Guard officer on the roof-top parking deck of our Sausalito home. Little did I know that he would eventually father my child, and one day, many years later, take me away from the life that Lisa, then also Vera, and I had created."

All this while, Carolyn had her hand on my leg. I listened without question or comment, I wondered how many times she had told herself that story. Now, I could see tears forming in her eyes. I said, "Carolyn. As far as I am concerned, you never need to tell that story again. If I could undo those years of your suffering, I would. But you are who and what you are now. If you still feel a need to give yourself to Lisette, I will understand." We made love slowly, as I kept telling her how much I treasured her.

— — —

Once the shoots started, everything changed, at least for me, and especially for Carolyn who had at least one role in virtually every shot. Even if she was not in it, those shots needed to fit with the story being told of Paris first revealing itself through Carolyn to her "New Family." The different fashions for the times of day mattered, as did the fittings themselves (Children just seem to grow in spurts at times!). Plus, since all of the shots were in public places, everyone had to be ready from the moment we took over the site.

We shot for six straight days. Then it started to rain: a hard, sometimes driving, monotonous winter rain, often accompanied by wind. We did all the inside shots that we could. But it kept on raining, and the forecast was for more of the same. We went to *Versailles*, but we could do only interior shots. Some good news: I was able to keep up my legal work as the shooting schedule's intensity slowly collapsed.

Some of the shoots proved more memorable, even in the relatively short time which we spent in Paris; for instance, our two days at the *Louvre*. Because of the press of tourists and spectators, even during the Winter Holiday season, we only had limited time and opportunities. Probably, the *Mona Lisa* is the most famous single piece exhibited: but it is fairly small, and despite *Robert*'s best efforts, even a close-up with Carolyn did neither her, nor it, any real justice. But the shot of that piece was perhaps saved by Maeve and Meaghan on one side of it and Ingrid on the other with Carolyn, clustering around the picture while showing off their upper body outfits, hair and make-up.

My favorite scene was the family gathered in clumps of two or three around that 600 square foot most elegant painting, *The Coronation of Napoleon* as Emperor at the *Chapel of Cluny*, with Carolyn seemingly holding forth on the regal scene. As painted by *Jacques-Louis Davide* in the first decade of the nineteenth century, it depicts the whole French royal court with Napoleon about to receive the Emperor's Crown, and about to be followed by Josephine's Consecration as his Empress. The women, especially Carolyn, were elegant in their own right with the then-contemporary simplicity of their outfits for touring Paris while becoming familiar with some of its treasures. The men and boys, meanwhile, looked quite handsome in their high-end casual attire, most appropriate for touring such a famous museum.

Although it did not get past the cutting room floor, I greatly enjoyed watching the then-aging children revert to their earlier childhood on one rainy day in the Hall of Mirrors in *Versailles*, when they went racing from one point to another while contriving games utilizing those mirrors, albeit to limited sporting effect, but adding a great deal of laughter.

Then the *Eiffel Tower* in the wind was great sport for the first

15-20 minutes, but much wardrobe difficulty soon followed caused by that persistent wind. By then, we had any number of shots complete, but still some absolute must-haves remained. The gatherings shots at the base of the tower had gone without hitch, but the wind at the first level played havoc with both the ladies' hair-styles as well as their attire. Next thing we knew Robert had his crew set up a tiny makeshift dressing room/make-up area, doubling as a wind block on that most windy side of the deck away from the background target for the models. The spectators loved watching this organized chaos and one American woman said it was the best show she had seen in her two weeks in Paris, "...(W)orth the price of admission!"

In the midst of all of this activity, I tried to appreciate the children, as well as Kate and Ingrid, in the course of their posing and staging. I began to notice that Maeve was quite serious at times, especially with "her" young men. I also came to notice how tall Patrick Tyne was becoming. Then, perhaps 6'6" or even taller. Robert was also at least 6,' while Maeve must have been 5'8." The whole brood was tall, and bound to get taller. Ingrid and Kate were both 5'6" and barely taller than the Twins, Pat and Meaghan. They all wore their outfits well and were fastidious about them. They all wanted to please *Robert*, so that Carolyn would be pleased with them. For several shots in the *Louvre, Robert* was looking for proportional arrangement: Maeve seemed to grasp his wishes intuitively. She struggled to communicate with her two taller brothers who were supposed to flank her. Finally, she took each by an elbow and told them where and how to stand, and next how to pose. Her sister and Ingrid observed this and maneuvered the twin boy into position. Then, in a matter of two minutes, Robert and his cameramen must have gotten 10-20 shots with these varying poses. Maeve was watching Carolyn who was conveying silent instruction and she seemed to understand the nuances that Carolyn conveyed, while Carolyn was working with her two young men and

Meaghan for a complementary shot each time. I was impressed, but I needed to ask Carolyn what, if anything, all of that sign language and many of those facial expressions meant.

I tried to hold all of these goings-on together to explain our many activities in Paris to Dr. Arnaud, but so much went on that I'm not at all certain that I didn't omit significant events. The whole trip, but especially the shoots, with all of the work that Carolyn put in to make certain that everyone in the family had a chance to look out from a page of Vogue, created memories for a lifetime. Kate was in awe, but tired easily and missed some of the shoots, including the trip to Versailles (not sure that wasn't because the last time she was there was with my father, then almost 30 years ago). As for me, I admired Carolyn's energy, wit, enthusiasm and intelligence. In retrospect, I realized I would do this again under similar circumstances because it brought me more vividly into my wife's life, not to mention my enjoyment of my family! This reflection had another side, perhaps not quite dark, but certainly regrettable: I had failed to be as involved in Mollie's life as I had become with Carolyn. Most of all, I will forever treasure the looks on the faces of my children, also Kate and Ingrid, and especially Carolyn. What an adventure, as I related this all to Dr. Arnaud!

— — —

Robert got together with an assistant editor-in-chief for the USA and EU editions of the magazine. Carolyn was called in. They would make do with what they had shot. They asked if we would do *La Pavillion*, as *Vogue* had taken over the restaurant for that night (in two nights). I called Dr.Bignon. He and his wife were untroubled by the weather and would gladly appear. That became the final event. There were a few cancellations caused by weather-disrupted flights. Our family was strategically placed around the restaurant with people who spoke English.

Camille was enchanting, and *Vogue* senior executives were extremely impressed when they learned even more about Dr.

Bignon and his position as the titular "Chief" of *INSERM,* among the most highly regarded, if not the most prestigious, of the French medical institutions. The 'after dinner' co-mingling went on for more than an hour as the doctor and his wife became *Vogue* celebrities via their conversations with that magazine's executives, international advertisers, and other celebrities brought together for this occasion. As a result, the dinner became its own article in both *Vogue* and on the social pages of many newspapers, not just limited to France.

We did get to do another shoot or two, but the difficult weather would not abate. The great news was the whole family spent the better part of two days in *Musee d'Orsay,* pouring over the many works of all of those great Impressionists. Carolyn even staged a family shoot there to commemorate the hours of the original shoot which would certainly not include everyone in the family. The museum was most gracious in its cooperation (It seemed that Carolyn was regarded as an adopted French celebrity, even though she was an American. So, she could en-gender some rare Parisian kindness.).

Since the "Adoption Dinner" as it quickly became known, the family's spirits had been on the rise. With Christmas just days away, we all returned from a day of the Impressionists to find the living area of our main suite decorated with a Christmas tree. A small repast and several bottles of wine and sparkling water completed the tableau. We had decided to attend Midnight Mass on Christmas Eve at *Notre Dame* with the assistance of the Chief Concierge of *Le Meurice.* (A generous donation to the Cathedral as well as to that concierge succeeded in getting us reserved seat-ing on the floor of that ancient church, while allowing us the ac-cess needed to receive Holy Communion.) Thereafter, we were to return to the Bistro where Lisette and Carolyn had taken me that first night in Paris for our Christmas supper. (Not really a big surprise when Lisette was there with Celestine, Robert and DonaViva.) A fun-time was had by all!

It was an unforgettable evening, but exhausting. It was nearly 3 a.m. when we finished walking back and getting to our rooms. The children all went straight to bed as was our deal and so did Kate and Ingrid. So, when Carolyn and I finally walked into our suite living room, imagine our shock as we found piles of beautifully wrapped presents under and all around the Christmas tree and even more decorations in that room. Carolyn turned to me with tears in her eyes and said, "I never imagined they would do anything like this!" Then, she began to kiss me and steer me toward the bedroom, saying, "I can never love anyone more than I love you at this very moment."

We slept well until the first child awoke, then in a matter of moments, they were all awake and clamoring for Kate, Ingrid and us to join them.

The surprise of the presents themselves caused such a fuss that we barely got to make coffee and tea as the children went about sorting them all. The Patricks figured out that Patrick was the Tyne and Pat was the O'Neill (No Matter!). Kate and Ingrid had two each, while I had one and Carolyn three. We started opening with the youngest first, and that was Meaghan. She carefully preserved the gorgeous red bow which adorned her first package, but then went about destroying the paper. (Although there was a name tag, the gift-giver was unspecified!) Then she lifted the top and inside was her favorite outfit of all of those she had worn during her shoots. The card read, "To Meaghan, for all of your *patience and cheerfulness while we worked together. Merry Christmas, Vogue et Robert.*"

Each of the presents with the red bows contained similar gifts and a card with variations of the same sentiments. Even Kate and Ingrid got the same. Carolyn had two red bows and I had none. She opened the smallest first. A white silk shawl which she had worn to *La Pavillion.* The second had a card on top saying, "To be Opened Only When Alone With Ronan." So, she put the lid back on and said, "This one may be personal."

The second set of boxes all had dark green bows. We had Kate open the first, it contained a place setting of china and flatware from *Le Meurice's* Main Dining Room, the card told her "For a meal whenever you wish to remember us!" Carolyn's green bow was a smaller box, holding only a card which said, "To Carolyn & Ronan O'Neill, The balance of your settings, flatware and all serving dishes will be delivered to your residence in California. Thank you for being wonderful guests and for all of the great publicity which your stay engendered for our establishment! Merry Christmas!"

— — —

A few more rain-swept days, and we wished the family good-bye at *Charles de Gaulle* as they all flew non-stop back to SFO while Carolyn and I flew to London.

26

NO SUNSHINE IN LONDON

At wheels down on the Heathrow runway, the sky was dark grey and dismal, no hint of the sun. Thankfully, no rain and we caught a taxi and proceeded directly to the Grosvenor House. A message from Martha at the Front Desk said she would be arriving in two days and that we needed to meet with Corbett McDonald who was becoming more than a little reluctant, perhaps even recalcitrant, about coming to D.C. for almost a month for his deposition. I looked at my watch and decided to wait a few hours to call Martha to allay her worries.

Grosvenor House gave us a suite and asked if Martha should get the adjoining room when she arrived. Carolyn looked at me on that inquiry, and I leaned over, saying, "Would make it easier to coordinate things, the living area can function as an office, as needed." She nodded assent, then I turned to the Front Desk Manager and agreed. That manager took us to our rooms as was the wont of those grander hotels in London and Paris back then. In the main room, he presented us with a bottle of Scotch and two bottles of French red wine and one of Chardonnay. They were "honored" to have us stay with them, yet again, especially just after the Holidays.

Finally, he left. We unpacked, mostly hang-ups for me. Carolyn filled the balance of the armoire and our luggage racks took care of her other bags. Carolyn excused herself to the bathroom. Ten minutes later, she re-appeared dressed in a diaphanous garment that covered her from neck to knees, showing bare arms, but hiding little. "This was your Christmas present from *Vogue*, my instructions were to give it to you when we were truly alone." I thoroughly enjoyed unwrapping that present as the remainder of my day brightened immeasurably!

— — —

We dined at Wheeler's that first evening with our friends on its staff. Nothing fancy, just their marvelous Dover sole and a bottle of good French Chardonnay. The next morning at 10:30, I met with Barclay and Madeline to go over the final formal documents for the new LTL Ltd joint venture and to assure that they would meet with Desert Mutual's approval. (It did not take very long for me to realize what a very real conflict of interest could occur here if anything went wrong. At the end of our meeting, I mentioned this to DMIC's two UK partners. They looked at each other and both smiled. Madeline spoke first, Bradley clearly deferring, "We have discussed that potential several times. Neither of us sees any real possibility. This may go on for any number of years, but it will end. As long as you are part of it, neither of us is concerned. Are you, really?"

I looked Madeline straight in the eyes, saying, "Does Bradley know?"

She smiled back, ever so slightly, saying, "Do you know that you do not know everything?" My eyes widened. Madeline went on, "Gabrielle, Bradley and I have a very open relationship at any number of levels. There, now, you know; and, by virtue of knowing, you also know you have nothing to fear. However, our final question for you to take back to DMIC concerns their precise role in this venture. Now that they have decided to be an investor, or "silent partner as you seem to infer, should we offer to expand this 'Securing Names to Pay' relationship to other U.S. insurers through Cheshire & Booth, if the situation presents itself?"

Gabrielle joined us for dinner at Simpson's, as did Carolyn. There were a few toasts, a great deal about our time in Paris, and other catching-up conversation. As the meal began to wind down, I felt a tension, perhaps sexual, from the three Brits. But if they were looking for a clue as to moving their disclosure forward with us, I was most careful to give them nothing. When we agreed on a "last call," that sensation bordering on anxiety seemed to dissolve and our last twenty minutes were given over to "good feelings!"

Martha arrived the next day and we immediately turned to seeing Corbett in order to resolve his uncertainties about his deposition in Tinker's office on NW "K" Street in Washington, D.C. in a matter of weeks. Mercifully, Alison was in that meeting. She was finally persuaded to fly to D.C. to help Corbett get settled at the Mayflower and to encourage his final preparation. Then, she would be off to Montreal to see three of her children, all MDs, two of whom were clinicians, and the other a researcher. All were associated with Magill University Hospital. All three were married and all had at least two children. It sounded like "GrandMa's Heaven." (Martha and I pointed out to Corbett that if a need arose, flights between the D.C. and Montreal airports were very frequent and the flying distance was relatively short.) Meanwhile, Carolyn was busy with packing as she was briefly going on to Milan, then back home one day ahead of me to organize everything post-trip and see that all was well with 'back to school.'

Carolyn joined Corbett and Alison, as well as Martha and me for a steak dinner at one of the two 'feuding steak houses' a few storefronts apart on a mews just off Berkeley Square. Corbett had told me about them. He was fond of them both and went to each in-turn. The interiors were virtually identical. Upon entering, you would encounter displays of meat and seafood. You would select your appetizer, and either your actual fresh seafood or your cut of steak or chop from those huge displays. Starting with two rounds of drinks at the outset was mandatory lest your meal sequence be disturbed. A good time was had by all, but the sticker shock was ever-present before departure. (Unlike most UK dining establishments, these warring entrepreneurs affixed a twenty per cent surcharge for their service!)

Taxis took us in different directions. I asked Carolyn if I could talk to Martha for twenty minutes or so, then come right up. She agreed. Martha and I repaired to the Red Room Bar where we ordered our usual double-double Scotch Whiskeys. We did a quick assessment of Alison, she was beginning to fail, even more, and as to Corbett, most of his nervousness was doubtless about her well-being. Then, Martha raised her glass and clicked mine, "Ronan, it's been so long! To tomorrow night!!"

Carolyn was leaving early to catch the first flight of the day which would allow her a full day and a half in Milan. Taking a later flight that second day would allow her a lengthy nap to undercut the massive time change flying west to SFO, and to plunge ahead with all the tasks which would be at hand in her days immediately ahead at home.

Martha and I, together with Quincy, Bradley and Madeline had a three hour stint at Cheshire & Booth, including a physical review of the search area itself, a meeting with Jason Turnbull, Jr., and a meeting with Stanley Booth to finalize the relationship between his brokerage house and the new Joint Venture, LTL Ltd. We all parted friends and repaired to Bradley's office where Madeline had doubtless anticipated our visit. Cocktails, a light late lunch and some excellent wine were shared among the five of us. By 5:30, I was ready to go, and looking at Martha, she nodded ever so surreptitiously, and we began the process of excusing ourselves. Madeline pulled me aside, and I gave her the disappointing news that we might have to await my next trip. A moment's frown, and she was over me!

Back at Grosvenor House, we repaired to Martha's room for "our reunion," as Martha put it. (*Having spent such a glorious time with Carolyn and the Family, did I feel a sense of "guilt?" I asked Dr. Arnaud about this when next I saw her, and she practically laughed in my face.)*

Martha brought news on several fronts: first, the Defense in SCHOOLS was having issues on the Writ Petition drafting to Recuse Judge Kelly, and the Southern California Counties were now trying to formalize their mass joinders by county. More issues to ponder for the flight back to reality!

The next afternoon and evening, we spent with Julian Peto getting him ready to come to D.C. in little more than a month. Then to my surprise, Martha said that Mary was going to fly over and they were planning to meet in Paris for a long weekend. Would I mind if she checked out before dinner tonight?

Martha was gone within the hour and Madeline readily moved into my bedroom within 30 minutes of Martha's departure. We had an excellent fourteen hours, but got little work done!

— — —

EPILOGUE

I had been home for four days and was planning my time in the East for Corbett's final deposition preparation and an outline of the key points on Direct Examination, the next National Coordinating Counsel Meeting, the South Carolina Defense Counsel Meeting for the COLLEGES Class Action, and Julian Peto's time in D.C. I had come home not to get away from all of my pending commitments, but to work out how I was going to meet all of them. Then, I got a call from Lily. She wanted to know if I would take a call from Jim Downing, the Plaintiff counsel on the *Hobart* family matter.

I said YES, and she put him through. Jim had been busy with Judge Forestall in getting the three component defendants to come up with significant settlement contributions. Jim spent a few minutes reviewing the evolving settlement status. Apparently, the other four defendants (the fourth being the tank company) were now ready to contribute up to a few dollars short of what was needed to fund the structured settlement for the Hobart Family and to pay his fees. Jim confided that he had cut his fee to try to bring this matter to a close (Jim also had previously confided that this was his last case and he wanted to get on with his retirement, his vineyards, and his wine brand, *Cobb Mountain*). He hated to ask since our client and its carrier had proven instrumental in bringing this matter to a relatively quick conclusion, but could we come up with another $5,500? They were both in New York state, so I told him I would try, and be back to him tomorrow, if possible, and explained that I only had Friday before I would be gone the entire next week. (It proved to be an adventure. I did get that money, and the settlement was completed.)

I was just getting those two phone numbers together to make those Friday calls, when Carolyn knocked on my 'office door.' I asked her to come in and she looked at me with a "funny look." Then, she smiled sheepishly. I became concerned, and asked her, "Are you alright?"

Carolyn's face lit up with that, followed by a bit of a chuckle, as she said, "Did you know that your partner, Phil, has proposed to our Ingrid?" I looked at Carolyn askance. Then, she added, "Oh, by the way, Ronan, you'll never believe this: I'M PREG-NANT!"

I think I almost fainted!

— — —

ROSS CHARACTERS

(includes most from SAUSALITO and MILL VALLEY)

These pages display the main, recurring characters from SAUSALITO, MILL VALLEY, and this novel, ROSS. The organization is by relationship to Ronan, then by place or event.

THE O'NEILL'S and Other MAJOR CHARACTERS

Robert Emmett O'Neill, Ronan's father, who dies in *Sausalito*

Mary Katherine (Kate) Garrity O'Neill, Ronan's Mother, Twice Widowed

Rose Mary (1940), Meaghan & Mary Clare (Twins, 1948), Ronan's siblings

Ronan Joseph O'Neill (1943), Autobiographer

Mollie Phelan (1945), Ronan's Wife and Mother of their four children;
   Her brother, Chad (1943), a basketball teammate of Ronan at Georgetown;
   Her father, a widower, marries Kate later in life

Ronan & Mollie's Children: Maeve (1977), Robert (1979), Patrick & Meaghan (Twins, 1981)
   Au Pairs: Yolanda (their first) & Ingrid (throughout this series)

ROSS

— — —

Carolyn Tyne (1954), a fashion model and Ronan's first acquaintance in SAUSALITO with whom Ronan becomes friendly, and casually romantic;

> Unknown to Ronan for some time, she has a son by him, Patrick (1975);
>
> Lisa/later Lisette- Carolyn's mentor and first lover, works in Paris
>
> Vera-Carolyn's Connecticut lover and Patrick's "other mother"

Sandra Allen (1949), UC Hastings law student, becomes engaged to Ronan; her father,

> Ken, is senior partner in large San Francisco law firm; (dies in MILL VALLEY):
>
> Both serve as lead counsel for Wallboard Corp.

Margot Arnaud, M.D., Ronan's psychiatrist for forty years; on her death,

> Ronan received all of her notes & tapes on their therapy sessions.
>
> Those materials provide much of the basis for these novels.

Joel Tinker (1942) marries Elaine, Sandra's law school roommate, both UC Hastings grads.

> Ronan's best friend and classmate during USCG active duty. Lived in Sausalito.
>
> Assisted Ronan in getting his first law job at Klein Kelly in Oakland.
>
> Moves to D.C. to practice law to accommodate his wife and maintains long friendship and working relationship with Ronan and Klein Kelly.

Jerry Klein & Sean Kelly, founding partners of Ronan's law firm at Jack London Square, Oakland.

Ronan's Team at Klein Kelly

Reggie Fox (wife: Ginger), Partner; Mary Smith, Partner; Phil Hassard, Partner; Martha Walsh, Senior Associate (Ronan's long -time mistress), becomes Partner in ROSS; Joshua Small, Associate Attorney; Deirdre, Senior Paralegal; Lily, Team Administrative Assistant.

— — —

Tinker's Team in D.C.: Mace Snow, older litigator; Tod Clifford, younger litigator; both partners

— — —

Society of Insurance/Civil Defense Counsel (SIDC)—Invitation only/Vetted Honorary Organization –Ronan becomes a member in MILL VALLEY

— — —

RONAN'S MAJOR CLIENTS

DESERT MUTUAL INSURANCE COMPANY (DMIC) – Scottsdale, Arizona

Charles Ezra Sewell, President (CEO)
John O'Sullivan, Senior Vice President & Chief Actuary (COO)
Dudley Chisholm, Vice President, Chief of Claims
Larry Decker, Assistant Vice President – Claims
Emmanuel (Manny) Garcia (wife: Esmeralda), Senior Manager, Major Claims

Geraldine (Gerry) Dwyer, Chief, Casualty Claims (leaves for
The Hartford)
Angela Lenovo, replaces Gerry Dwyer
Richard (Richie) Goldberg, Claims Coverage

CAL BOARD PRODUCTS, INC. (CAL Board) – Sacramento,
California (Ronan's major client along with DMIC, its Insurer):
Austin Smith, JD, Vice President and General Counsel

HANEY PUMPS, INC.—AUBURN, New York (Largest Submersible Pump Manufacturer in U.S.A.)
Carey Crawford, VP and General Counsel

— — —

WALLBOARD Corp. vs SF CASUALTY et al. ("Wallboard")
Iconic Insurance Coverage case, venued in San Francisco
Coordinated with four other similar matters under Order of
CA Judicial Counsel

WALLBOARD Corp. – San Francisco; Millard Granger, former
Risk Manager

SF CASUALTY, San Francisco, immediately prior primary insurer (to DMIC) of WALLBOARD for many years

Hon. Isadore Greenberg, Judge, San Francisco Superior Court,
jurist on the *Wallboard* and ultimately all other California Coordinated Asbestos Bodily Injury Insurance Coverage Litigation

Ken Allen, National Coordinating Counsel and Lead Trial Attor-
ney for Plaintiff WALLBOARD
Sandra Allen, Ken's Partner and daughter, Co-Lead Attorney for
WALLBOARD

Ronan O'Neill. Lead Trial Attorney for Defendant DMIC

— — —

Other NATIONAL COORDINATIONG COUNSEL (NCC) for Certain Other Defendants

NATIONAL GYPSUM – Abbott & Tweed, Philadelphia
    Alicia Goines, Lead NCC Coordinator
    Leonard Tweed, Co-Lead NCC

UNITED STATES GYPSUM – Bigstrom & Steel, Philadelphia
    Fred Talcott, Lead NCC
    Melinda Sykes & Adam Morris, Co-Lead Counsel

W.R. GRACE – Black, Weiss & Marsh, New York City
    Alan Maycroft, Lead NCC
    Dexter Wells, Co-Lead Counsel

INTERNATIONAL ASBESTOS BROKERS—Williams, Spencer
& Wright, Philadelphia
    Brad Eustace, Lead NCC and Lawyer Liaison to Third Circuit
    Court of Appeals

— — —

ASBESTOS IN BUILDINGS MAJOR CASES ("BUILDINGS CASES")

MULLEN CLASS ACTION, Martinez, California Superior Court
(Dismissed on Defendants' Joint Motion in *Sausalito*)

Judge: Hon. John Kendall

Marvin Jones, Plaintiff Lead Attorney
Ronan O'Neill for CAL Board, Co-Lead Defense Attorney
Ken Allen for Wallboard, Co-Lead Defense Attorney

— — —

LOS ANGELES UNIFIED SCHOOL DISTRICT ACTION (LAUSD), Los Angeles, California Superior Court, Central District

Judge: Hon. Bernard Weitzman
Charlie O'Reilly, Plaintiff Lead Attorney
Abel Stoneman, Co-Lead Attorney with O'Reilly
Avery Schein, Glass, Schein & Shea for National Gypsum, Lead Defense Coordinating Attorney
Rod Gorman, Glass Schein, Co-Lead Defense Trial Attorney
Ronan O'Neill for CAL Board, Co-Lead Defense/Trial Attorney

— — —

CONSOLIDATED SCHOOLS CLASS ACTION (SCHOOLS), U.S. District Court, Philadelphia, PA.

Judge: Hon. James McGirr Kelly, Article III Judge
David Berger, Lead Attorney for Plaintiff Lancaster School District
Ron Motley, Lead Attorney for Plaintiff Spartanburg School District
Scott Kelly, Lead Local CAL Board Attorney
Ted Darrow, Co-Lead Local CAL Board Attorney
OTHER NCCs, above, plus Ronan O'Neill as NCC for CAL Board and
Ken Allen and Sandra Allen as NCC for Wallboard

— — —

CENTRAL WESLEYAN COLLEGE CLASS ACTION, replaces the dismissed (in MILL VALLEY) CLEMSON UNIVERSITY CLASS ACTION (COLLEGES), U.S. District Court, Charleston, SC.

Judge: Hon. Solomon Blatt, Jr. replaces
  Hon. John Anderson, District Court Judge, Charleston, SC
  Ron Motley, Lead Plaintiff Attorney
  Arthur Miller, Harvard Law Professor, appearing specially
  for Plaintiff
  Josh Smoulders, Lead Local CAL Board Attorney

— — —

OTHER LOCAL CAL BOARD ATTORNEYS

WA: Tom Felix
OR: Lucy Baines.
AZ: Bob Hoover
TX: David Simms.
NV: Joyce James

NYC: Reggie Black
NJ: Barry Brown
MA: Ramona Kingsley
MD: Alan Kinnard

— — —

EXPERT WITNESSES

FOR THE PLAINTIFFS; Irving Selikoff, M.D., Epidemiologist, Mt. Sinai, NYC
  And other Medical Scientists, many associated with Mt. Sinai Hospital
Consulting for CAL Board: Jeremy Nobel, M.D., Harvard School

of Public Health
    Sir Richard Doll, M.D. (wife: Eugenia), Epidemiologist, Oxford, UK
    Mary, his Executive Assistant, Ratcliffe Infirmary, Oxford
    Julian Peto, Ph.D., Mathematics, Oxford & U. of London
    Alison McDonald, M.D., Epidemiologist, U. of London
    Jean Bignon, M.D. (w: Camille), Chief Physician (CEO), INSERM, Paris

ALSO FOR CAL Board: J. Corbett McDonald, M.D., (wife: Alison) Epidemiologist, McGill   University, Montreal & University of London, Schools of Medicine/Epidemiology

— — —

DMIC REINSURANCE POLICY RECOVERY PROJECT
In LONDON/LLOYDS INSURANCE MARKET

WELLINGTON CHASE, Brokers for U.S. Clients/ London Placements with Lloyds Brokers,
    (Defunct, Undertook DMIC Reinsurance placements over many decades to Lloyds Placing Brokers)

CHEHIRE & BOOTH, LLOYDS Placing Brokers
    Stanley Booth IV, Chairman of the Firm
    Frederick Booth, one of Stanley's sons, Policy Document Search Leader
    Grayson Turnbull, Jr., Retired Employee and Consultant to DMIC for their Search

PIERCE FIELDS, Solicitors, The City, London
    Frederick Pierce, Jr., Senior Partner/Grandson of Founder, For Chehsire & Booth
FOR DMIC: TWENTY KING'S BENCH WALK CHAMBERS,

Barristers, The Temple, City of London
Quincy Franden-Jones (Q), Senior Barrister For DMIC
Wilfred Smythe, Chief Clerk of Chambers

ALSO for DMIC: THORNTON, CAMPBELL & THORNTON,
Solicitors, Lime Street, The City, London
Bradley Campbell (wife: Gabrielle), Senior Partner/Founder's
Son,
Madeline Myles, Bradley Campbell's Executive Assistant and
Eventual COO of Long-Tail Litigation, Limited (LTL Ltd.),
London

— — —

BOSLEY HOBART, JR. et al.
vs HANEY PUMPS, INC. ("BO HOBART" Case)

JUDGE: Hon. Hiram Forestall, California Superior Court Judge,
Calaveras County

Ruth HOBART, Lead Plaintiff, *Guardian ad Litem* for/and wife of
Bosley HOBART, Jr. ("BO") Plaintiff, severely incapacitated in
water pressure tank explosion

James (Jim) Downing, Walkup & Downing, San Francisco,
Counsel for the Hobarts

Carey Crawford, VP and General Counsel for Haney Pumps,
Auburn, NY
Ronan O'Neill, Lead Counsel for Haney Pumps
Strom Nordquist, Senior Adjuster, Cayuga Mutual Insur-
ance, Pasadena, Primary insurer for Haney Pumps

Ross Weatherbee, uninsured installer of allegedly defective

pumping system,
> Including the Haney submersible pump and the water pressure tank supplied by Haney

Stanley Pressure Tanks, Kansas City, MO, alleged actual manufacturer of the subject water tank
> Cross-Defendant of Haney Pumps
> Howard Shein, Counsel for Stanley Pressure Tanks

ABOOKS

ALIVE Book Publishing and ALIVE Publishing Group
are imprints of Advanced Publishing LLC,
3200 A Danville Blvd., Suite 204, Alamo, California 94507

Telephone: 925.837.7303
alivebookpublishing.com